BARLOW LAID BARE

by

John McAllister

For Trish
And
Daniel who acts as unpaid researcher
And
Lucie, my publicist

And
my Guru, Kevin Hart

Published by Glenlish Publications & Portnoy Publishing

ISBN: 978 0 9956338 5 8

Chapter 1

Station Sergeant Barlow was on his second mug of tea and wondering if he should have stayed on the sick, when Constable Wilson burst into the Enquiry Office. 'Sarge… Sergeant you've got to come.'

'Oh I do, do I?' But he was already on his feet reaching for his cap. He paused, cap in his hand. 'Are you going to tell me or do you want me to guess?'

Wilson caught his breath. 'She's dead.'

'So you smashed down the door?'

'There was a key hidden under a flower pot.'

'There always is.'

He kept watching Wilson. The young officer was upset at finding the old woman dead but he was holding himself together. *There's a lot of hidden steel there.* But he knew that already.

Wilson made his report formal. 'Mrs. Cosgrave didn't answer the door though Constable Gillespie knocked several times and yesterday's milk was still on the doorstep, as the milkman said. The downstairs curtains were all drawn and the neighbors, when questioned, said that they hadn't seen her in a couple of days.' Wilson consulted his notebook. 'Friday lunchtime was the last definite sighting we've got.'

'So you found a key and let yourselves in, and…?

'We found her in the living room. She'd fallen, striking the back of her head on the fire irons.'

'So you ran down to tell me of an accidental death?'

Wilson developed a blank expression that junior officers – and most senior ones as well – tended to display when dealing with Barlow. He carried on with his report.

'Constable Gillespie took charge of the death scene. Susan… WPC Day is talking to the neighbors to see if they saw or heard anything. I was sent to fetch you.'

And to get you away from the dead body, thought Barlow.

He threw the car keys at Wilson. 'Bring the car round.'

With the duty car gone the detectives would have to lug their murder bag up the hill.

It'll do that lazy lot good.

Barlow walked down the corridor to the detectives' office and pushed the door open without knocking. He found only Detective Sergeant Leary at his desk. Leary was overweight, or needed a height of seven foot instead of his five foot eight to make his waist look slim. He also looked strained.

Barlow told Leary, 'There's death to look into, a Mrs. Cosgrave.'

Leary's eyes went wide. 'Not Deputy Commander Cosgrave's mother?'

'The same.'

Deputy Commander Jack Cosgrave of New Scotland Yard had died some years earlier of cancer but the death of his mother was bound to hit the national papers.

Leary looked ready to cry with exhaustion and strain. 'Do you remember the good old days when the only crime around here was the Dunlops trying to make some easy money to tide them over the holidays?'

'I'll send the car back for you,' said Barlow and walked on feeling surprised at his own generosity. *I'm getting soft in my old age.*

He dug a constable out of a cushy hidey-hole and told him to man the Enquiry Office. As a reluctant afterthought he fetched his gun belt out of his locker. He hated the implication of life and death that its weight implied, *but regulations are regulations.*

Wilson was waiting for him at the front door. Barlow slid into the passenger seat and said, 'Don't go straight up Princes Street. Curve around the town and come in by the other way.'

'Yes, Sergeant.' They drove off. Wilson dared ask, 'Why?'

'For a man who doesn't ask questions you're awful curious.'

Wilson's face went blank as he waited for the proper answer.

'Gillespie and you two have been up the hill to Balmoral Avenue. It never hurts to look at things from a different angle.'

'I'll remember that,' said Wilson as they reached the Pentagon and took the first road on the left.

'You didn't remember that you weren't supposed to be on duty until tomorrow at the earliest.'

Barlow made it sound like a threat and waited, hoping the answer would come.

'Money!' said Wilson like it was a bad word. 'Eleanor wants me to resign from the police and sell life insurance. She says that she has the contacts. Between us we could make a fortune.'

'So?'

The young officer blushed. 'It seemed wrong somehow, all that bedroom stuff when we weren't going anywhere.'

Barlow phrased it more crudely in his mind. Eleanor Packenham of *the Packenhams* of Kells Water was happy to keep Wilson as a bit of rough on the side. But marriage to a police constable? No way!

Somehow it made him rethink his own relationship with Louise Carberry. The possibility of her seeing him as a bit of "rough on the side" hurt more than he cared to admit.

Chapter 2

***Barlow stood in the front door of the police station** and chose an imaginary sweet to chew on the weary walk home. After seeing a man trapped in a burning vehicle, and unable to help, he hadn't the spirit left to growl an objection when the Police Doctor insisted that he take a few days off.*

A mint, he thought, and squared his cap on his head. He hardly registered a car pull up beside him or a window being rolled down.

A woman's voice said, 'John Barlow. John, are you going my way?'

He blinked to bring his mind into focus and saw Mrs. Carberry leaning out the car window. A fine woman, he thought of her. Kept her figure neat and dressed stylishly on a small budget. They'd had discussions recently about certain goings on. *Give Louise her due, she'd been more concerned about saving a friend's marriage than protecting her own good name.*

Barlow said, 'I could be Mrs. Carberry - Louise. I could well be.'

She smiled, leaned back into the car and pushed the passenger door open. He walked around the back of the car and got in. Couldn't resist a sigh of relief as his body eased into the bucket seat.

The bungalow that he now called home came up too quickly because it meant he had to move, to think his way out of the car.

'Thanks missis.'

'Louise.'

'Aye.'

He opened the door and hauled himself out of the car. Even bending down and nodding his thanks took a conscious effort. The walk up his short drive interminable.

He pushed at the front door then remembered that people on the Ballymoney Road kept their windows shut and their doors locked.

Now in Mill Row…

He shook his head to clear the memory of another house with its own nightmares, and hunted out his keys.

Stepping into the tiled hallway was stepping into the house of his dreams. Yet what he needed right then was the familiarity of the old mill house, and the salvaged rocking chair with the cushion to make it comfortable, and the rim of the cast-iron stove where he could rest his stocking feet. This new house was still full of other people's souls and his daughter, Vera, wasn't there to give him the comfort of family.

A hand came around his waist, another hand grasped his elbow and urged him on. 'John, you're done in.'

'Bucked,' he said.

Then he was in the kitchen and she was easing him into a chair.

'When did you last eat?' Louise asked.

'I'd a cup of tea sometime...'

'I thought so,' she said even as he wondered why she'd put him sitting at the table when there were more comfortable chairs. On one of those he could put his head back and - nothing. He knew he was too wound-up to sleep.

She came back, he didn't know she'd been gone. 'I've the kettle on and there's eggs and bread. I'll make you some scrambled egg on toast.'

She's fussing over me, and her as well-bred as any titled lady in the land.

It made sense in an odd sort of way.

She was gone again. He heard footsteps walking around his bedroom. He'd know the crack of that floorboard anywhere.

He was too exhausted to feel annoyance.

Then she stood before him, holding his pajamas. 'Put these on while I cook your eggs.'

She unclipped his uniform tie. Not practically like a nurse or erotically as a lover. Like a friend, with her nice bit of perfume and a peck of a kiss on the nose to show her concern. She unlaced his boots and slid them and his socks off his feet, then she eased him out of his jacket and pulled him to his feet. She unbuttoned his shirt, first at the wrists and then down the front, slid it down his arms and off.

He gripped the top of his trousers rather than risk her starting there.

She said, 'If they're not off by the time I have the eggs scrambled, I'll do it for you.'

'You're a desperate woman.' He had to be saying something.

She went back into the scullery and he heard the cooking start: the crack of the gas sparking on and the scrape of a wooden spoon as she stirred the eggs in the saucepan. Vera did that sort of thing for him, this was different. Vera played house, it was all new to her. Louise brought practiced ease to the same task and a feeling of normality that he hadn't experienced in half a lifetime.

He was still securing his pajama trousers when she came in with two mugs of tea. He sat down again and she reappeared with two plates, one for him, one for her: the bread de-crusted and lightly toasted and soaking in butter, the eggs moist, and a rasher of bacon stretched over the lot. The food slipped down his throat almost without chewing. Only when his fork kept stabbing plate did he realize that he was finished. Some of the cold void had gone out of his stomach.

'Bed,' she said.

'Aye.'

He ached for bed and sleep, but feared a sleep haunted by a man's screams as he burned to death. Realized he hadn't the energy to argue with her.

'I'm right behind you, John,' Louise said and dogged his heels the whole way up the corridor and into his bedroom.

The bedclothes were already turned back. All he had to do was crash into bed. He did and she pulled the bedclothes up around him.

He looked at her, she looked at him. He couldn't ask her to stay and come between him and those screams. He closed his eyes. Heard her shoes slide and the rustle of her dress. Opened his eyes to confirm that she was gone and it was too late anyway.

Louise stood facing him in her brazier and what he thought might be French knickers.

'There's a bit of malingering there, Barlow,' she said.

Even curling into the soft heat of her body took effort. Tensions drained out of him. Try as he might he couldn't keep his head up or his eyes open.

Chapter 3

Mrs. Cosgrave's home was a post-war council house, one of a terrace of similar houses in a quiet cul-de-sac at the top of the hill. As the milkman had said, yesterday's pint of milk still sat on the doorstep.

The hallway looked fine. That was Barlow's opinion as he stood at the front door. A length of matting covered the basic tiling supplied by the council. Gillespie and WPC Day stood beside him. Once Gillespie had confirmed death and realized that it might not be accidental he'd cleared the house to leave the potential crime scene uncontaminated for the detectives.

'She's in the sitting room,' said Gillespie.

Barlow looked at the Yale key in the door lock. 'There could have been fingerprints on that.'

'And this is one of your better days,' said Gillespie.

Barlow merely looked at Gillespie, a glare was wasted on the man. Any extra weight Gillespie carried was muscle, muscle that he'd used more than once to back Barlow when everything seemed against him. Not that they ever had a good word to say about the other. Not from the day when a fresh-faced Constable Barlow caught teenager Gillespie scrumping apples. Instead of showing remorse the young Gillespie offered to sell the stolen apples to Barlow at a bargain price.

Barlow walked into the house and stopped in the sitting room doorway. The room had a suite of furniture, casual tables, a china cabinet and a fitted carpet.

A fitted carpet! Now that takes money.

Not that he thought Mrs. Cosgrave had spent that sort of money on her own comfort. More likely her son, the late Deputy Commander, had insisted on buying everything for her while on a visit.

Mrs. Cosgrave lay crumpled on the fireside rug, her head

among the scattered fire irons. Congealed blood stained the blue rinse in her hair. Her hands were up to protect her face, the knuckles and joints knarled by Rheumatoid Arthritis. Barlow sniffed and got household smells overlaid with a tinge of sweet decay. The body had lain there for day, maybe two.

He asked, 'Did you touch anything: lights, curtains?'

'The curtains were drawn, the lights on.'

Barlow pointed into the corner. 'And the television?'

'Off,' said Gillespie. 'At first I assumed she'd fallen and hit her head when turning it off.' He shrugged, belittling his honed instinct for trouble. 'It's still possible.'

They retreated to the front step where WPC Day waited. Wilson had gone back to collect DS Leary.

'Well?' he asked the WPC.

She said, 'Nobody saw anything, heard nothing.'

'Keep at it. Find out when she was last seen.'

He turned to watch the arrival of the murder team, Leary and one man. 'Is that the best you can do?'

'It's all we've got,' said Leary. 'Harvey is bitching about overtime and budgets so I gave the rest of the team the weekend off.'

Wilson stuck his head out the widow of the car. 'Sergeant, you're wanted on the radio.'

'Tell them I'm busy.'

Wilson pulled back into the car and spoke into the radio. His head popped out again.

'There's an urgent message for you from the Fire Brigade. They're attending a fire on a farm.'

It's bad luck when things go quiet. It's only trouble stored.

Wilson kept talking. 'It's a rick fire on a farm belonging to an Arthur Somerton. They assumed it was caused by spontaneous combustion but they've found a body.'

Chapter 4

Barlow felt that he was crumbling inside. *A body!* Whose? No one had been reported missing. Not yet anyway. *I should have stayed at home.* He hadn't signed in yet. Maybe he should sneak off and leave things to Acting Sergeant Gillespie. *Let him earn his money for once.*

Leary looked ready to cry with exhaustion. He said, 'Pray God it's an old tramp who died of exposure.'

'We wouldn't have that sort of luck,' said Barlow and sorted things with Leary. 'You stay here, this is a definite crime scene. I'll go check things at the farm.'

They were still discussing the details when a Saab turned into Balmoral Avenue. It stopped.

'Now there's my dream car,' said Leary as the driver reversed the Saab back into Princes Street and drove off the way he had come. According to the Highway Code, the Saab driver should have reversed into the side-street and driven out, but Barlow had enough on his plate without worrying about a minor driving infraction. *Especially when I'd have to chase after him.*

He growled, 'Next time,' as he swung himself into the passenger seat of the squad car and reached for the RT speaker. He ordered the constable manning the Enquiry Office to ring Inspector Foxwood at home and tell him that he was needed at Balmoral Avenue. Foxwood would not be pleased at being called back into work on his weekend off.

The call finished Barlow growled at Wilson. 'Why are we sitting here? The Ballymoney Road, and fast if you want to be back in time for dinner.'

Wilson perked up. 'The bell?'

'But not the speed.'

They drove off, their bell ringing nice and loud, demanding a clear road ahead.

Barlow settled himself in the seat and found time to select an imaginary sweet – *something to chew on* – while he thought things out. He selected his favorite, a wine gum.

He reckoned the body had to be that of a man. A missing woman would have been reported by now. Either way it could complicate things for him.

Private things.

Chapter 5

Arthur Somerton lived in a two-story but ageing farmhouse. A disused water pump stood at the front door and electric cabling stitched the air from out-building to out-building.

Nobody waited for them in the yard, nor was there a fire engine to be seen. Barlow did a left/right in his head. Wheat field one way, haystacks the other.

'Go right,' he told Wilson.

Wilson turned right down a laneway between the farmhouse and the outbuildings. The laneway ran straight between hedgerows for a hundred yard before turning and climbing out of a hollow. Wilson braked to a halt close up to a fire engine.

'How did you know which way to go, Sarge?'

'I saw a whiff of smoke,' said Barlow and got out of the car before Wilson could ask any more awkward questions. The rick fire was well and truly out, the hay scattered and soaked until not a curl of smoke showed. Firemen were rolling up a hosepipe.

Wilson didn't hurry out of the car with Barlow, but he didn't blame the boy. Realized in fact that he should have brought some other constable with him. Only days before all he and Wilson could do was stand and listen to a dying man's screams.

And now?

The strengthening wind was coming over the wheat field towards the haystacks. That meant that the smell of burnt flesh would mainly go east towards Slemish Mountain. Barlow put his head into the car and said, 'Drive back to the farmyard and take the laneway leading off to the left.'

'I'm all right, Sergeant,' said Wilson, though clearly the thought of going close to another incinerated body was eating at him.

Barlow scowled like he was annoyed at his orders being

questioned. 'Remember what I said about coming at things from a different angle?'

Wilson turned the car in the open ground and drove back down the rutted track at a speed likely to snap a spring.

Barlow nodded to the firemen as he walked up the side of the fire engine and into the field of haystacks. The rick nearest the gate had burned out and now lay in a charcoal circle. In the center of the circle was the remains of a human being. Barlow swallowed hard when he looked at the blackened corpse. A man, he thought, big and beefy in life but now well burned through. A full head of teeth sparkled white in the middle of the burnt flesh.

It'll take those to identify the poor sod.

Two men were waiting to speak to him: the Leading Fireman and Arthur Somerton, the farmer. Both men were quiet though both were used to death in their own way. Dealing with bodies was part of the Leading Fireman's job. Every autumn Arthur Somerton killed-out a bullock and stored the meat in one of the new chest freezers to tide the family over the winter.

Barlow tramped up to the two men. The ground felt hard underfoot, not doing any damage to his uniform. It would be a different matter when he walked over charcoaled hay and water-soaked grass to get to the corpse.

The Leading Fireman nodded towards the body. 'Sorry about this, Mr. Barlow.'

'You didn't find a suicide note or anything?'

The Leading Fireman looked surprised. 'No?'

'That would have saved us some paperwork,' said Barlow and turned his attention to Arthur Somerton who gave a nervous dry cough.

'Are you all right, Arthur?'

'I am,' said Arthur though he looked shaken.

Arthur was more wiry-thin than small. Even on a summer's day and after a dry spell he still wore Wellington boots and had a stockman's coat held closed by a length of bailing twine. He had a curved pipe hanging from the corner of his mouth and puffed hard at it as they spoke to keep the smell of death at bay. Every so often he'd take the pipe out of his mouth and give a dry cough. 'It's the hay,' he explained. 'It catches me throat all the time.'

Barlow held back a "does it now?" This was no time for thoughtless sympathy. 'Maybe you'd tell me what happened.'

Arthur sucked hard at the pipe then used the stem to point to cattle and sheep in the surrounding fields. The sheep had retreated to the furthest corner. The cattle were rubber-necking over the hedge to see what was going on. 'I was having a read at the paper when I heard the animals being restless. I thought there might be a dog up to no good so I went to have a look and saw the smoke.'

He went back to sucking on his pipe.

Barlow had no intention of filling in the silence with speculation. 'And?'

Arthur had another suck. 'I phoned the fire brigade and I called for our Willie to come over.' Arthur again used the pipe stem, this time to point at a garden hose lying near a water-trough. 'We did our best to keep things damped down until the brigade arrived.'

Barlow made his look-around pointedly ponderous. 'And where's "Our Willie" now?'

'He went back to Anna. She gets a bit nervous when things like this happen.'

Willie Standish was Arthur's brother-in-law. He had married Arthur's twin sister when they were both in their mid-forties. Anna was what Barlow would describe as a nervous wee woman who stayed hunched into herself and only gave strangers a fleeting glance.

Somehow, in spite of their ages, Willie and Anna had managed to start a family. Twins again, now teenagers. The girl, if Barlow remembered right, attended the Tech. The boy was at Greenmount Agricultural College, learning about modern farming methods.

Barlow said, 'When did you discover the body?'

Arthur shook his head. 'Not us.' He nodded to the Leading Fireman. 'Your man there.'

Barlow turned back to the Leading Fireman who said, 'You'll need to take a look yourself.'

That was the last thing Barlow wanted to do but he was obliged to report that he had examined the body and confirmed the possibility of death by fire. Only the police doctor could actually say that the man was dead and the pathologist how he died. The police doctor was already busy at Balmoral Avenue, *or should be.*

Barlow went over to the body. He tried to make it appear a casual wander. He'd done it often enough during the war when serving in a bomb disposal unit. When things went wrong and a friend died, it was his job to find enough bits to justify a funeral.

The Leading Fireman went ahead of him, using his rubber-encased feet to shove burnt hay aside so that Barlow wasn't wading through a sea of charcoal. They stopped just short of the body. Thankfully, the smell was more charcoal than cooked flesh.

The man's arms were up as if protecting his face to the end. He had been tall, *maybe over six foot.*

What did come as a surprise was the remains of a knife buried in the man's neck.

Chapter 6

Barlow knew that he'd stared at the corpse and the knife far too long to pretend indifference.

'What a way to go,' he said.

The Leading Fireman nodded his agreement. 'I reckon he bled out.'

'So not the fire then?'

'Perhaps a contributory factor, but I doubt it.'

Barlow looked in distaste at the burnt and water-soaked hay under his feet. He could be standing on a pool of blood and he certainly didn't want that on his clothes.

'Now here's a funny thing,' said the Leading Fireman.

'What?'

'No matter how bad the fire there's always evidence of clothes: collars, belts, shoes. Now this one…'

'A right turn up for the books,' said Barlow as if he'd noticed it as well. 'Naked as a Jay Bird he was.'

He pulled at the Leading Fireman's arm and they stepped back from the corpse and off the circle of charcoal hay. He encouraged the Leading Fireman to get his men out of the field altogether, this was now an official crime scene. Though what Leary and his men were going to make of it was beyond Barlow.

Give Leary his due, if there's anything to be found they'll find it.

He himself felt sick and shaken. Times like this he used to recite John Dunne's *Desiderata.* But over the years he'd realized that the man had got it wrong. Each death he had to deal with didn't "diminish" him, it tore out another piece of his heart.

He walked back to the gate and the waiting Arthur. On the way he eyed the garden hose. The hose was attached to the standpipe used to fill the drinking trough. In this case an old claw-footed bath.

Just like the one I bought for my wee house.

The loss of that bath still rankled with Barlow. He'd spent a lifetime of marriage in a house with only a tin bath for bathing in. Then he'd managed only one long soak in a proper bath in a proper bathroom before it got blown up around him.

Something about the ground at the bath or, rather, poking out from around the standpipe, caught his eye. Mud stained grass, he presumed, and then thought he'd better take a closer look because the mud looked unnaturally dark.

He hunkered down and rubbed the grass between his finger and thumb. Red rather than brown came off on his fingers. He couldn't swear it in a court of law, but that was blood. He used the water in the old bath to rinse the blood off his fingers. And something else he noticed now his suspicions were aroused.

He called for Arthur Somerton to come over. 'Tell me, Arthur, when did you last clean out a drinking trough?'

Arthur backed away. 'I'm for the house. I can't be doing with this anymore.'

He hurried out of the field and disappeared behind the fire engine.

Barlow stepped out of the mud patch that surrounds any drinking trough. Between Arthur and his brother-in-law, the firemen and now Barlow himself, the chances of finding a footprint belonging to the murderer was unlikely if not impossible.

All the same, someone had washed themselves in that trough and then scoured the old bath inside and out to wipe away all traces of blood. The water in the bath was pristine, so that someone had gone to the trouble of refilling the bath.

He looked between the field of wheat, and the burnt hay, and the bath, and tried to make sense of what had happened

The dead man goes or is enticed into the hayfield where he is stabbed to death and hay pulled down to cover the body. Then the murderer had used the water in the drinking trough to wash off the blood. Maybe even bathed in it. Then the murderer had taken the time to wipe the bath clean of bloodstains and refilled it.

One thing puzzled Barlow. If the murder had taken place the previous night, how come the fire had only started that morning?

The only thing he knew about fires is that they were funny things that never did what was expected of them. How many times had he put a match to paper in his own fireplace only for the sticks and coal not catch?

He went out of the field and leaned on the five-barred gate and studied the layout of the surviving stacks of hay. Arthur Somerton had been lucky, the rick that burned had been well away from the rest and close enough to the standpipe for him to fight the fire until the Fire Brigade arrived. It also occurred to him to wonder where Wilson had gone with the car.

He was supposed to go into the wheat field.

Though when he thought about it, he hadn't actually told the boy to do that.

Anyway…

The Leading Fireman came over and leaned on the gate beside Barlow.

Barlow nodded in the general direction of the body. 'If someone put a match to that hay last night and it didn't catch, could it smolder until this morning and…'

The Leading Fireman interrupted him. 'Easy.'

'Easy what?' Barlow sounded sharper than he intended, not liking his almost musings interrupted.

The Leading Fireman pretended to light a match and throw it onto a bed of hay.

'The hay catches fire but it's damp.' He didn't say "damp with blood" but it was in their minds. 'The flame goes out. Even so there could still be a glow off hay cocooned underneath the rest. Then when the wind got up this morning, away it went.'

Barlow hadn't thought of that.

The Leading Fireman finished by saying, 'It's a good thing Mr. Somerton was at home and went to investigate when he heard the cattle being restless. He could have lost the lot.'

Barlow didn't care about Arthur Somerton and his crop. He kept thinking about himself and Louise.

Chapter 7

On the previous Friday afternoon, Barlow's stride down the Ballymoney Road might have been purposeful but his mind dithered between public phone boxes: which one to use and what, in the name of heaven, was he going to say to Mrs. Carberry.

'Louise,' he growled inwardly.

There was a call box at the Pentagon but Vera could easily head that way. And then wouldn't there be nosey questions. The one on Broadway, at the junction of the two shopping streets. With half the town watching?

The call box at the top of Warden Street, he decided and cut up Fountain Place. The hill in Springwell Street knocked the puff out of him. Made him realize just how hard the last few days had been on him. Wondered if there was a bit of age there too, but decided in the end to blame Vera and her heaped plates of food and the WPCs with their boxes of buns out of Matthews Bakery.

At the chosen call box he looked around suspiciously for anyone watching him. The call box sat at the junction of five roads: the Cushendall Road, Broughshane Road, Warden Street, Broughshane Street and the Market Road. He also had to contend with the Catholic Church angling into the junction and all the Holy Marys coming and going from there.

There was a phone book in the kiosk. The next worry, was Louise listed or was her number one of those X directory ones that crooks resorted to?

Her number was listed under: Carberry L. He stacked his pennies on top of the telephone and wiped again at his forehead. The call box felt over-hot for the time of day.

He lifted the receiver, put a penny in the slot and dialed. Her phone started to ring. His heart pounded and he puffed breath. The ringing stopped and the beeps came down the earpiece. She'd answered. He pressed the A button, the penny dropped and he could hear her voice saying "Hello.'

'Mrs. Carberry.'

'Mister Barlow.' With emphasis on the "Mister".

She sounded like a snotty member of the blue-rinse brigade with a bad smell up her nose. He found himself smiling.

'Louise.'

'John.'

'Yesterday, I couldn't have got through it without you.'

'Is that a thanks for the lift home or the meal?'

'For everything.'

Maybe that was a bit forward, maybe it would give her the wrong notion why he'd called.

She said nothing back. He stumbled to fill the silence. 'I wanted to thank you properly.'

'Flowers then.'

He could see himself walking through the town carrying a big bouquet and the raised eyebrows that would cause.

He said, 'I was wondering if we could have dinner?' For some reason to do with the nightmares still in his head he added. 'Not Caufields.'

The last time he was in Caufields, Vera had treated him to dinner there. Minutes after leaving the café Vera had been shot.

Louise was laughing. 'I agree with you there. Caufields make the best coffee in town. But for dinner? No.'

And that was the gap between them that frightened him. She and her friends went in for this Cordon Bleu thing of eating and what he called snobby living: dining out and drinks in the garden, strawberries and cream. Champagne! He hadn't even thought about champagne, and that cost more than a Station Sergeant's pay.

'Where had you in mind?' she asked.

His feet danced a jig. *I'm worse than a teenager.* He'd nowhere in mind. The Castle Arms Hotel or Leighinmohr House? He had dined there at times, an occasional treat for Vera when she was growing up. But Louise, with half the town *watching them? It would spoil things, make the whole evening awkward.*

He realized he'd been standing silent while she waited for an answer. And he hadn't one. 'Is there any place you'd particularly like to go?'

She said slowly, like it was just coming to her, 'If it's not too far, what about the Manor House Hotel in Ballymoney?'

Frig! Ballymoney was sixteen miles away. How was he going to get her there? Johnny Scullion and his taxi would cost a fortune for the evening. They could take the train and walk up from the station. He didn't think that would do either.

'Aye,' he said. Someone was coming up Warden Street. He made himself look them in the eye and give them a nod as they passed.

'Aye, the Manor House Hotel, no better place.'

He wiped what seemed a gallon of sweat from his forehead.

She said, 'The owner's a cattle dealer, so the meat is top quality.'

Her voice wasn't quite right either, he could tell that, especially when she rushed saying, 'My car's a bit of a rust-bucket but it will get us there.'

She'd just saved him a fortune in taxi fares. Better than that she'd been hoping that he would call and had planned where they could go.

Is she like me and wants a quiet evening or is she ashamed to be seen with me*?*

He found himself saying, 'You don't have to come if you don't want to.'

Totally the wrong thing to say because she went silent.

'I mean... I just... I don't know... Sorry.'

She said, 'Tomorrow night then. If I was at your gate about seven you could take over the driving from there.'

'That would be prefect,' he said and thought her a great lady. She'd said all the right things while he'd stumbled from one bloomer to another.

But she wanted to go with him. He confirmed the arrangements and remembered to ask after her health and thank her again for yesterday. The thought of them in bed together was in the air between them. What was really in his mind was her sitting at his kitchen table and fitting in like she belonged there.

Chapter 8

At long last Wilson and the squad car came up the track, bouncing from rut to rut. Wilson pulled up and joined Barlow at the gate, his face flushed with the pleasure of having discovered something.

Barlow said, 'You're a lot more careful with the springs of your own wee car.'

'Yes, Sergeant.'

He couldn't fault the tone of Wilson's reply. Even so he didn't like it. One other young constable used to talk to him like that and he went on to be so senior that even District Inspector Harvey called him sir. In the meantime Wilson was turning into a competent young officer who needed the odd slapping down. *That Gillespie's a bad influence on the boy.*

Barlow realized that he had been scowling while he was thinking. Now Wilson didn't look so confident. *That'll teach him.*

'Wait there, son. The Fireman will give you an update while I call up Leary and give him the good news.'

Barlow swung himself into the patrol car and got the Controller to patch him through. He thought the fat detective sergeant was going to cry when he told him of a second death. A death apparently induced by an external force. In this case a knife in the throat.

He also spoke to Inspector Foxwood. Foxwood was intrigued with the fact that the man had been found naked and no sign of his clothes lying around. He said he'd be right out after he'd contacted District Inspector Harvey at home.

There was no doubt in Barlow's mind that Harvey would run his interfering overview of both murder investigations from his office. From there he was also available at all times to talk to the press and to keep the big chiefs in Belfast constantly informed of his progress in apprehending the culprits.

'Well what did you find?' he eventually asked Wilson when he was back at the five-barred gate. The top rung was higher than the counter in the Enquiry Office but it did save a man's back while he talked.

Wilson pointed to a shaded rise beyond the wheat field. 'I believe the fight started up there. There's signs of a struggle, and I think we may have fingerprints as well.'

Chapter 9

It took all Barlow's strength of will not to show emotion. 'A struggle, you say? Fingerprints, you say?'

Wilson grew animated. In his mind he'd all but solved the murder.

'Yes, Sergeant. There's an area where the grass is flattened and lumps of fresh moss have been torn out of the ground.'

Right beside the fallen tree, Barlow was thinking.

'Are you all right, Sergeant?'

Barlow hurriedly brought himself back to the present. 'Fine. Go on.'

The "go on" turned out to be the fingerprints that Wilson had found, or rather pieces of paper that might contain fingerprints: a menu guide for a box of Milk Tray and the plastic wrapping.

'Maybe even tooth marks,' said Wilson. He sounded proud of what he'd found.

And pleased. That sort of thing, properly accredited, could earn him an early transfer to the "Plain Clothes" branch. Not only was the work of the detectives less routine, results tended to be noticed and awarded with promotions.

'Teeth marks?'

'I found two Turkish Delights thrown away and a sweet half bitten through.'

'And all this evidence is still lying there?'

But Wilson was shaking his head. 'I put them all in evidence bags. They're in the boot of the car.'

'Well done.'

Barlow refused to let Wilson's excited face upset him. *I hate boy scouts.* Instead he pointed directly at the wheat field where he had intended Wilson to go in the first place. 'Have a look in there. See what you can find.'

Wilson was like a greyhound in a trap waiting the order to go. 'And when I find something there?'

When! God help us.

Barlow pointed way across the fields. 'The man didn't walk here to get himself killed. There's an old bog road over there that I want to check out.'

Barlow saw Wilson off, making sure that he walked this time. Barlow knew who Harvey would blame if a spring in the car snapped. He wondered what the chances were of Wilson's 'evidence' disappearing. *Maybe a bolt of lightning in the right place?*

He went back into the hayfield and walked the boundary of the field. Downwind, the smell of death was particularly strong. It made Barlow realize that time was getting on and he could do with his dinner.

He let himself out a gate onto the old bog road and had a good look at the compressed vehicle tracks before stepping onto the mound of grassed earth in the center. He had to go slowly because the mound was uneven, with unexpected stones to turn the unwary ankle.

At least it's getting the mud off my boots. And the blood.

The bog road was sheltered by marching hawthorn trees that over hung the path. Here and there in damp patches he saw tire tracks. Mostly a collage of images but occasionally a tire track showed clearly on its own. A job for Leary and his men to take plaster casts but it was nice to know they were there. Not that Barlow had much hope in that direction but there was every chance that the last car to leave was driven by the murderer.

Barlow came across an open gateway on the other side of the bog road. In the field, parked along the hedge where it wouldn't be easily seen, sat a black Rover car. A car so painfully new that he didn't recognize it nor could he guess at the name of the owner.

Barlow walked around the car. No evidence of damage to its paneling. No blood caking its gleaming paintwork nor any signs of a hasty wash down. Lying in a crumpled heap on the backseat was a man's suit, with socks and underwear perched on top.

'Well, well,' said Barlow. 'You'd have been in less of a hurry if you'd known how the night would end for you.'

He tried the door. The car was unlocked and it opened. He used finger and thumb to drop the underwear and socks into the foot-well. Pushed the trousers and shirt aside and picked up the jacket.

He pulled the jacket out of the car and held it up. Brown tweed, but a light material so therefore expensive. *Very expensive, going by the car.*

He patted the jacket down and felt a wallet in the breast pocket. He recognized the wallet as soon as he had it in his hand. Only lately he'd been accused of stealing fifty pounds from it. Still he had to open it to be sure. He found a piece of paper with a name on it that he dreaded to see.

Ezekiel Fetherton, the owner of the local dairy. Fetherton was currently facing trial for watering down milk supplied to schools. Several of the children had contracted gastroenteritis from the contaminate milk. Fetherton, allegedly, had once offered his soul to the devil if he could get Barlow jailed.

If there was ever a man Barlow felt justified in hating it was Fetherton. Now Fetherton was dead, murdered.

District Inspector Harvey would do his damnedest to pin the killing on Barlow.

Chapter 10

***Come Saturday evening** Barlow had haunted the sitting room waiting for Louise to arrive. He paced the floor from the door to the corner of the fireplace wall, from there he could see down the road. It was either that or stand at the window like a lovelorn swain and be on view to every Tom, Dick or Harry passing.*

He spotted the car at long last. She was punctual almost to the minute. He ran out into the hallway, almost forgetting the corsage and box of Dairy Milk.

'I'm away,' he shouted at Vera who, pointedly, had remained in the kitchen.

'Okay,' she called back.

No "good luck" no "enjoy yourself"

Vera had been like that since he'd arrived home from making the phone call, his arms ladened down with parcels.

Vera kept delving. 'Shirt, tie, shoes socks.' She stood in the middle of discarded wrapping paper and asked. 'Why now, why all of a sudden?'

He had no clear answer for her, not anything he could put into words. 'You see...'

I eat policemen for breakfast, I've District Inspector Harvey well on his way to developing an ulcer, and my own daughter can reduce me to a quivering wreck.

'Have you got a date?'

Her tone was light but there was hurt in her eyes.

Be a man say it out straight.

'Mrs. Carberry - Louise, tomorrow night, Saturday.'

This needed a proper discussion. He sat down on the settee. Your mother and I, there's nothing there now, love.'

Vera said, 'Mum's so much better. She's even goes swimming.'

It sounded like an accusation, of him betraying Maggie when she was in recovery. And there's her swimming again. *In* the early days of their marriage she had given up swimming rather than wear a revealing swimming costume in his presence. The only times he had seen her naked was when he'd teased the clothes off her body. Then he'd thought it shyness. Hadn't realized it was learned terror, a legacy of her home life.

Vera pulled free of his hands, went to the window and stood looking out. He doubted if she was seeing much. From where he sat he should be able to see slate roofs across the way and the tops of car passing, and couldn't because moisture in his eyes put everything in soft focus. Louise had worked her way into his hoped-for future. In his heart he didn't want Maggie to get better.

Eventually Vera turned to face him. 'So long as I don't have to be nice to them I'll not stop you from seeing Mrs. Carberry or anyone else you fancy. But Dad, you promised Mum "for better or worse. For better or worse."'

The arrival of Louise's car at the gate put Vera out of his mind.

Louise got out of the car and stood waiting for him, keys in hand. She was wearing a different dress, turquoise green this time, and her lipstick shone bright in the setting sun.

'You look great,' he said and stood with the corsage in one hand and the box of chocolates in the other and wondered if he should kiss her. And if so, whether on the lips or on the cheek?

He hesitated and the moment had gone.

She exclaimed in pleasure at the corsage and said she'd pin it on in the car. Thanked him for the sweets and handed him the keys. Her hands were busy holding his gifts. She smiled at him and he remembered to open the passenger door. Made a point of staring somewhere between her eyes rather than down the swell of her front as she eased into the seat.

He got into the driver's seat and started the engine. At the town boundary, in fact way beyond Fairbairns Hatchery, he realized that he hadn't spoken since they'd driven off.

'I'm a bit out of practice at this,' he said.

'There's nothing wrong with your driving,' she said back.

He glanced her way, her eyes were laughing at him.

'You're an awful tease,' he said.

'And you're an awful man. You never mentioned my hair.'

'You got it washed and trimmed in Christine's.'

Now she looked startled.

'You always go to Christine's,' he said.

'That's the worst thing about you,' she said. 'You'll know what I'm doing almost before I do it.'

He liked the hint that she was thinking of a relationship beyond that evening.

It was only sixteen miles to Ballymoney and the Manor House Hotel. They were in good time so he used the setting sun getting into his eyes as an excuse to keep the speed down. Talk was sporadic. She as busy with her thoughts as he was with his. He was feeling his way and trying not to make a mess of things.

I should just be myself, he thought, and didn't really think that a good idea. Not when he hadn't noticed her perfume until then. It sweetened every breath he took and there was no smell of smoke in the car. He liked that in a woman. Somehow cigarettes seemed to diminish them.

She accepted his arm as they stepped across the pavement and walked up the steps into the Manor House Hotel. They were given a table against the inner wall and well away from the windows. He had a good look at the fellow diners before he settled, and didn't recognize any of them.

She said, 'The Ballymena Observer will carry an article next week about us dining together.'

'Would you stop reading my mind.'

'And would you stop worrying about me being seen in your company.'

Chapter 11

Barlow checked the rest of the mysterious Rover car, even peering into a boot that gleamed from non-use. No women's clothes, no personal papers. The wallet was thick with money, and that worried him, just as it would, justifiably, worry his superiors.

He found the car keys in Fetherton's trouser pockets. Locked the car and walked back to the five-barred gate, which had become his unofficial assembly point. Inspector Foxwood had arrived and was waiting for him. Wordlessly Barlow handed him the wallet.

Foxwood looked inside and saw Fetherton's name. 'Oh!' He handed the wallet back to Barlow. 'Count the money, Sergeant, and make a note of the other contents.'

'Aye.' He felt he had to say it. 'There's a fair bit of money in there, sir. I'd like you to pat me down just to be sure.'

'Certainly not,' said Foxwood in his best Southern English accent.

Inspector Foxwood was an English man who had married a North Irish girl and transferred from the Metropolitan Police to the RUC. The man was good at his job though cowed by authority, as personified locally by District Inspector Harvey.

Foxwood asked for an update on what else Barlow had found or observed.

Not that much, Barlow had to concede to himself. The wrapping paper from the box of sweets stirred Foxwood's interest. If only because the person or persons up there might have seen something.

'That stuff could have been there for days,' said Barlow trying to quell Foxwood's enthusiasm.

Wilson was back in time to disagree. 'It rained yesterday morning and everything was dry.'

'It was hardly a skiff,' said Barlow, wishing he could wring the young officer's neck.

Wilson wanted Foxwood to go and inspect a circle of tramped down wheat in the adjoining field and the footprints of naked feet on odd patches of soft ground.

'No burn marks or anything?' queried Barlow.

Foxwood shuddered, completely misunderstanding the reason for the question. 'Do you think there's more bodies waiting to be discovered?'

'You'd never know,' said Barlow.

Foxwood and Wilson went off into the wheat field. Barlow used the bonnet of the squad car as a table while he counted the money in Fetherton's wallet – ninety pounds in fivers and four singles – and listed the other contents.

He locked the wallet in the squad car and walked after Wilson and Foxwood, intending to have a look around the wheat field himself. However, when he reached Arthur Somerton's farmyard he found a car parked there. One of the new Opel Rekord P2's.

He walked up to the farmhouse, gave the outer door a thump, a lesser thump on the inner door and walked into the kitchen.

Arthur Somerton was an aged bachelor living on his own. Other than electricity being run in, there appeared to have been no work done to the house since his parents' time.

The kitchen floor was still flagged and the fireplace had the hooks for cooking pots and pans still in place. A butcher's block sat tight against an internal wall, with a selection of knives and cleavers hung in hooks above it. The room had two small windows, one overlooking the farmyard and the other the fields behind.

Arthur was sitting in a high-backed wooden chair while Doctor Ingram tapped his back. When Barlow was young he though Dr. Ingram old. Now Dr. Ingram was positively ancient and still practicing in spite of a stoop and a habit of screwing his eyes into slits to keep people in focus.

Sitting in a similar chair and looking comfortable with a glass of something amber in his hand was a middle-aged man. Barlow thought he might be Dr. Ingram's much younger brother, a cousin anyway, because there was a family resemblance.

'Have I come at a bad time?' he asked to be polite.

'Not at all, Young Barlow, we've just finished,' said the doctor.

Arthur pulled his shirt down over bony ribs and got to his feet. 'You'll be taking a drink, Sergeant?'

'Not on duty but thank you for the offer' Arthur looked like he'd got over his upset in the field, but still the doctor was there. 'Are you feeling okay? Is there a problem?'

Arthur said, 'I'm fine. Anna is shaken, her nerves you know, and Willie asked the doctor to call.'

Dr. Ingram stuffed his stethoscope into his pocket and sat in a chair opposite Arthur. Picked up a glass of amber liquid and held it tight to his body against an early Parkinson's shake in his hands.

'Make sure you take your pills,' he told Arthur.

'I'll be fine,' said Arthur and coughed.

'You should be taking it easy,' said the Doctor.

His brother/cousin laughed. 'You're one to be talking.' He stood up and shook Barlow's hand. 'Keith Ingram, I'm the unpaid and un-thanked chauffeur at weekends.'

He popped an antacid tablet and sat down again.

Dr. Ingram said, 'If you stopped taking the drink you wouldn't need the tablets.'

Keith said, 'At least I know to take time off and enjoy life.'

Brothers, Barlow decided because their tones were half humorous, half chiding.

'You're retired then, sir?' he asked Keith.

'I wish.' Keith shrugged. 'Sort of, though I like to keep my hand in.'

Dr. Ingram said, 'If you're looking for life insurance, Keith's your man.'

'I'll put you in touch with the right people. Other than that…' Keith shrugged again.

Dr. Ingram finished his drink. He stood up and told Arthur, 'You have an early night and don't be worrying about Anna. Willie and the children are there, keeping an eye on her. Anyway, she's fine. Remarkably so in the circumstances.'

He and Keith left. Barlow heard the Opel Rekord start up and drive out of the yard.

He sat down on what had been Dr. Ingram's chair and aimed his toes at the open fire. Not that his toes were cold on a find August day, but it was a comforting old habit. Anyway, an old flagged-floor farmhouse, built long before damp-proof courses had been invented, was never warm.

Arthur said, 'I saw you looking at the knives?'

'I'm reckoning they're a better quality than the one stuck in the corpse.'

'They are that. We used to do our own butchering and we were forever sharpening the cheap ones.'

'You're right there,' said Barlow glad Arthur didn't have to justify a gap in the row of knives.

He told Arthur. 'This unpleasantness, we'll get a written statement off you tomorrow.'

Arthur said, 'Not tomorrow. The weather's going to break and I need to get that wheat in.'

If there was a cloud in the sky that day, Barlow hadn't seen it. 'What makes you think that?'

'The birds, Sergeant. Always watch the birds. There's going to be a run of bad weather, though it may change with the next full moon.'

Barlow didn't care. Most of his job was indoors and he always had his cape and a stout pair of boots.

He told Arthur, 'For now I'd like you to run me through what happened and when. Let's start with yesterday evening, did you hear or notice anything unusual?'

Chapter 12

Questioning Arthur didn't take Barlow long. Arthur had seen nothing and heard nothing until he went out to investigate what was making the cattle restless and saw the smoke. The previous night he's gone to bed early because the "age was in my bones".

'You're not that old,' said Barlow. He reckoned Arthur and his twin sister had to be about sixty, but the years hadn't been good to Arthur. He could have passed for a wizen old man of seventy.

'Old enough,' said Arthur.

Barlow said, 'You were reading the newspaper when you realized something was wrong. Did you see anyone hanging around when you went to buy it?'

Arthur dug the newspaper out from under his cushion, Saturday's *News Letter*. 'I'm always a day behind. Willie leaves his up when he's done with it.'

Now that is tight.

Arthur said, 'I knew the fire was bad so I rang for Willie. Then I ran out the hosepipe and we did our best until the Fire Brigade came.'

'When did you get the…' Barlow realized that to say "smell" was possibly upsetting.

Before he could find the right word Arthur added, 'Grand boys the firemen these days. Them and their hoses, they'd the fire out in no time.'

And when did you all realize…' He still couldn't find the right word.

'We thought it was maybe a nest of rats trapped in the hay. Then when the firemen spread the ashes we saw him.'

So he's avoiding the word as well.

'We think it was Ezekiel Fetherton,' said Barlow.

Suddenly Arthur was animated. He spat in the fire and

wiped his mouth with the back of his hand. 'Bad luck to him for watering down the children's milk.'

At that, Barlow thought it time to go. Arthur had nothing of interest to tell him. Someone would have to talk to Willie and Anna but it was hardly worth his while to tramp over there. Not when his stomach was thinking more about the lunch waiting for him at home: boiled ham, carrots and parsnips and flour potatoes. His mouth watered.

He didn't think they'd get much out of Willie or Anna, but they had twins, young teenagers, a boy and a girl. They might be worth talking to. He'd mention it to Leary, *or maybe not.*

Barlow went looking for Wilson. He thought it time he got the young constable well away from the body and put his mind to something else. By the time he got back to the five-barred gate Detective Sergeant Leary and his man had arrived. Wilson was talking animatedly to Leary about the suspicious wrapping paper and half-bitten sweet he'd found on the little hill.

When Wilson went off to recover the "evidence" from the boot of the car, Leary gave Barlow a pained look. 'Thanks to you I've already got a pile of work on hand. Now you've given me another murder and a suspicious death to look into.'

'It's hardly my fault.'

'You're a scunner, that's what you are.' Leary watched Wilson coming back with the evidence bags. 'I've a mound of forensic evidence choking the labs and now this Boy Scout wants me to check out stuff he found in the next county.'

Leary didn't seem to know whether to cry or spit and Barlow didn't dare comment.

'Don't discourage the boy,' he said and went off to get Foxwood's permission for him and Wilson to head back to the station.

Chapter 13

When Barlow arrived back at the station, Acting Sergeant Gillespie wiped a hand across his mouth to make sure that no traces of food remained on his lips. He also gave a polite belch. In reply, Barlow's stomach rumbled empty.

'I'm away for my break,' said Barlow.

'The DI wants to see you.'

Wilson had already disappeared down the corridor towards the kitchen and couldn't hear them.

Barlow said, 'You haven't seen me.'

'I think you'd better,' said Gillespie.

'Bollocks.'

Barlow knocked on Harvey's door and went in without waiting for the command to enter. Instead of giving his usual glare at the sight of Barlow the edges of Harvey's lips softened. The nearest he ever got to a smile.

'Well, Barlow, what do you think?'

'Sir?'

'The Dunlops. They rob the brewery every August, and always before the Hibernian Parade on the fifteenth. That's what I have against you, Barlow, you haven't the intelligence to see the obvious.'

'And you caught two of the Dunlops, sir, the grandsons?'

'Red handed.'

Harvey paused, obviously waiting for Barlow to congratulate him. It didn't come. Instead Barlow nodded and wandered to the door.

He stopped with his hand on the handle. 'I was wondering, sir. Does Captain Denton know yet?'

Harvey preened himself. 'No, he's taken the family to Dublin for the weekend, but I'm sure he'll be delighted.'

Barlow said, 'He'll have something to say. You can be sure

of that,' and went back to the Enquiry Office where Gillespie greeted him with a raised eyebrow.

'You're a double bollocks,' Barlow informed him as he reached for the Duty Roster and flicked through the pages, stopping every time he came to came to Gillespie's name.

So you're off the last Saturday of the month?'

'I am.'

'And tomorrow, the fifteenth, as well?'

'That too.'

'You'll be telling me next that your feet and your back and your shoulder and your chest are giving you bother.'

Gillespie tried to look hurt. 'Have I complained?'

Barlow reached for a pencil and wrote Gillespie's name down for duty the next day: early morning too late in the evening.

'Now hold on, that's a shift and a half,' said Gillespie.

Barlow went over Gillespie's name with the pencil, making sure it stood out. 'If you're not fit to guard the members of the Ancient Order of Hibernians when they assert their right to march, then you're not fit to tramp through the working area of the town with your friends in the Royal Black Institution.

Gillespie pretended annoyance. 'We don't tramp, we parade through the town on our way to the Field.'

'Sure you do. Making sure the working man knows his place and doesn't dare step out of it.'

'You're a typical Taig, looking for trouble where there isn't any.'

Barlow reached for his cap, needing to be out the door before Harvey could think of some reason to delay him. 'You mean a typical Taig who still hasn't got the promised poached salmon.'

Now Gillespie really looked annoyed. 'Flaming Harvey, he saw the fishing rods one day and demanded to see my licenses.'

'So no poached salmon then?'

'Salmon yes, poached no.' Gillespie looked sour. 'It doesn't taste the same.'

Barlow good humor was restored at the thought of Gillespie having to pay for a fishing license. It wouldn't kill the man to dig into his pocket for a few bob, though most of his wages was spent generously on rearing a big family. Gillespie never asked for the job. In fact he always made it seem the biggest bother, but he took great delight in using the overtime earned from escorting the Nationalist Hibernian parade to fund his membership of the Loyalist Royal Black Institution.

Now where did he learn that bit of awkwardness, wondered Barlow. Then he heard DI Harvey's tip-toe footsteps on the corridor. 'Are you looking for something, sir?'

Harvey appeared. 'What were you two talking about? Why aren't you getting on with your work?'

Barlow said, 'We were talking about poachers.'

Gillespie added, 'The Water Bailiffs don't do their job properly.'

'Turning a blind eye to family and friends, and them without licenses,' finished Barlow, with an eye on Gillespie who looked like butter wouldn't melt in his mouth.

'Well, yes.' Harvey huffled and shuffled. 'Barlow I've just had a word with Inspector Foxwood. The detectives are overstretched as it is. This new murder on the farm and the old woman – Headquarters say they have already loaned us every detective they can spare.'

Barlow guessed the way things were going and determined not to make it any easier for Harvey. 'We're shorthanded ourselves, sir, and don't forget we've got the Hibernian Parade tomorrow and then the "Black" Men at the end of the month.'

Harvey cleared his throat in a determined way. 'This old woman…'

'Mrs. Cosgrave,' prompted Barlow.

'There's no sign of a break-in and her purse was untouched.' Now Harvey felt he was on firmer ground. 'In my opinion, you overreacted calling out the detectives to what is obviously an accidental death. Wasted their time in fact when they are already busy with extremely pressing cases.'

For "Extremely pressing" Barlow took to be Harvey wanting the "Murder Book" to be ready for the DPP in record time. A quick trial for cases already solved, with the consequent newspaper coverage, would do wonders for his career.

'What are you suggesting, sir?'

Harvey hesitated. He had intended to give his orders from on high and brook no argument. Now Barlow had an opening to query points.

'I want the Uniform Branch, in fact you personally, to deal with this allegedly suspicious death of Mrs. Cosgrave.'

Barlow nodded. Harvey was deliberately adding to his already heavy workload in the hope that something would go wrong and he could be blamed. 'I'd need a constable on it full time – not Wilson.'

Harvey brightened because he saw Constable Wilson as his man. 'Wilson. Definitely Wilson. I want him working closely with you on the case.'

'I need an experienced constable,' said Barlow.

'You have your orders.' Harvey marched off.

Barlow nodded, pleased. Junior Constable Frank Wilson had already sent a Station Sergeant to jail and Harvey had hopes that Wilson would do the same to Barlow.

What Harvey didn't realize was that Wilson was painfully honest. He would report Barlow for any crime he came across but he wouldn't have any part in fitting him up for something he didn't do. It was a fine line but Barlow liked treading it.

Chapter 14

The frost in Vera's manner at Barlow daring to date another women had only deepened with him being late home for lunch. A note propped pointedly against the tomato sauce bottle informed him that his "ruined" lunch was being kept warm in the bottom oven. Vera herself had disappeared into the world of "out" inhabited by teenagers.

The gravy had gone rock hard and the potatoes needed a chew to break them down but it still tasted good to a hungry Barlow. After half a lifetime in a mill house he still found it strange living in a spacious house with spare rooms. Sometimes he even found himself heading outside to go to the toilet when he had an indoor bathroom.

He ate facing out the kitchen window, looking down the concrete yard. *Twelve feet wide, if it's an inch.* Beyond the yard was a back lawn. The garden ended at the boundary wall of the convent belonging to the Sisters of St Louis. Against the wall was the makings of a vegetable patch that he still had to put a spade into.

A back garden, a front garden, a garage, sheds and a bath with plumbed in running water. He thought the house should be renamed "Heaven". But having arrived at "Heaven" instead of giving thanks and being grateful, his restless soul yearned for something else.

The house was empty so he said it out loud, 'Louise.' He said it again, louder this time as if she was somewhere handy and he wanted her to come and join him at the table. He even left a forkful of food on the side of the plate, wanting her to taste it and see how good a cook Vera was.

Chapter 15

Still sitting at the kitchen table, the thought of Louise and the night before made something like butterflies flutter in Barlow's chest. 'I'm going soft in the head,' he said, and made himself eat the food he'd put aside for Louise. Anyway, Vera tended to get huffy if he didn't scrape the plate clean.

He put the plate in the sink. *Time to get back to work.* Really he should phone Louise but there was no time to go to the call box at the top of Warden Street. *Maybe after work.* But he knew good manners dictated that he should call before then.

There was a phone in his hallway. Or rather the disconnected carcass of one left over from a previous tenancy. On his way out the door he lifted the receiver to check and got silence instead of electrical static. Tomorrow, definitely, he'd see about getting it reconnected, then he could ring Louise whenever he wanted.

Vera and her friends?

He remembered the complaints of other fathers, how their children ran up huge phone bills. Thought he should set ground rules as to when and how long the telephone should be used.

All the same, Vera was out most evenings. He and Louise could talk for hours and not be overheard. *If she wants to.* He still had to make that "thank you" call to her. It partly worried him, partly warmed his thoughts as he went on.

He had left his bicycle leaning against the front door. The back wheel caught on two sticks as he tried to mount it. Small sticks cut from a blackthorn bush, but big enough to risk a puncture if he rode over them. *Now where did they come from?* He threw the sticks into the hedge.

Nearing the gate he saw a patch of turned earth in the flowerbed under the trees. The weeding had been done around only one plant. In fact the plant itself looked new, like it had been set in in a gap between the existing flowers. *Vera making her mark*. He rather liked its tall stem of blue flowers.

He cycled on, happy that Vera had settled into their new home. On impulse he detoured up Mount Street, just to make sure that the men foot patrol were where they should be.

Edward Adair appeared out of Hill Street and nearly ran into him.

'My apologies, Mr. Barlow, but one is running a trifle late.'

Edward was back to wearing his worn-out army greatcoat. His face sprouted a day's bristles and a sucked peppermint barely concealed the smell of stale drink.

Barlow stared at Edward in disappointment. 'You're drinking again and I suppose you're back to living in that shack under Curles Bridge.'

Edward looked annoyed, like he had been accused of something unsavory. 'Weekends only, old boy. From Monday am to Friday teatime, one is otherwise engaged in commerce.'

He made "commerce" sound like a bad word.

Edward had started life as the heir apparent to the Adair estate, had gone to war both bankrupt and expecting to die a gentleman in the service of the King. Instead he returned as an honored war hero and was now the town drunk living in a wooden hut under Curles Bridge.

Edward's only sibling, his sister Grace, had gone to Australia rather than face the sniggers at the Adair family's downfall. Recently she had returned on a brief visit, wanting to see her hometown one last time before she died of cancer. Barlow had Edward barred from every public house in the town to keep him sober during her stay. He had also talked Captain Denton, who owned his commission and, indirectly, his fortune to Edward, into listing Edward as a director in one of his companies.

Somehow the non-job with Captain Denton had become a permanent post.

'What about Mrs. Anderson?' Barlow asked. Meaning how was she coping with a man reluctantly drying out five days a week.

The Adair nose rose haughtily at Barlow's implied criticism. 'On this occasion, weekend liberty has been restricted. One has a meeting of the Church Lads Brigade that one must attend.' Edward made a play of looking at his watch. 'Time is of the essence. Due to unforeseen circumstances one is running late. The good lady will be getting anxious.'

Barlow let Edward go on. At that point he had enough problems of his own without getting involved in Edward's complicated lifestyle.

Chapter 16

Back at the station Barlow discovered that DI Harvey had gone for the day. *Now there's a blessing.* He popped into the detectives' office where bags of "Evidence" crowded the desks and stray fingerprint powder stained surfaces and paperwork. Barlow decided it safer to stand near the door rather than risk his uniform being contaminated.

DS Leary was sitting at his desk, staring glassy-eyed at the new mess in his office. He looked up when Barlow appeared. 'If you've another suspicious death, hide the body until the middle of next week.' Normally Leary was abrasively arrogant with the Uniform Branch – as they were with him.

Rather than show sympathy Barlow asked, 'Is there anything I should know?'

'Yeah, your boy scout isn't that good. He was too busy chasing sweetie papers to see the real McCoy.' Leary pushed a well-dusted baked bean tin towards Barlow. 'I found this shoved down a rabbit hole.'

The tin looked fresh, the label unstained by weather. Rather than get fingerprint powder on his hands Barlow leaned forward and looked into the tin. He saw the butts of cigarettes. Some of the ends were stained with lipstick. Not all the same shade of red, he noted.

Leary said, 'Get closer, have a good sniff.'

Barlow did as he was told, though he was already getting the smell of tobacco and… He remembered standing, watching the glow-worm effect of cigarettes being handed from hand to hand. He took a guess though he had never smelled it before. 'Is that hashish?'

'It is, so you know what that means?'

Barlow pretended to ponder before answering. 'Harvey will raid every Chinese laundry in the area looking for opium dens.'

'Organized drugs are here.' Now Leary looked like he could cry. 'Not just the occasional gabshite coming back from London with a few in his luggage, but a man who's going to sell them to your kids and mine.'

'Then we get him, lock him up and throw away the key,' said Barlow suddenly worried for Vera and he kept on worrying as Leary updated him on the case.

The police doctor had officially declared Mrs. Cosgrave dead and had provisionally estimated death somewhere between 24 and 36 hours before they'd found the body. Somewhere between Friday night and Saturday mid-day.

From an initial examination he thought that the lady had fallen into the fireplace, striking the back of her head against the fire-irons, with fatal results.

'So a clear case of accidental death?' prodded Barlow looking for Leary's opinion.

'The doctor wouldn't say, not without a post-mortem.'

Leary made up a bundle of initial reports and statements for Barlow to take with him. 'Have a good look around yourself and then we'll discuss it.'

Barlow nodded and went on. Leary was holding back on details but no way would he lower himself to ask. One thing he did know, Leary didn't agree with Harvey's quick assessment of an accidental death. Or at least, like Barlow, the old police instinct of "everything too neat" had kicked in.

Barlow told Wilson and WPC Day to follow him up to the house. What he really needed was time in that house on his own. Something he couldn't do, didn't dare do in case there was money lying around or should have been lying around. Harvey was quick to blame him if there was a question of money having gone missing. A feeling of something not quite right in the house was tugging his memory.

He told the young officers to finish their lunch and then follow him up. He needed a few minutes of privacy because on the road up to the house, and well out of sight of the police station, was a public telephone box. He could ring Louise from there.

Chapter 17

Louise didn't answer her telephone although Barlow let it ring twenty times and then another two for luck. *Is she out or is she avoiding me?* He found Frank Wilson's crumbling relationship with Eleanor Packenham eating at his own confidence. *I'll be nobody's bit on the side.* At the same time, part of him was willing to exchange pride for Louise's company. *Bloody women!*

Mrs. Cosgrave's house was locked and the windows secured. With Barlow's arrival, faces that first showed behind drawn curtains appeared in doorways and exchanged opinions with their neighbors. Barlow let himself be drawn into conversation while he waited for the young officers to arrive.

'It's a terrible thing,' he agreed. 'A decent woman like that lying dead and no one knowing.'

'Kept herself to herself,' said an old gossip.

'Too good for the likes of us,' said one less charitable woman.

'It's bad luck to speak ill of the dead,' said the first gossip.

'Huh! Her and her airs and graces. The best of them drowned, and him thieving at the time.'

'You don't say,' said Barlow.

'Before your time, Sergeant. You wouldn't have been more than a nipper yourself when it happened.'

The arrival of Wilson and WPC Day saved Barlow from having to answer. With them on his heel he let himself into the house.

He told WPC Day, 'Have a look around upstairs. Let me know if there is anything I should look at.'

Wilson was instructed to stay with him. A woman like Mrs. Cosgrave would have something put by to bury her. Probably cash. Leary and his man hadn't found it so it had to be well hidden. In those circumstances it was better to have two men as witnesses for each other.

Wilson dogged Barlow's heels into the living room. At least the body had gone, carted off to the hospital. The mantelpiece and surrounds, in fact every surface that could take it was now stained with fingerprint powder. Wilson stood looking around, curious yet tense.

'Is this the first time you've been in the house?' Barlow asked him.

'It is. Acting Sergeant Gillespie told me to go talk to the neighbors.'

Barlow nodded approval at that. Gillespie had got the young officers offside while he dealt with the body itself. He made a sweeping gesture. 'Starting here, look for things.'

At least Wilson didn't ask what to look for, Barlow noted with satisfaction. He himself didn't know what he was looking for but he'd know when he found it.

The body had gone, the fire irons bagged and taken for forensic examination. Blood stained the hearth, *but not much.* Either the woman's heart had given out with the shock or the brain had bled internally.

Wilson checked cushions and delved down the sides of the chairs. Flicked through library books and that week's *Woman* magazine. Barlow stood in the center of the room and watched Wilson work while he tried to force his brain to tell him what he'd missed that first visit. He kept his hands firmly behind his back rather than risk distracting his thoughts by lifting things up.

A brass ashtray sat on a ledge at the hearth. Its base was grey from stubbed out cigarettes but no cigarette butts or tobacco ash remained in it.

He asked Wilson, 'Have you come across any cigarettes or a box of matches?'

'No.'

He supposed they could be in Mrs. Cosgrave's apron pocket. They'd look for that in the kitchen. And even if the woman didn't smoke herself, people always kept an ashtray for visitors.

All the same, he remembered Leary having to tell him to lean closer to the bean tin to get the smell of drugs. He bent over the brass ashtray, sniffed and got the same smell of hashish.

'This town is going to the dogs.'

'Celtic or Dunmore?' asked Wilson, risking a joke by mentioning the North's two leading greyhound tracks.

'The dog pound, where you'll be if I hear another crack out of you.'

Wilson wisely kept his head down and tried the drawers in the sideboard. Needles, bits of wool and knitting patterns bulged out of the first one.

Barlow said, 'Empty every drawer out. People hide things in the daftest places.'

He noted that the ashtray had been dusted for fingerprints but no prints showed. Yet the ashtray looked as if ash and butts had been thrown out and the base rough cleaned.

Now alert to what he was looking for he ran his eye along the hearth and over worktops and the edges of shelves. Large areas were stained by black fingerprint powder but surprising stretches showed no fingerprints. Either Mrs. Cosgrave was in the middle of cleaning when she tripped and died – *late at night, near midnight?* – or someone had been trying to destroy all traces of their visit.

'Sergeant.'

Wilson was holding a book out for Barlow to see. 'I found this at the bottom of the drawer. Sort of hidden under a pile of envelopes.'

Barlow growled his answer, 'I'm not surprised,' rather than show his sudden unease.

The book was *The Superstitions of Witchcraft* by Howard Williams.

'Carry on,' he told Wilson and tried to get back to his musing about what could have happened to Mrs. Carberry and when. It was almost a relief when WPC Day shouted from upstairs, 'Sergeant, would you mind having a look?'

He took the stairs two at a time and peeked into the spare bedrooms and the bathroom before he joined WPC Day in the front bedroom. The main bedroom walls were bare of photographs and paintings. The wallpaper was ancient and water stained where a tile on the roof had slipped during a storm. The bed sagged in the middle, the springs creaked when Barlow pressed down hard on the bedclothes. The bedclothes themselves were layers of old blankets worn down to near useless.

Barlow shook his head in despair. The rest of the upstairs rooms were like that, yet downstairs everything was fresh and comfortable. Obviously the generosity of the son – the late Deputy Commander – had only extended to the parts of the house that visitors saw. Or more likely the old woman refused to let him spend the money. He didn't have to look in the kitchen cupboards to know that they held little more than a loaf of bread and butter, eggs, bacon and sprouting potatoes.

Pride's a funny thing, thought Barlow, and turned his attention on WPC Day who was standing at a dressing table with the middle drawer partly open.

'So you found something you didn't like?' he asked.

She pointed at the drawer. 'Don't touch, just have a look.'

The drawer was stuffed with washed-out underwear.

'And?' he asked.

She said, 'DS Leary was called away before he had time to do more up here than check for fingerprints in the bathroom.'

'And,' he asked again.

'I'll swear someone's been through these drawers.'

'Mrs. Cosgrave looking for something?' He was playing the devil's advocate, trying to shake her conviction.

'No, Papa Bear, it's the same in every drawer and the clothes in the wardrobe are pushed to one side.'

She called him "Papa Bear" when she was in an especially good mood. Like now when she felt she'd come across something important.

She pointed to the wardrobe. 'There's a box-file of papers in there. One of those cardboard things with hanging folders.'

'You think someone's been at it?'

'The way the folders are hanging, yes. I didn't touch it.'

'Good girl.'

He had a good look at the box of hanging folders. The hook on one folder overlapped its neighbor. Barlow used his pen to push the folder open. It was empty. *Now what would that have held?*

Rather than contaminate what was now a definite crime scene, they went downstairs.

Barlow found Wilson staring at the ashes in the grate.

'I was wondering, Sarge.'

'Aye.'

'A woman like Mrs. Cosgrave always has enough money put-by to bury them.'

'True.'

'And they usually put it somewhere safe like a tea caddy or stuffed behind their good crockery.'

Barlow knew what he meant. People wanted their "burial money" easily found if anything should happen to them. No one wanted the dishonor of going to a pauper's grave because it was too well hidden.

Wilson pointed to the remains of the coal fire. On top of the cinders lay the incinerated remains of what could have been a crumpled up envelope.

Pure instinct for trouble, that's what the three of them were going on. The sort of thing that made a good policeman. Gillespie had it. Now Wilson and WPC Day were displaying it as well.

I've got a great team.

Chapter 18

Barlow ordered the crime scene, the house in Balmoral Avenue, closed and sealed until Leary and his men had time to go over it in detail. He left Wilson on guard at the front door, with a curious neighbor offering him a cup of tea in exchange for information.

With nothing effective to do, Barlow went back to the station. WPC Day went with him so he couldn't use the public phone to call Louise. He tried to think of an excuse to send Day on ahead without arousing her curiosity, and couldn't think of any. The woman was naturally nosey, which right then he thought a disadvantage.

Back at the station he had a word with Leary. Leary like him was uneasy at things as they stood. Unfortunately the only solid – if they could call it that – thing they had to go on was the mysterious absence of fingerprints. Leary, like Barlow, had also noted no cup or mug lying on the draining board in the kitchen. People living on their own tended to rinse a cup and leave it handy for the next time.

Mrs. Cosgrave's only surviving child, the Deputy Commander, was dead. Barlow had a vague memory that the Deputy Commander's only child, a girl, still lived in London. He rang New Scotland Yard and got speaking to a sergeant there, a Yorkshire man from Hartlepool. They talked of fishing and flies and shaded pools with clear running water. The sergeant knew vaguely of the Deputy Commander and of his untimely death from cancer. He had no knowledge of the daughter but would try and get a message to her through Personnel.

He spent the rest of his shift at the kitchen table catching up on paperwork – and in wondering what to say to Louise.

WPC Day appeared to make tea for the Enquiry Office staff.

'Acting Sergeant Gillespie sent a man to relive Frank at

Balmoral Avenue,' she informed Barlow.

'What did you say Woman Police Constable Day?' ask Barlow.

'Sorry, sorry, Constable Wilson has been relieved at Balmoral Avenue and is now back in the station.'

'Thank you, Constable.'

It seemed a petty victory over an underling and Barlow knew he wasn't changing with the times. Off duty, officers could call each other whatever they wanted. But in the station surnames were to be used at all times.

WPC Day had flushed prettily and not because of the correction, Barlow realized. A few months back Barlow had caught her and her beau in a compromising embrace in a car under Curles Bridge. The boyfriend claimed that he and Susan Day had just become engaged to be married. Overwhelmed by the excitement of the proposal and acceptance they had been carried away by their love for each other. Not that Barlow believed a word the boyfriend, a second-hand car salesman, said but Susan had finally got her ring. Barlow wasn't the least surprised when the boyfriend left for England and wrote from there breaking the whole thing off.

Now Susan Day, one of his broken hearts, had a notion of his other broken heart, Frank Wilson.

'We're a police station, not a lonely hearts club' he told her and went back to his paperwork.

It was well after eight before he finished giving the incoming Duty Sergeant an update, then he got on his bike and pedaled up through the town to the call box at the top of Warden Street.

The five-road junction was quiet, the Sunday evening service in the Catholic Church safely over and the church doors closed for the night. *Thank the Lord, no Holy Marys.*

He again stacked his pennies on top of the coin box and dialed a number now etched into his brain. Louise answered on the second ring.

‘It’s me,’ he said.

‘And this is me,’ she said.

He wanted to say “Bitch” but it was too early in their relationship for that. ‘It’s John,’ he said, his voice pitched higher than normal.

She said, ‘Thank you for last night.’ Then she paused a breath before adding. ‘The prawns were absolutely delicious.’

He said, ‘For me it was the relief of not getting a Turkish delight.’

Now they were laughing at themselves and each other. The little pile of pennies rapidly disappeared into the coin-box. On the last penny, without giving any gruesome details, he told her about the body being found in the haystack. He needed her to put names to as many of the local devil worshippers as she could.

Chapter 19

Birds chittering on the tree outside his window woke Barlow early the next morning, Monday the fifteenth of August and Hibernian Man's Day. He lay stretched diagonally across the bed, hands behind his head and enjoyed the stillness of the town before Ballymena's version of the rush-hour started. Times like this he could imagine Geordie Dunlop and his ne'er-do-well family taking time off from thinking up trouble. DI Harvey's ambition was to have all the Dunlops in jail at the one time. Harvey reckoned that if – or as Harvey himself put it – when he achieved that goal, crime in the area would drop by at least fifty percent. A guaranteed career making result.

In a way Barlow wished Harvey success. Then the town would be shot of the man's running interference and they could get back to regular policing. The current spate of murders might even stop.

Gradually that day's problems worked their way into his consciousness. Rather than spoil the pleasure of the lie-in, he went downstairs and made his breakfast while the emersion warmed the water for his shower. The emersion, to his relief, had a mechanical timer. He had a horror of it being left on all day with a resulting big bill from the Electricity Board.

He took Vera up a cup of tea. She was due back at Woolworths for nine o'clock.

'Dad, it's the middle of the night.'

'It's nearly half seven.'

'That's what I mean.'

He left her, head and all curled in under the blankets, and went on. On his way to the station he passed a milkman from Fetherton's dairy. The man wore a black armband so the news was out that their boss was dead.

The Hibernian Parade wasn't due to start until ten-thirty,

which gave him time to do some work on the Cosgrave case. Among the "documents" collected by DS Leary was Mrs. Cosgrave's prescription tablets for blood pressure. If evidence of foul play was found at the post-mortem then the tablets might have to be examined for signs of being tampered with. The label on the bottles gave the name of the issuing chemist, Alex McCoy of Ballymoney Street. Barlow phoned Alex who told him that Dr. Ingram was Mrs. Cosgrave's GP.

Barlow picked up his cap and was on his way out the door when the phone rang. Wilson answered the call, then he put his hand over the receiver and called after Barlow, 'Sarge, it's Mrs. Cosgrave's granddaughter.'

Not a call he wanted to take but that's what he was paid to do.

He went back and took the receiver off Wilson. 'Station Sergeant Barlow speaking,' he said.

A woman's voice, with a southern English accent replied. 'This is Mary Jo Cosgrave, Mrs. Cosgrave's granddaughter. I believe that granny is dead? Was it a heart attack?'

Mary Jo Cosgrave didn't sound particularly upset. There was no reason for her to. With living in England much of her life she could hardly have known the woman. All the same there was an impersonalness about the tone that cut off Barlow's words of sympathy.

He said, 'We'll know better after the autopsy, but Mrs. Cosgrave appears to have fallen and hit her head on the fire irons.'

'Did she suffer?' Now there was an edge of concern in the voice.

'No, the lady never recovered consciousness.'

Mary Jo talked on about how she hated her granny living on her own in case something like this happened. The old lady refused to even consider going into Wilson House, the retirement home near Broughshane. Refused to have a telephone installed in case of an emergency. Stubborn on principle, was the impression Barlow got from Mary Jo's rush of memories. Maybe even a little regret that she hadn't done more for her granny.

Finally Mary Jo said that she'd be on that afternoon's BEA flight into Nutts Corner. That she had a key to Balmoral Avenue and would stay there once Forensics had done their work. They exchanged a few pleasantries before Barlow was finally able to hang up and head to Dr. Ingram's surgery.

Chapter 20

Dr. Ingram and his family lived in a sprawling old town house set in its own garden. The waiting room had originally been the sitting room and the dining room was now the consultation room.

The waiting room was a large square room with a gas fire set in a dark marble fireplace. Two large sash windows overlooked the street. Blinds half-drawn against the morning sun made the room dull and colourless. Patients waiting to see Dr. Ingram sat on wooden chairs set around the wall. Heart attack or sore finger they saw Dr. Ingram in the order of their arrival at the surgery.

The buzz of talk in the waiting room ceased with Barlow's arrival. That day about a dozen people waited to see Dr. Ingram. A handful of workers looking for sick notes; Barlow was almost surprised not to find Gillespie among them. Mostly old ladies and worried parents with children. The old ladies sat close together, two small groups of them, separated by one chair.

Dr. Ingram's brother, Keith, came in the door. He held it open for an old lady following close behind. She shuffled in, leaning on a stick. The old lady looked at Barlow almost guiltily and sat quickly with her friends. He was used to that reaction when people unexpectedly came upon him in uniform. *She probably put a washer in the gas meter when she was short of change.*

Another old lady asked her, 'How's the hip now?'

'Much better.' Having put down her stick she picked it up again. 'In fact I'll not bother waiting for the doctor.' She gave Keith a smile and left.

Keith nodded to her and then to Barlow and took what was apparently his seat between the two groups of ladies.

'I didn't expect to see you here?' Barlow asked Keith, looking for information.

Keith gave a wheezy cough. He looked tired and strained.

'This time of year, anything to do with farms or gardens kills me.'

'And your brother makes you queue with the rest?'

'It puts in the time when you're retired.'

Barlow took a seat near the door into the consultation room. The door opened and a patient came out. A mother fussed her school-age child off a seat, obviously she was next in line to go in. The child looked more malingering than ill.

Barlow stood up. 'If you don't mind, missis, this is police business.'

Without waiting for a reply he walked into the consultation room and sat down on the chair beside Dr. Ingram's desk. The room was long and narrow. The walls were covered with photographs of children: boys on one side, girls on the other. Many of the photographs had faded with age.

Dr. Ingram said, 'Well, Young Barlow, I can guess what you're here about.' He sounded sad as he indicated the photographs. 'I brought all these into the world and I've buried a good number.'

'You've been at it a long time, Doctor.'

Maybe too long for his own good, Barlow thought. One of Dr. Ingram's grandsons was already at medical school. Hopefully, the young man would join the practice and spell the old doctor from the long hours he insisted on working.

Dr. Ingram got up and fetched two A5 folders from a cabinet: one bulging with papers, one thin. He opened the thin folder first and pulled out three sheets of paper. 'I see you're never out of this place,' he told Barlow.

'I'm not here about me.'

He was ignored as Dr. Ingram held the base of his stethoscope against the palm of his hand to warm it. 'In the past year you've been stabbed and shot, you've been blown up and you've inhaled enough smoke to kill half the patients waiting outside.' He tried to look fierce but only came over as a favorite uncle. 'Jacket off, shirt up. I'm checking your lungs, blood pressure and urine. After that I'll tell you about Mrs. Cosgrave.'

Doctor Ingram had treated the young Barlow for free when he was a runaway from the Workhouse and before the formation of the National Health Service. Vera's photograph was somewhere up on the wall with all the other children he'd delivered at the Cottage Hospital. He had also spent long hours counselling Maggie with her mental health problems.

'You're a terrible man,' Barlow said, but did as he was told.

Chapter 21

Certified fit for duty if not stress free, Barlow tucked his shirt into his trousers and sat down again.

Doctor Ingram perched his reading glasses on the edge of his nose. He picked up the folder with Mrs. Cosgrave's name on it but didn't have to open the file to tell what was needed.

'Mrs. Mary Elizabeth Cosgrave née Carouth. She had mild if chronic bronchitis of the right lung, blood pressure, intermittent tinnitus and early stages of Alzheimer's.'

'Treatment?' asked Barlow.

'Tablets for the blood pressure, antibiotics when the bronchitis flared up and a bit of understanding for the Alzheimer's.'

Barlow had only a vague understanding of Alzheimer's disease. He knew that people with it could remember what they'd got for their third birthday but not what they'd had for breakfast that day.

He said, 'They forget things, like eating properly, and being argumentative.'

'Very much so,' said the doctor, looking pointedly at the clock.

'I'm grateful for your time,' said Barlow standing up. He made as if to go to the door then turned back as if something had just occurred to him. 'Anna Coulter, Arthur Somerton's sister?'

The doctor became cagey. There was no offer to pull out her folder.

Barlow said, 'I understand she's a bit nervy.'

'She's a fine woman,' said the doctor.

'I didn't say she wasn't,' said Barlow, noting the change in tone to defensive. 'But we'll have to interview her.'

Doctor Ingram relaxed and smiled. 'I trust you, Barlow. Just be your reputedly ignorant self, but take a woman constable along with you.'

'I'll do that,' said Barlow and let himself out.

All the way back to the station he wondered what Dr. Ingram was trying to hide from him.

I'll get it out of the old man yet, see if I don't.

Chapter 22

Barlow arrived back at the station in time to see Gillespie and a handful of constables preparing to set off for the Hibernian parade.

'You escort them, you don't march with them,' Barlow warned Gillespie.

'Right into the river if I'd half a chance,' said Gillespie looking sour. Then he swung a bundle of papers Barlow's way. 'Sign those and I'll get them off before we leave.'

'Sign what?' asked Barlow flicking through a sheaf of forms.

'Just be grateful I saved you the bother,' said Gillespie producing a pen, a Parker biro.

Barlow signed without checking the forms. They were all routine reports and he could trust Gillespie to tell a good story. The man was a better bluffer than he was. All the inspectors and above, right up to the Chief Constable himself, thought Gillespie wonderful, a model officer destined for higher things.

'If you'd do the promotion exams,' said Barlow, finishing his thoughts out loud.

'What, with the grouse season barely started?' Gillespie looked horrified.

Barlow poked him in the chest to make his point. 'The next time I see Wilson and WPC Day studying and you not there, you'll be on foot-patrol for a week.'

Right then the front door slammed open and a tall man with plenty of fat-enhanced muscle stormed into the Enquiry Office.

The man pointed at Barlow. 'You, come with me,' then he ploughed through the rank of waiting constables and stalked down the corridor leading to the back of the building.

The constables reformed rank and disappeared out the front door as fast as they could. Gillespie hitched his gun belt comfortable and was right on their heels, a smirk on his face.

Barlow had barely started down the corridor after the angry man, when he had a thought. He went back and told the Duty Constable. 'Ring the Telephone Exchange and tell the girls that I want my house phone reconnected.'

The constable grabbed a pencil and a piece of paper. 'What's the number, Sergeant?'

'Use your initiative,' said Barlow who hadn't a clue what the number was.

He walked on quickly because he could hear Captain Charles Denton, Managing Director and owner of the Ballymena Brewing Company and Chairman of the Local Policing Board roaring, 'Harvey, you're an idiot.'

Barlow was barely in Harvey's door when Denton turned on him. 'You too, you should have known better.'

Harvey was on his feet, trying not to wring his hands. 'What's wrong? What have I done?'

Denton roared, 'You arrested the Dunlops. What the hell were you thinking of?'

'They were robbing...'

'They do that every August, dammit!'

Harvey went grey around the jawbone.

'Every August,' roared the Chairman. 'And while you were charging the young bucks, the rest of the family broke in and stole a lorry load of whiskey.'

The Chairman was almost dancing with rage. Harvey's grey started to look bilious.

Barlow was tempted to fold his arms and rest a shoulder against the doorpost while Denton shredded Harvey's pride. Instead he found himself explaining to Harvey, 'Sir, it's an understanding between Captain Denton here and the Dunlops. He allows the Dunlops take what drink they need for Connie's birthday party. She's their grandmother. That way they leave the brewery alone for the rest of the year and they make sure all the other hoods do the same.'

Denton snapped, 'Barlow you should have told Harvey this.'

Maybe I should have, Barlow thought. He was quite sure that some of the older constables would have tried to talk Harvey out of the arrests, but Harvey wasn't a man to listen to advice.

Denton jabbed his face hard against Harvey's. 'Don't forget, Harvey, you're promotion to District Inspector hasn't been confirmed yet. Another cock-up like this...' He bulled past Barlow and disappeared up the corridor, still growling his fury.

Barlow and Harvey stood looking at each other. Harvey was shaking. Barlow wasn't too calm himself. In over forty years he'd never seen Charlie Denton is such a rage.

Harvey's voice trembled as he asked, 'Why doesn't he just give the drink to the Dunlops?'

'Sir, have you ever seen Geordie Dunlop or any of his lot doing things the easy way?'

At that Barlow left, giving Harvey privacy while he rebuilt his rancor and pride.

He had barely taken a step towards the kitchen and much needed cup of tea when he heard Inspector Foxwood call, 'Barlow, a minute please.'

Foxwood's door was ajar. Barlow went in and found himself waived into a chair. Foxwood's face was carefully bland. If he had heard the confrontation next door, and he could hardly not have, he wasn't letting on.

The posters on the wall behind Foxwood had changed. The regulations regarding the pulling of ragweed, the sort of information needed by a city trained officer now transferred to the country, had been replaced by ones dealing with prohibited drugs.

Barlow nodded at the new posters. 'I'd hoped never to need those.'

Foxwood nodded in agreement. 'The idiots that take them say they're recreational.'

'So's Russian roulette.'

They discussed the possibility of a regular supply of drugs

coming into the town. They were going more on rumors than hard facts. Barlow was careful to not even hint at devil worshippers sharing round cigarettes laced with hashish.

Foxwood said, 'They're getting into the North via the postal service.'

He said this with such authority that Barlow asked, 'Are they?' to encourage him on.

'You're not to say but, as I presume you know, Post Office parcels destined for the Province are sent by ferry from Liverpool to Belfast. Recently, a trailer-load of parcels was left on the quayside to be collected by the Post Office. They got caught in a downpour before the van arrived. One of the packages disintegrated and out poured a rather nasty selection of drugs.'

'And the delivery address led the Belfast boys to…'

'Nowhere. The ink had run, the address was completely illegible.'

'That's bad luck.' Not that Barlow was surprised. If there'd been an arrest like that news of it would have been around the stations like a dose of Andrews Liver Salts.

'Which gets us on to something more or less related,' said Foxwood. He eyed the papers in front of him instead of looking at Barlow. 'The body in the haystack. We've made a positive identification from his dental records.'

'And?'

'It was as you thought, Ezekiel Fetherton.'

Foxwood's tone was so casual that Barlow went straight on guard.

Chapter 23

Inspector Foxwood continued not to look at Barlow. He made a play of flicking through the file in front of him. 'We're still waiting for the pathologists' report of course, but in the meantime we're treating Fetherton's death as a case where foul play is suspected.' Finally he looked up at Barlow, seeking a reply.

Foxwood was trying too hard to appear chatty, talking colleague to colleague. Barlow chose his words carefully. 'Normal procedure.'

'It's the stab wound,' continued Foxwood. 'Given Fetherton's current problems, if the knife had been driven straight into the throat or a sliced jugular, the chances are it would be suicide.' He made a fist and pretended to stab himself in the neck. 'The angle of entry was all wrong.'

Barlow frowned as if that thought hadn't occurred to him, and was careful to neither nod nor shake his head.

'So you see, it's murder,' said Foxwood.

'I see what you're saying, sir.' Barlow kept his head up, eyes facing to the front. He focused his gaze on the posters about drugs coming into the Province. In his innocence, he had believed there were only two drugs to worry about: hashish and cocaine. The posters gave a list of drugs he'd barely heard of.

Foxwood's voice became even more false-casual. 'So now it's the old routine: who he was with, when he was last seen and by whom. We want to eliminate his relations, his friends, anyone he's had a run-in with recently.' He kept looking at Barlow expectantly. 'With Fetherton being the mayor of Ballymena there'll be a lot of publicity attached to the case. And even more criticism of the police if we don't get a result soon.'

Barlow felt that he had to appear helpful. 'It seems a bit funny, Leary finding that tin of cigarette butts close to the body.'

Foxwood nodded, clearly anxious to keep on Barlow's

good side by agreeing with him. 'It's something we're looking into. There's different lipsticks on the butts and with Fetherton being naked we have to assume there was some sort of shenanigans…' He paused, like he'd heard the word "shenanigans" but had never before used it himself.

'You're getting the local lingo, sir.'

'Yes.' Foxwood didn't seem enamored with that thought.

'And you were saying something about Mr. Fetherton's business being in trouble?'

'Apparently the bank wants his overdraft cleared. In fact they told him to take his business elsewhere.'

Which didn't surprise Barlow. Not only had Fetherton been caught watering down milk going to schools, there was also the suspicion that he had been responsible for the theft of cattle from several farms. Farms belonging to fellow members of the City Club, as did the bank manager.

'Anyway,' said Foxwood, fighting off Barlow's attempt at changing the subject. He poised his pen over a fresh sheet of paper. 'As I was saying, we're checking the alibis of everyone associated with Mr. Fetherton.' He wrote "Station Sergeant John Barlow" at the top of the page. 'To start with, Sergeant, you were off duty from eight o'clock on Friday night until eight o'clock yesterday, Sunday, morning.'

Rather than reply Barlow stared hard at Foxwood.

Foxwood said the words as he wrote them down. "I left the station about eight-thirty on the evening of Friday the twelfth and went…' He looked at Barlow expectantly.

'Why do you need an account of my movements?' asked Barlow.

'Mr. Fetherton was an important man locally, being mayor and all that.' Foxwood kept his pen hovering over the page. 'We need to be seen to be doing things correctly and with your history with Mr. Fetherton…'

'What history?'

'The confrontations.'

'I'm not with you, sir. It was the previous District Inspector, may he rest in peace, who charged Fetherton with watering down the milk, causing an outbreak of gastroenteritis among the school children. I only did the paperwork. As for the cattle, I didn't accuse him of stealing them. It was Captain Denton who did that, right in front of all of their friends in the club. I just happened to be there at the time.'

'And the stolen money?' asked Foxwood, tight lipped.

'I recovered the wallet but so far as Fetherton was concerned only myself or the pickpocket could have taken that money. The man wasn't to know his wife had been at the wallet before he left the house.'

'It nearly cost you your job.'

'So Mr. Fetherton made a mistake.' Barlow shook his head in sorrow. 'An apology would have been nice, but…' He shrugged.

Foxwood slammed the pen down. 'Barlow I know you of old.' He leaned forward, trying to intimidate by physical nearness. 'I want to know, minute by minute, what you were doing between Friday evening and Sunday morning.'

'And I'm not telling you,' said Barlow.

'I have a right….'

'You have no right. The rules say I don't have to tell you anything until I'm charged, if even then. He stood up. 'And I resent being considered a suspect.'

He slammed his way out the door.

Chapter 24

I'm not furious, more annoyed, Barlow had to admit to himself at Foxwood's questions. In the circumstances it was fair enough of the man to make sure a subordinate was not implicated in a suspicious death. Especially as bad blood between the two men was well known.

Even more annoying to Barlow was the mistake he had made during the interview. He hadn't asked where Mrs. Fetherton had been on Friday night – because if anyone knew where her husband was and what he was up to, she should. Barlow realized that he hadn't asked because he already knew. The omission of that question would register with Foxwood eventually.

What now? He needed to keep out of Harvey's way for as long as possible. *Attend Mrs. Cosgrave's autopsy*? DS Leary had delegated a detective constable to be present at both hers and Fetherton's, *so not that.* Leaving the station to check on foot patrols would look like he was trying to avoid his superiors, *exactly what it would be.* He had no reason to be in court, the Hibernian parade probably had more police covering it than actual marchers and the last thing he wanted was another body turning up, requiring his attention.

Bollocks!

He checked his watch. *Barely past tea-break time.* He had to talk to Louise, the grass at home was overdue a cut and, even more, he needed a chance to get things straight in his head. He scooped up his hat from the cupboard in the Enquiry Office and stalked out. He was gone and *Harvey can thole it.*

His determination lasted until he got off the bike at Louise's house. He stood looking at it, his heart fluttering with uncertainty. It was a big red brick house. Louise lived on the ground floor: the upper story had been converted into two self-contained flats. Both let to bank clerks, whose managers would have them posted if they misbehaved.

Placed sideways, Barlow's bungalow and garden would have fitted into Louise's drive and front lawn. Her car stood at the front door so the chances were she was at home.

Barlow parked his bike against the wall of the house and drew breath while he thought things through. He needed information off Louise but he couldn't go at it bluntly the way he did with ordinary people. Louise meant something to him that he couldn't put into words. With her he had a feeling of completeness; something he had never felt before.

He rang the bell. Saw her shadow through the inner stained-glass door as she came up the hallway. The motif on the glass was unusual. It looked like three bishops' mitres run together in a Celtic design. Each miter was a different color: red, green and blue. The edging of the glass was unusual as well, runs of black and white, where he'd have expected something more cheerful.

How Louise greeted his unannounced arrival meant a lot to him. And what should he do? Shake her hand? Kiss her? *Certainly not!* Say something casual "I was passing", *an obvious lie.* "Any chance of a cuppa?" Not when he hadn't been in the house before.

The door opened and Louise stood there. She was wearing a blue silk dress that caught her curves without clinging. The enquiring lift of her eyebrows changed instantly to a smile. 'John, how lovely.'

Her pleasure at his unexpected arrival dispelled his doubts. Whatever words he'd intended to say left him.

'Is it all right, you don't have visitors or anything?'

'If I had I could always slip you in by the back door.'

Why do I keep wanting to call her "bitch"?

She stood back and he walked in. She closed the door, with her eyes on him not on the road, looking to see who might have spotted his arrival. Somehow it seemed right to hold her loosely by the waist and share that impossible kiss. They broke hold by mutual consent when things threatened to get out of hand.

He found himself looking around the hallway. Up until

recently he'd never had a hallway to call his own. Hallways, he had begun to realize, defined a house. This one had wide stairs and an even wider passageway. The sitting room door was ajar and he could see embossed wallpaper, chintz and heavily padded chairs. The chairs held cushions in different pastel colors that should have clashed, but didn't. The whole thing wasn't really Louise but then, if he remembered right, she had inherited the house from an aunt.

'You'll take a cup of tea?' she asked.

He felt he had to be bluntly honest. 'It's not entirely social.'

'No, poor old Ezekiel. What a terrible way to die.'

'Aye.' Even with her he needed to be noncommittal. There was every likelihood that she'd be questioned about what he'd said.

'Did he suffer?' There was anxiety in her voice.

He thought about the way the body had lain, stretched out flat. 'No.'

By then she had taken his hand and was leading him into a small sitting room at the back of the house. French doors led onto a patio that stretched into a lawn ringed with mature shrubs. The room had "Louise" written all over it. Wallpaper painted over in cream. A light blue settee, with pastel yellow and green cushions, set squarely in front of a white marble fireplace. A glass vase held flowers picked from her garden and on the hearth sat a long thin glass jar filled with white and black stones. The stones were oval shaped and smooth. There was a jar and its contents exactly like that in his own sitting room.

He sat on the settee with her. He had to, she still held his hand. It was warm and soft in his. He hoped she'd never let go. He smiled at her and they enjoyed a second lingering kiss. He was afraid she'd think he'd only come for sex and broke kiss first. Put his arm around her. Her head seemed to fit naturally into the angle between his neck and shoulder.

He loved the room, everything in it was used-comfortable. A room friends came to, the sitting room kept "good" for visitors.

There was no sign of glasses or bottles hastily put away and her kisses tasted of lipstick and salty bacon for breakfast. No alcohol, not a hint of it on her breath. He realized that he didn't know her drinking habits, *though it's early enough in the day for that.*

'I get depressed sometimes,' she said as if reading his mind.

He knew what depression was, of life seeming to slip by and no happiness coming from it. *Contentment at best.*

It seemed impossible but what he felt for Louise was love. They'd only met casually over the years, mostly business, and had one date. He let himself daydream of living in this house with her. With his salary she could stop taking in tenants and they would have the whole house to themselves.

'What?' she asked.

He realized he'd been staring at her and that his hand had somehow managed to cup itself around her breast. Hers rested on his hipbone.

'You're a good woman,' he said.

'Now there's a compliment.'

'I hope you're not one of those militant women the girls in the station are turning into?'

'I'm the flag carrier.'

'I thought you might be.'

They sat on in silence.

Something else surprised him. In a few months he had gone from living in a two up-one down mill house to wondering what it would be like to live in "nobs" row. The neighbors might be cautious at first but they'd soon learn that when Station Sergeant Barlow took off his uniform he also took off his authority.

Which brought him back to work and the reason for his visit.

Chapter 25

Barlow sat up straight. He removed his hand from Louise's breast and hers from his hip.

'Business,' he said, all stiff and formal.

Her fingers played with his lips. 'Do you cuddle all the ladies to soften them up before the interrogation starts?'

He nibbled her fingertips. Fought down the urge to take things further. 'Every time.'

Still sitting on the settee, she turned away from him and stretched for a notebook sitting on top of a casual table. He couldn't resist running his hand from shoulder to flank. She didn't stiffen at his touch so she didn't mind. Something she liked, he'd have to remember that.

She sat up. 'Men!' She was smiling as she held the pad between them. 'I thought it would help if I did two lists: one of people I'm sure are still involved, and one for those who might still be.'

He had counted ten or so devil worshippers. In all she had listed twenty names. He took the miniature pencil attached to the pad and ticked the names of the Fethertons.

That leaves eight to identify for sure.

'Well done,' he told her and earned a smile.

Louise had put question marks against one couple.

He pointed to the question marks, 'What are those for.'

'Mrs. Fetherton claims that as far as she knew Ezekiel had gone to the club. Rather than spend the evening on her own she visited the Smythe-Harringtons.'

'Did she now?' he asked rhetorically. He had recognized Mrs. Fetherton as one of the devil worshippers. 'And the Smythe-Harringtons confirm this?'

'When I went round to Fethertons to pay my respects, they were both there organizing the wake. They said that they and Mrs.

Fetherton shared a couple of bottles of wine so, rather than let her drive home, they made her stay the night.'

A good alibi or a conspiracy, he wondered. A good alibi, he reckoned. The Smythe-Harringtons were ex-army, recently moved into the town so they would have no grief against Fetherton.

He put a tick against the Smythe-Harringtons' names.

Four identified, six to go.

Louise said, 'I'm told the Smythe-Harringtons have an extra-wide bed.'

'Who told you that?'

'The husband.'

Now she was looking at him anxiously, afraid her reputation with men would drive him away.

He said, 'It would be a lucky man you set your cap on.'

'I only wear a hat in church.'

She was thinking in terms of marriage and he already had a wife.

She must have seen his hurt, uncertainty at least, because she leaned into him and whispered, 'John, we're both damaged goods.'

He said, 'I survived, you rose above it.'

'That's the nicest thing…' A tear rolled down her cheek.

He brushed the tear away with his thumb. 'I call things as I see them.' At that he got to his feet. 'I must be going or Harvey will have search parties out looking for me.'

And that, he realized, could very well be true.

She came with him to the front door. 'Will I have to make an official statement?'

'Nah, I'll take care of it.'

She said, 'Don't get into any trouble on my behalf. I'll only be embarrassed at what we did, not who I was with.'

Somehow she could see through him, the impenetrable Sergeant Barlow. He liked that, being seen for what he was, not the image he had created to hide hurt and rejection.

Her eyes were still moist as they stood at the front door, unwilling to open it and end something special between them. Their hug became intimate, their goodbye kiss lingered. The dining room, now her bedroom, only a step away.

She was willing but he couldn't take that step. He had to show that she meant more to him than sex.

He broke kiss and grip, used the mirror to set the cap straight on his head. 'Some house this, you don't even get the cup of tea they offer you.'

A hand flew to her mouth. 'Oh my God, I didn't.' Then she swung the door open. 'Out! You're trying to start a row.'

He grabbed a final kiss in passing, *and devil take any nosy neighbor*. She waited on the top step while he settled himself on the bicycle.

'John, you'll come for dinner some night?'

'I'd love that.'

'If it's a good night we can sit out on the patio.'

With the neighbors watching our every move?

He didn't mind if she didn't. He found himself smiling at the comfort of being courted by a good woman.

Chapter 26

Barlow had told Louise not to worry, that he'd sort things out at the station. However he had already put himself in the wrong by not admitting to being at Somerton's farm on the night of the murder. His and Louise's evidence would disprove Mrs. Fetherton's claim that she was elsewhere when her husband was murdered. Which made her the prime suspect.

But Mrs. Fetherton's witnesses were the Smythe-Harringtons, recent blow-ins into the town and not related in any way. He could understand the Smythe-Harringtons being unwilling to admit to prancing around Skyclad, but he couldn't see them concealing Mrs. Fetherton's involvement in a murder.

The murderer, he reckoned, had to be someone under a great emotional strain, maybe a jealous rage? *There were enough male hormones floating about the field that night.* A person that upset wouldn't be fit to clean themselves properly afterwards, let alone scrub the bath pristine. Someone somewhere knew the truth. It was only a matter of knowing where to apply pressure.

All this thinking had got him down the Galgorm Road as far as the railway bridge. Straight on was the police station with a couple of constables just heading out on patrol. Chances were they had instructions to tell him to report straight back to the station. Barlow stuck out his arm to signal a right turn and sped into Waveney Road.

At the junction with the tin bridge he turned into Bridge Street, a route he usually avoided because the climb up Bridge Street, followed by Church Street took the puff out of many younger legs. This time on this route, he hoped to see two men.

He spotted Geordie Dunlop straight away. Geordie was standing at the Bridge Bar, his face flushed and his hands clenched. Always a bad sign. Geordie was an ageing man, whose heavy muscle was turning to fat. Even so, his right fist still finished many an argument.

Barlow stopped the bike and put a foot on the ground for balance. 'You've started early today, or did you stop at all?'

'I never had nothing to do with it.'

'Do with what?'

'Whatever you're accusing me of.'

'Keep drinking like that and you won't be around to be accused of anything.'

Geordie drew a hand across his mouth. 'A good Protestant like Gillespie having to escort those Fenian gits.'

'They're better employed walking down an empty road than getting pissed in a bar.'

'Wankers. Scum like yourself.'

Barlow prepared to move on. 'You served in the same regiment and you drink in the same bar, and they didn't steal the Captain's whiskey.'

'Not my idea,' said Geordie.

'Maybe not, but you're enjoying the benefits.'

He pushed off.

By the time Barlow struggled up the rest of the hill to where Bridge Street became Church Street, it became a choice between a heart attack and loss of pride. He got off the bike and walked as far as Woodside's chemist shop where the road dipped down towards Broadway.

A two-man patrol saw him come and stepped onto the street to block his way.

'Sarge, you're wanted back at the station.'

'Why, has Gillespie started a riot with the Hibernians?'

Not a smile cracked the lips of either man. 'The DI's shouting for you, and he's in one of his moods.'

'I'm on my way,' said Barlow and sensed them watch him, checking the route he took, as he cycled on. Instead of turning down Wellington Street towards the station he went around the roundabout and down Broughshane Street. Being disobedient, disobeying orders and doing a runner gave him a thrill.

Now I know why I have to chase after the wee devils.

Nearing O'Hara's Fruit and Vegetable shop he came across the second man he was looking for, Edward Adair. This time Edward wasn't the town drunk recovering from a night on the tiles. He was Major, the Honorable Edward Adair GC MC, returning from taking the salute at the Hibernian march past.

Barlow parked his bike against a lamppost and guided Edward into O'Hara's entry. 'I'm looking for a bit of your nob knowledge.'

'My dear chap, if I can be of assistance in any way.'

Barlow had a good look at Edward while he hunted out the list of names Louise had given him. Edward looked well, Mrs. Anderson's cooking was putting some weight on the man's bones. Seeing Edward sober and wearing a good suit, fresh white shirt and regimental tie, made Barlow realize why Captain Denton had kept him on the books after his sister had gone back to Australia. The man exuded a quality that Denton could never achieve.

The only downside about Edward was the dark rings under his eyes. Staying dry during the working week couldn't be easy, especially for a man who had drunk day and daily for decades.

Barlow showed Edward the list. 'You've heard about Ezekiel Fetherton?'

'Most unfortunate but, sadly, not one whose demise will be mourned.'

'That attitude makes you another suspect.'

Edward looked concerned. 'Do I take it Sergeant Major that you also…? Oh dear.'

'Oh dear indeed,' said Barlow, ignoring the fact that Edward was still in his wartime military mode. He chose his words carefully while he explained about the list. It would appear… perhaps… it was rumored… devil worship…

'Not devil worship,' Edward corrected him. 'It was a celebration of the Lughnasa festival by which one pays homage to the male aspect of the great She Goddess.'

'Is there anything or anyone you don't know?'

'One has participated in certain events in one's youth.'

'Has one?'

Edward looked at him patiently. 'Sarcasm does not become you, Sergeant Major.'

Barlow passed the list to Edward. 'See if you could tick any other names on that list?'

'And what makes you think that one may be of service in this matter?'

Sometimes Barlow thought he preferred Edward drunk. He said, with a patience he didn't feel, 'Because you take an interest in people. They tell you things they wouldn't tell their granny.'

Edward finally relented. He folded the list and put it carefully in an inner pocket. 'One has one's contacts.'

Barlow knew he should keep a copy of that list, but didn't want anything written down in his official notebook. He trusted Edward not to lose it.

Chapter 27

At the hospital Barlow parked his bicycle against the curving wall of the Nissen hut used by the Pathologist, and went in.

Before he could speak, the nurse at reception smirked and said, 'Go on in, he's expecting you.'

Barlow walked on tempted to ask her if the reported "goings on" at the monthly dance in the Nurses' Home, really did go on.

He gave the Pathologist's door a brief knock and looked in. 'You were expecting me, doc?'

'Doctor, and your Cause of Death will read "Curiosity".'

Barlow sat across the desk from the doctor. The doctor was a tall, lean man. No amount of food could put bulk on his bones. Starvation rations while a prisoner of war of the Japanese had done something to his Thyroid. Those years had also taught him to walk slowly and to think before he spoke.

The doctor patted the files in front of him. 'What do you want to know?'

'Everything – in words of three syllables or less – about with Mrs. Cosgrave.'

He thought it best to start with the case he was on officially.

The doctor said, 'The lady fell and banged her head. Unconsciousness was probably instantaneous. Shock, heart, compressed fracture at the back of the skull with internal bleeding.' He touched what had to be his official report. 'It's all there.'

Barlow pretended a sigh of relief. 'Well that's one off my desk.'

'Except.'

Barlow frowned. 'Doc, I don't like your "excepts".'

'Bruising around the wrists as if someone had grabbed and held them. There is also a fresh bruise on the back of the left leg, just above the ankle.'

The second sigh was involuntary. 'That makes it assault, manslaughter, aggravated burglary.' The list of possibilities was endless.

'Only probably. Another pathologist may disagree with my findings.'

It would be a brave man.

If the Pathologist had a reputation for anything it was exactitude.

Barlow pulled out his notebook. As much to have proof of being busy in the cause of justice than needing notes to keep things fresh in his mind. He wrote down the facts as the doctor had said, then he looked up expectantly.

He said, 'Now that you've examined the body…'

'Would you care to see it?'

'Not before my dinner.' He hoped to be moving into Louisa's social set so he corrected himself. 'My lunch.'

The doctor steepled his fingers. 'You want me to move away from facts into the realms of speculation?'

'You're pretty good at it.'

'Buttering up will get you nowhere.'

All the same the doctor looked to the side. In his mind he saw through the wall into the room where the autopsies were carried out. That way he could again see the bodies laid out in front of him.

'This is pure speculation, Barlow, but there was a row, an argument of some sort. Mrs. Cosgrave lifted her hand, her right hand, to strike, and was stopped by someone grabbing the wrist and holding on tightly. Then the other person grabbed Mrs. Cosgrave's left wrist and held both hands up and away from them. There was a struggle. Whoever it was back-heeled Mrs. Cosgrave to put her off balance. Maybe they intended to push her into a chair, maybe they panicked – the outcome was still the same.'

Barlow nodded, 'That's the way I read it.'

The doctor pretended indignation. 'If you'd said earlier it

could have saved me half an hour in there this morning.'

'But, doc, we need your big words for the Coroner.'

'Doctor,' said the Pathologist. He closed the file and looked expectantly at the door as if Barlow should be away.

Barlow ignored the subtle hint and visibly relaxed in the chair. 'Doc, now I'm here, what can you tell me about Ezekiel Fetherton?'

For the first time the doctor showed real emotion, embarrassment. 'Nothing I'm afraid, Barlow.' He flicked a list attached to a second file. 'Mr. Harvey's specific instructions. The autopsy and anything relating to it can only be discussed with named officers. I'm sorry, but your name is not on that list.'

Chapter 28

Barlow took his time cycling back into town from the hospital. So far as he was concerned he was in no rush to the station and another confrontation with Harvey. *But needs must.* At Broadway he turned down Wellington Street. Given a fair wind and no pedestrians getting in the way, he could freewheel to the bottom of Wellington Street, turn right into Mill Street, left at the Pentagon and on down the Galgorm Road to the station itself without having to touch the pedals.

At the bottom of Wellington Street a young woman stepped out in front of him. He stopped with the front wheel at the toe of her shiny black high-heels.

'Missis, have you any idea how much paperwork a death by suicide involves?'

'I do, Mr. Barlow,' she said.

She had an English accent.

He looked at her puzzled for a moment, then he recognized her. 'Young Mary Jo Cosgrave,' he said.

'Not as young as I was the last time we met.'

The last time they'd met she'd been a stroppy teenager with split-ends. Now the hair had been tamed. The teenage face had lengthened and thinned, and lines of experience, not all good, were etched around her mouth and eyes.

He said, 'I'm sorry about your granny and your father before that.'

'Thank you.' She still blocked his way. 'Have you time for a cup of tea?'

'Aye.' He'd time for anything that gave Harvey an opportunity to have second thoughts and not go at things in his usual headstrong way.

He pushed the bike up Mill Street to Caufields. She walked beside him.

'You made good time getting here,' he said.

'As soon as I heard of granny's death I went straight to the BEA offices in Cromwell Road. I was lucky and caught a flight ready to leave.' She motioned at her clothes: a black jacket and skirt and a white blouse. 'Anything I need I can buy here.'

She was mid to late twenties, if he remembered the years right. She flashed a weary looking Warrant Card at him and then put it away.

'You're in the police? Good on you, keeping it in the family.' He nodded at her shoes, the high heels. 'You'll not do much patrolling in those.'

She said, 'I'm no longer in uniform.'

'A detective then? You're doing well.'

'Not that either, at least not the way you think.'

By then he was parking his bike on the kerb outside Caufields. She went in ahead of him. He joined her in one of the padded booths, his interest aroused.

Before he could speak she touched his hand. 'Please don't ask, I can't tell you anything.'

He'd heard of these almost unofficial units in the London police: officers detailed to deal with armed robberies and an endemic of wage snatches. What she faced made the Dunlops look more like piggy bank thieves than a crime gang.

When she lifted her head to look at the continental décor around the walls he spotted a scabbed cut in her neck. Nothing much, he'd done worse to himself before safety razors came onto the market.

He pointed. 'Did you get that shaving?'

She made a face at him. 'I was doing a ladies thing with tweezers and a mirror, and I sneezed.'

'No beauty comes without pain.'

Their tea came. They talked as they drank. After her father's death, Mary Jo had moved into a small flat in Notting Hill, with a convenient tube station across the road. She hadn't seen much of her mother since her parent's divorce many years back.

Mrs. Cosgrave, her granny, was the nearest thing she had to a relation.

He expressed his regrets again.

It gave her the opportunity to ask, 'What happened to granny, did she take a turn or something?'

Even with Mary Jo being in the Metropolitan Police he couldn't be fully open with her. 'All we know at the minute is that she fell and hit her head on the fire irons. That's the probable cause of death but the Pathologist is a bit of an old woman and he wants to run further tests.'

She'd been in the job long enough to spot evasion when she heard it. 'What sort of tests?'

'Tests. He told me what ones, but once words get beyond the third syllable…' He threw his hands out as if in despair.

To change the subject, and knowing that money could be tight he suggested she have a word with DS Leary. If Leary's team had finished doing forensics she could live in Balmoral Avenue rather stay in a boarding house.

Impulsively, she grabbed both his hands in hers. 'You're really thoughtful, Mr. Barlow.'

His eyes were on the picture window and the street outside. Louise stood there, looking in at them. Barlow couldn't get a hand free to indicate for Louise to join them. By the time he did she had walked on. He knew she was in a rage.

All those double-dealing men. Now she's me down for one as well.

'Bollocks!'

'What?' asked Mary Jo.

He jumped to his feet, 'Sorry, I've got to go.'

At the same time he couldn't just walk out on the woman. He had to wait for the bill. Mary Jo insisted on checking it. 'It's something you have to do in London. The over-pricing that goes on in the best of places, you wouldn't believe.'

It took time to extract himself from Caufields. By then Louise was out of sight. Guessing she was heading for the shops he cycled up Wellington Street again. No sign of her. She had changed out of the blue dress. There were plenty of colors in the street but no one wearing a white skirt and a yellow jumper. He guessed that Louise had gone into a shop to avoid meeting him.

At that point he got thick. 'Bloody woman. I'm not going to spend the rest of my days explaining everyone I talk to.'

He didn't dare go back to the station in case of a run-in with Harvey. At that point he was mad enough to take the little runt by the throat.

Chapter 29

Still looking for excuses to delay the confrontation with Harvey, Barlow decided to head home for an early lunch.

He went by Clarence Street. Not necessarily the most direct way but it greatly lessened the chances of running into a patrol. . The last section of his route to home suited him: a quarter-mile straight, with the gentlest of slopes in his favor. It gave him time to collect his thoughts for the difficult afternoon that lay ahead.

He walked into their bungalow to find Vera standing in the hallway, her head and shoulders twisted into an awkward shape.

'What's wrong?'

'It's so wonderful,' she said.

She straightened and held the telephone receiver out to him. *She's all right. It's the way she was holding it.* He took the receiver off her, listened and heard electric static.

Vera said, 'The engineer, Hughie someone, was at the door when I got back from my split shift. He said he was passing anyway and he owned you a couple of favors.'

'Aye.' He knew who Hughie someone was and it was decent of the man to give them an immediate connection. All the same, there hadn't been time to talk to Vera first about the cost of phone calls, especially before the evening cheap rate.

He carefully placed the receiver on its Bakelite rest. He had done it thousands of times in the office, yet for some reason this placing seemed special. Vera was wiping at her eyes. If he'd known a phone had meant that much to her he'd have got one put in years ago.

He pointed to the telephone. 'Money doesn't grow on trees, you know, so I want you too…'

'Be a bridesmaid,' she said. Now Vera was beaming, her face flushed with happiness. 'I was so happy for her I cried.'

'Who is? Which one of your friends?'

A rushed wedding? The very thought chilled him. It could easily happen to Vera with that Cameron boy hanging around. Not that his parents would let him marry her. *Not grand enough for them.*

'Ough Dad, Aunt Daisy.'

He looked at her in surprise. Daisy, his sister-in-law, getting married? 'How do you know that?'

'Telephone Enquiries gave me the number and I rang her at work.'

Barlow had helped Daisy get over sexual abuse she'd suffered at the hands of her father. Abuse that had continued well into adulthood. A night with him had taught Daisy that she could finally feel pleasure in giving herself to a man. Now her widowed boss was going to reap, was reaping the benefits of that night.

He knew he was being illogical, especially with Louise apparently setting her cap on him. *You can't have it both ways, son.*

'I'm delighted for her,' he said, and really meant it. It would be his job to give Daisy away so he'd have to do some sucking up to Harvey to get the time off. 'When's the big day?'

'In a couple of weeks. They read the banns last Sunday.'

'That quick? She's not pregnant, is she?'

'Da!'

'She's not that old.'

Daisy was past child-bearing but it didn't hurt to remind Vera what happened when people got carried away with desire.

Vera gave Barlow a quick peck on the cheek and virtually ran out the door. If she hurried she had time to have a quick look in the dress shops on the way back to work. As a bridesmaid she needed to wear something good and, according to her, everything in her wardrobe was pure rags.

Barlow shuddered as the glass door slammed behind her. Daisy's wedding gave him a worry that hadn't occurred to Vera. Maggie, his wife and Vera's mother, now lived with Daisy. Would she move into the big house with Daisy and her beau or would she continue to live in the family home on her own. Could he afford the upkeep of both houses?

He found himself staring at the telephone. It might have to be disconnected again before he'd even the chance of a goodnight chat with Louise.

Thinking of Louise's reaction at seeing him with Mary Jo put him off lunch as such. He chewed a crust of bread while he went on through the house into the back yard, and muttered 'The wedding season has started early,' when he pulled the mower out of the windowless shed.

A broken pink candle in the shape of a heart lay on top of the mower. He picked it up and looked at it. 'Now where did that come from?' He lobbed the candle into the dustbin and set too.

He got the front lawn cut before he felt he should go back to work, and planned to do the back lawn that evening. On the way out the gate he looked at the weeds in the flowerbeds. 'That's a weekend job.' At the same he wanted to laugh at himself. Before he'd even put a fork in the soil he'd begun to realize the weariness of gardening.

He bent down and ran his hand up the stem of the blue flower, somehow it gave him connection with Vera who had planted it. 'Nothing is too much trouble for you love.'

Chapter 30

Barlow cycled to work with the sun on his face and black clouds piling up on the horizon. The wet weather Arthur Somerton had predicted was coming, but he didn't care. He felt curiously light-headed and out of touch with things he should be worrying about.

At the station he turned into the back yard and, with rain threatening, ran his bike under cover. Wilson and WPC Day sat on the back step, apparently deep in a manual of procedures: what to do when, and what standard forms to use. All the same, the laughter he heard as he came round the corner of the station had more to do with a boy and girl enjoying each other's company than serious work.

They made room for him to pass as he approached the back door. He stopped, envying their fresh-faced innocence.

He asked, 'Any news yet of Captain Denton's whiskey?'

WPC Day shook her head. 'A patrol found the lorry lying abandoned near Kells Water. Whoever it was even took the tarpaulin.'

Wilson said, 'It's a big loss. There's already talk of people being laid off at the brewery.'

Sometimes Barlow didn't like Charlie Denton's methods, but no way would Denton lay a man off, especially an old soldier, unless cash flow was critical. With DI Harvey taking personal charge of the enquiry he had little hope of the whiskey being found.

He told Wilson what he intended to tell every officer. 'Any Dunlop anywhere, anytime. I want to know where they came from and where they go to.'

'Yes, sergeant.' Wilson hopped to his feet. 'I've still twenty minutes left of my lunch break. I'll take a quick turn up the town in case any of them are around.'

WPC Day jumped to her feet. 'I'll go with you.'

She became aware of Barlow's eye on her and colored.

Barlow walked on into the station and took his time pacing through the building to the Enquiry Office. The light-headed elation had gone. In its place he felt bone weary at the thought of another confrontation with Harvey.

The sight of Sergeant Pierson's white face at the window, watching people coming and going outside instead of getting on with his job, did not help.

Barlow bulled up to him. 'Have you nothing better to do?'

The internal phone rang. Pierson backed off an answered it. 'Yes, sir. He's here, sir. Right away, sir, I'll escort him personally.'

He hung up. 'Mr. Harvey wants to see you right away.' He almost cooed the words, 'You're for the high jump.'

'Well while I'm jumping,' Barlow pointed at a pile of files on the counter. 'This is a police station, not your home. Put those away. '

Chapter 31

Without waiting for Pierson, Barlow walked back down the corridor. As well as the lassitude his stomach now hurt. *I should have eaten something.* He scratched an itch and entered Harvey's office without knocking.

Harvey was small and kept thin by his nervous ways. His modern desk and chair clashed with the Victorian cornicing and the flocked wallpaper. Barlow stopped with his toes touching the base of Harvey's desk. He snapped to attention, honoring the portrait of the Queen on the wall behind Harvey.

'You wanted to see me, sir?'

'Back a step, Barlow.'

Barlow took a decent step back, satisfied that he had made his point. *No surrender!* Anyway, he was more concerned at the presence of two other men in the room. They were seated to the left of Harvey. Inspector Foxwood he'd expected but not the Representative from the Police Federation. Harvey really did mean business this time.

Barlow knew it spoiled the effect but he just had to flex his shoulders to get at an itch in the small of his back.

The Representative from the Police Federation looked apprehensive. He'd been present on other occasions when Barlow and Harvey went toe to toe. At least with him here, Harvey could only sound sharp and impersonal. He wouldn't dare display the blazing hate he usually showed for Barlow.

Harvey motioned to Inspector Foxwood to keep the minutes of the meeting. 'Barlow, we are currently investigating the murder of our mayor, Alderman Ezekiel Fetherton. This morning you were asked by Inspector Foxwood here,' He nodded in Foxwood's direction, 'to give an account of your movements last weekend. This you refused to do.'

Barlow's fingers were tingling, he was suddenly sticky

with sweat. He rubbed his fingers against his trouser leg to ease the discomfort. Now he wanted to scratch his arm.

Somehow he'd lost the thread of what Harvey was saying. Had said. Harvey had stopped speaking and was looking at him expectantly. For once the little gabshite looked happy. He thought he had Barlow cornered. *I've news for you.*

'Well, Barlow?'

'Sir, I didn't refuse to answer…'

'That's a lie.'

Barlow ignored the interruption and kept on speaking. '...Inspector Foxwood's questions.'

'You did.'

'I wanted to know why he thought it necessary to ask them in the first place.'

The light in the room was suddenly so bad that he couldn't see Foxwood's face clearly. However, he did see him nod to the Federation Representative. Rain hammered off the window. They'll be soaked, he thought, remembering that Wilson and WPC Day had headed up the town looking for Dunlops to follow.

The tingling in his fingers had now extended beyond his wrist. The air in the room so muggy that his breathing began to strain. He wanted to scratch his back. A creepy-crawly must have got down the back of his neck while he was cutting the grass. Maybe it would drown in the sweat.

Harvey said, 'Barlow, where were you between Friday evening and Sunday lunchtime?'

Barlow asked, 'When did Fetherton die?'

'That's for me to know.' Harvey opened a file and pushed a piece of paper Barlow's way. 'A report from Forensics. Fingerprints on plastic found near the scene of the crime match your fingerprints on file.'

Near the scene? Barlow wanted to laugh. 'We…' He managed to stop himself in time from saying, "We were a full field away". He didn't know what was wrong with him, nearly walking into an admission like that. He hoped that Wilson and his boyish enthusiasm got soaked on his way back to the station.

Rather than risk a silence being taken as an indication of guilt he asked again, 'When did Fetherton die?'

Harvey thumped the table. 'Answer the question.' The Federation Representative pretended not to hear Harvey's *sotto voce* aside. 'Now you can see for yourself Barlow's deviousness and obvious guilt.'

The tingling had extended to Barlow's shoulder, so many creepy-crawlies were under his clothes that he didn't know which part to scratch first. And if someone didn't open the window or door he'd choke from lack of air.

He said, 'Inspector Foxwood accused me of bias towards Fetherton.' He went hard up against Harvey's desk and eyeballed Harvey as close as he could. It also gave him the chance to squish some creepy-crawlies on his thigh. 'Harvey, what about your obvious bias against me. In this last year you've done your best to have me fired or jailed for crimes you invented.' He had to take a deep breath before he could continue. 'I'm betting the Pathologist can't say with any accuracy when Fetherton died.' He took another breath. 'Which leaves you free to claim he was killed sometime when I've no witnesses…' Another breath. '...as to where I was and what I was doing.'

Foxwood asked, 'Barlow, are you all right?'

'Fine.'

Barlow's legs gave way. He could only watch Harvey push back in alarm as he fell over the desk. From there he slid to the floor, taking files and the telephone with him. At least Harvey had a square of carpet in his room and not the linoleum that covered the rest of the building. The carpet was comfortable to lie on. The bristles pushing into his face killed off the creepy-crawlies there, but more quickly took their place.

Someone said, 'He's having a heart attack.'

Chapter 32

A gang of doctors and nurses were waiting for Barlow when the ambulance men wheeled him into the Emergency Ward.

A doctor put a stethoscope to his chest. The white-haired sister leaned over him, checking his oxygen mask. 'Mr. Barlow, you're getting to be quite a regular.'

Up until a year ago he only ever been there in his professional capacity. Since then he'd been stabbed, shot and blown up. He remembered he owed the sister a parking fine for sending the best looking nurse in the hospital to rub nappy cream on his scorched backside.

Right then he hadn't the energy to smile. Even with oxygen, breathing was a choking effort and the creepy-crawlies had to be red ants because they were tearing holes in his skin. His arms hung heavy, numb.

A line of circular light-fittings passed by as they rushed him into a room. The sister squirted a thick liquid onto his chest then played around with electric cables, attaching one end to him and the other to a cream-colored box. Other nurses did things to his arms. What, he didn't know or care about. The cream-colored box churned out a piece of paper, the sort bookkeepers used when totting up lines of figures.

A doctor held the piece of paper up to the light. 'Definite ventricular arrhythmia.'

A nurse said, 'Blood pressure eighty-five over fifty-three.'

The nurse holding his other arm said, 'BPM 58.'

After that things got vague, especially when they gave him morphine to ease his breathing distress. Rooms and equipment and people swirled around him.

Darkened

Came bright again. He was somewhere else now, somewhere quieter with no one fussing over him. The oxygen mask was chaffing his face. He got an eye open and saw Vera's face. It was blotchy, her eyes red. He couldn't speak, felt his lips crack with dryness when he tried to say, 'Hi love.'

Someone stood behind Vera – Camilla Denton. He managed a jerk of the head by way of thanks. No matter what happened to him, Vera would be taken care of.

Vera kissed him, moving very gently to avoid touching him with anything but her lips. He managed a smile. Vera was talking to him, Camilla's mouth moved as well. He could hear sound but not the words themselves.

Someone leaned over him from the other side. Louise. She kissed his forehead, he could see her hold his hand. Only that morning he could have died with happiness in her company. Now he was really dying. Except for Vera it didn't matter.

He got his eyes open again. A nurse was there, shooing the visitors out. They all kissed him goodbye, including Camilla who was obviously worried about passing on some dreadful disease to her children. This time he managed to press his cheek against Vera's.

The nurse fussed around doing tests, making notes. He closed his eyes and let her get on with it. She lifted his oxygen mask and rubbed salve onto his dry lips. He was thirsty but couldn't be bothered to drink when she held a glass with a straw to his mouth. He thought she'd never go away. Finally she left only to come back with a doctor. They stood over him looking concerned. Another doctor, an older man, came and stood with them. They were talking to each other not to him.

They did the tests again. '78 over 47,' said the doctor. He seemed to be confirming something.

The second, older doctor, said, 'BPM 51, he's gone into relative bradycardia.'

The nurse said, 'I've checked, the results of the blood tests aren't back yet.'

'We're losing him,' said the younger doctor.

Barlow closed his eyes and wished they'd go away.

He had hardly sunk into a doze when the ward door burst open, slammed hard against the wall. It got him awake. Louise stood over him, her face a mixture of worry and anger. She was shouting at him, a lot of words. Two he understood because they were repeated and repeated: "flowers" and "touch".

He nodded to shut her up. Hell roast it, here she was worrying about him touching a flower. It's not as if he'd damaged it. Louise had turned into a mad woman. If she'd only go away and let him die in peace.

Instead of dragging her away and putting her in a straitjacket the medical people were listening to her. 'Wolfsbane,' she was shouting. 'Atropine, give him Atropine.'

Chapter 33

Barlow felt like death warmed up, except he wasn't dying. Dying had been much more pleasant: no pain, no aches, and an oxygen tank to do the breathing for him. According to the nurse his BPM – she'd translated that for his gluey brain as Beats Per Minute – was now steady at 63. He wouldn't have minded it being fifty or forty or even below thirty. Every beat sent a pulse crashing through an already aching head.

'You're getting better, you're grumpy,' the white-haired Sister told him when she came to visit.

'Grumpy is me in a good mood.'

The Pathologist called in. 'We nearly had you on one of my slabs, Barlow.'

'Only because your lot took their time checking my blood.'

'Well we fixed you up with a shot of Atropine.'

'What's that?'

'A derivative of Deadly Nightshade.'

Right then Barlow was too weak to shudder. Wolfsbane shut the body down, Deadly Nightshade speeded it up until it burned out from effort. He felt like one of those statistics he read about in the papers. Death at both ends and him the average statistic in the middle, barely alive.

Now that he was no longer dying visitors were restricted to Vera and Camilla Denton, and then only for a few short minutes. He'd lost a couple of days in an induced coma and they were still keeping him sedated to give his body a chance to recover. In his waking moments he watched the raindrops on the window gather into larger and larger drops until they ran out of sight.

And wonder about the Wolfsbane in his garden.

The only thing he knew for sure was that Vera hadn't planted it. She'd thought it was something he'd bought for Louisa, and then thought twice about it and stuck in his own flower bed.

Naturally she didn't mention it rather than start another argument about who he was seeing.

Nobody local had been struck down by Wolfsbane poisoning. Whoever had planted the Wolfsbane had known to wear gloves, which made it GBH at least, if not attempted murder.

So who and why?

The only person he knew who hated him that much was District Inspector Harvey, and not even Harvey would stoop that low.

It was a blessing when the Ward Sister finally removed the drip and restricted his sedative to a tablet at night to help him sleep.

'I never have any trouble sleeping,' said Barlow, not entirely honestly.

'It's for the night staff, to make sure you don't go wandering.'

On a previous stay in the hospital Barlow had slipped out of the ward to see the Pathologist about an ongoing case. It took a stretcher and an ambulance to get him back to the main building.

In a day or two he'd be fit to think up some way of pretending to take the sleeping pill. Meantime he gave into Sister's bullying and was fortunate that the afternoon visiting hour coincided with the fuzz of drugs finally clearing from his head.

Vera was working that afternoon so he wasn't expecting any visitors. The bell rang for the start of visiting hour. He heard hurrying feet passing his door, going to the ward beyond him, then a footstep he recognized. He pushed himself upright in the bed. He should have known that Louise would come when Vera couldn't. Vera might be grateful to Louise for saving his life but she still saw her as the other woman destroying their family unit.

He blamed the drugs for preventing him from thinking ahead. He could have at least combed his hair. And as for shaving…? His week-old stubble showed a streak of grey. 'That comes from rearing you,' he'd told Vera. All the same he didn't want Louise to see it.

The door opened and there stood Louise. She wore a black skirt and a white blouse. *Half alive, half dead.* A bit like me, he told himself as they hugged and slobbered kisses. He tasted coffee off her lips, not peppermint to conceal the smell of alcohol.

He made room for Louise to perch on the edge of the bed. One of her hands held his, the other finger-combed his hair tidy.

She said, 'They said you were dying.'

'I didn't, thanks to you.'

She stopped tidying his hair and brushed her knuckles against his beard. Especially the grey bit, he noticed.

He said, 'You look great.'

'I wish I could say the same about you.'

He pretended annoyance. 'You're supposed to tell me I look the picture of health.'

'If I tell you anything, it's that you're a walking disaster.'

'What have I done?'

'Wolfsbane!' she said like it was a dirty word.

'I take it, you didn't plant it as a housewarming present?'

'Hardly.'

Tears stood in her eyes. She pressed a hand over his heart. He touched hers and could feel her pulse race.

'It's all right,' he said.

'Someone tried to kill you.' A first tear trickled down her cheek. 'That house is one of the safest in the town and yet someone is using harmful spells against you.'

Harmful spells? He didn't know what she was talking about and what was particularly safe about his new home? It was just an ordinary post-war bungalow, *with every luxury I ever dreamed about.*

He didn't want to get into the mysteries of witchcraft and spells so he asked, 'What do you mean, the safest house?'

She wiped away that first tear and fought down others that threatened to follow. 'You aren't into Wicca.'

'Wicca?'

'Witchcraft, magic spells. Devil worship to an ignoramus

like you.'

She was using her feisty humor to keep things light.

He went along with it. 'I never got beyond Ali Baba and "open sesame".

He pulled her to him rather than see the look of hurt on her face at his near death. He wished they could lie together. He wasn't fit for anything sexual but he ached to have the comfort of her soft body against his. She seemed to feel the same need.

At the same he was listening hard to what she had to say because someone had tried to kill him. Could easily have killed Vera or anyone else unfortunate enough to touch the Wolfsbane.

She said, 'Did you even notice the cross at the front door?'

'I saw it.' He had, a plain wooden cross above the inner door. Two bits of wood well sanded down and expertly dovetailed together, but unvarnished and with no figure of Christ attached.

'The cross is made from the wood of a Rowan tree to guard the inhabitants against misfortune.'

'Okay.'

'And the trees in the front garden: Birch for a new start, Alder to remain true to oneself and Quert to make the right choice.'

He knew from the night of the devil worshippers that she had been involved in that sort of thing years back. A passing phase, he'd assumed, but this sort of knowledge he found unsettling. At the same time he couldn't believe that Louise practiced evil arts.

He remembered the glass jar of black and white stones in her house and a similar display in his sitting room, on the hearth.

'Those Carnlough stones?'

'Bring peace into your heart and into your home.'

He needed to know more but the poison still in his system was quickly draining away his energy. 'You spotted the Wolfsbane that day when you ran Vera home. Is there anything else in the garden that could be dangerous?'

'Dangerous no, but.' She pulled away from him and

reached for her handbag. Opened it, pulled out a sweetie bag and shook the contents onto the bed. First she pointed to the broken pink candle. 'That was lying in your bin.'

'Aye, I found it in the shed and put it there.' He picked up the two bits of the candle and held them together, making the shape of a heart. She picked up the pieces of blackthorn and held them out for him to examine them. They were the ones he'd thrown into the hedge.

She's got a good eye, was his first thought. 'Now what's significant about those?'

'They're for worse than bad luck to befall you.'

'They damn near gave me a puncture.'

'It's not funny, John.' She looked frightened for him. 'Someone is wishing evil on you, and they'll try again.'

Chapter 34

Louise saying that someone was wishing evil on him and would try again, frightened Barlow. Vera was on her own in that house and vulnerable. Whoever it was who wanted to do him harm didn't mind putting Vera at risk as well. He needed to be out of hospital and guarding her day and night.

He tried to jump out of bed. Louise held him back. 'Relax. I've arranged for Vera to stay with the Dentons until you're out of hospital. One of the estate workers will run her into work and collect her in the evenings.'

He sank back in the pillow, relieved. Charlie Denton knew how to handle a gun and Camilla was always grateful of Vera's help in dealing with three feisty children.

Again Louise delved into her handbag, and produced a book, *The Wicca Bible*, and held it out to him. He didn't know if he, a Christian, should even touch it.

She pushed it into his hands. 'Knowledge is defense. Know your enemy.'

Just then the door opened. Barlow shoved the book under the bedclothes rather than give a nurse the wrong idea. Louise scooped the broken candle and blackthorn into her handbag.

Instead of a nurse, Mary Jo Cosgrave came in. Her hair was uncombed and her blouse buttoned up wrong. 'I've just heard,' she said. 'Are you all right, John?'

She pushed Louise aside and gave him a hug. Her kiss on his lips lingered long beyond being social. Barlow could see past her to Louise. The skin on Louise's face went taut, her mouth narrowed.

Eventually Mary Jo backed off, which was a relief. Both for Louise's sake and the smell up Barlow's nose. Mary Jo's perfume was fresh applied and strong where Louise's was a quiet understatement.

Mary Jo wanted to know, 'When we were together… I mean you were so kind… I thought you'd ring, you said you would… Then I heard… I had to come straight away.'

Had he said he'd ring? *I might have.* He'd certainly intended to keep an eye out for her. She'd totally got the wrong idea of his kindnesses. And so had Louise, he could see it in her face as she retreated, handbag in hand.

'I have to go,' she said, her voice impersonal.

'Please stay.' He couldn't let her leave without trying to explain. She'd been hurt too often by men letting her down. He didn't want her to think that he was like the rest of them.

'Don't go because of me,' said Mary Jo.

It sounded more a social politeness than a real invitation.

'I must, I'm late already,' said Louise.

She stalked out in spite of his pleading, 'Louise.'

He found himself alone with Mary Jo who, *thank the Good Lord,* backed off and sat down on a chair. It had to be her English upbringing but she didn't seem to mind him being there while she unbuttoned her blouse. A silver pendant hung around her neck, it gleamed dully in the poor light. Barlow stared at the rain soaked window and tried not to notice the fine mesh bra as she buttoned-up again, properly this time.

'What happened? Are you okay?' she wanted to know.

The last thing he wanted to talk about was witches and spells. It could start a witch hunt around the town or, more likely, find him being referred to the local psychiatrist.

He said, 'I was gardening. I must be allergic to something I touched.'

'Oh you poor dear.'

She wanted to know the details of his illness: how he felt, had felt and what the doctors said. He played things down, but she was a policewoman and therefore a trained interrogator. It was an utter relief when Charles Denton thumped the door and walked in.

Denton stopped in the doorway and surveyed the room. His eyes lingered speculatively on Mary Jo who sat too close to

Barlow's bed for Barlow's comfort.

'Camilla didn't want you lying on your own during visiting time,' he announced, still eyeing Mary Jo.

'It's damn near over,' said Barlow and tried not to sound relieved at having someone to block Mary Jo's probing questions.

He made the introductions. After a few minutes Mary Jo said she had to see her granny's solicitor, and left.

Denton took her chair and shook his head at Barlow. 'How does a grumpy old git like you pull them?'

Barlow said, 'You did everything but ask for her London address.'

Denton said, 'I never play near home.'

'You wouldn't dare.'

Camilla had inherited a temper from her red-haired ancestors. Her and Denton's rows were legendary. They started when she was a visitor at Adair Castle and Denton the undergardener. He got fired for being rude to a guest. Out of guilt Camilla made her father give Denton a job in the family brewery. When Hitler invaded Poland, Rifleman Denton went off to war and came back Captain Denton, DSO. He also brought with him a lorry load of smuggled champagne that earned him a junior partnership in the brewery and Camilla's hand.

'I've been hearing rumors,' said Barlow, who had heard nothing since he'd been in hospital.

'Aye,' said Denton. 'Geordie.'

Chapter 35

Even mentioning Geordie Dunlop's name brought a burn of temper to Denton's face.

At primary school, with his family not much better off than Barlow's, Denton always dressed well with his shoes shining and his socks pulled up. Now, years on, even wearing Bond Street suits, that once poor boy still looked more like the family retainer than the owner of a growing empire.

That day his pinched look was that of a butler who has discovered that a case of the best wine had become "corked".

Barlow asked, 'Are things bad?'

'Thanks to the Dunlops, I had to pay Excise Duty on a lorry load of whiskey that disappeared into fresh air.' Denton used the palm of his hand to rub at tired eyes. 'This is the time of the year that pubs start to stock up for Christmas. I won't see the money until January and I've a couple of deals going that have taken me to the limit in the bank.'

'Surely the insurance?

'That fool Harvey told them that we'd left a window open and the alarm off. That negated the cover.' The temper built again. 'I'd happily give Geordie the drink for stopping everyone else from robbing me blind. But would he ask, would he hell. Every year he has to steal it for his wife's birthday party, then that excuse for a man, Harvey...'

Denton veered off the subject rather than criticize Barlow's superior. He talked about Vera staying in their house. 'She's no bother, in fact she's a great help with our little monsters.' He scowled at Barlow. 'You only had to ask.'

'Ask what?'

'Instead of her slaving in Woolworths, for me to get her a job in the Court House.'

Barlow had thought about it, but Denton liked favor for

favor and he was already in debt to the man. Twice in the past year Denton had prevented DI Harvey from having him discharged from the police force or jailed. From Harvey's point of view, preferably both.

Rather than harp back to a lot of troubles Barlow said, 'You did me a big enough favor giving Edward a job before his sister arrived from Australia.'

Denton knew him to well to pretend casualness so Barlow asked bluntly, 'She's been and gone. What's he doing still on the books?'

Denton said, 'Ninety percent of my time used to be taken up with personnel problems. Edward has the men eating out of his hand. Now they look for solutions instead of dumping the problems on my desk.'

More footsteps sounded in the corridor outside the room. Quick, tip-toe steps.

Make my day, thought Barlow as the door opened and DI Harvey marched in, all business.

'Good afternoon, sir. I hope you brought me grapes because no one else has.'

Harvey stiffened with anger but couldn't snap a reply because Denton was there, and Denton was the Chairman of the Local Policing Committee.

Inspector Foxwood followed Harvey in and stood well to the side.

'You're looking much better, Barlow,' said Foxwood.

'I am, sir, and thank you for asking.' The last part aimed at Harvey who obviously had more than Barlow's health on his mind.

Barlow had the impression that Foxwood enjoyed Harvey and him going ding-dong at each other, especially as Harvey usually came off second best. This time Barlow didn't think he could cope with Harvey. It had been a long stressful visiting hour and his stomach was already twisting into knots of tiredness.

Harvey said to Denton, 'It wasn't necessary for you to

come, sir, but I appreciate it.'

He didn't sound as if he did.

Denton said, 'I thought you could do with an independent witness.'

Harvey turned to Barlow. 'Barlow, I'll make this quick. The doctors hope to discharge you on Friday morning…'

'That's the first I heard of it,' said Barlow truthfully. 'Around here a patient could be dead and buried before they even tell him he's sick.'

Denton coughed back a laugh. Foxwood stared hard at the ceiling. Harvey made a gulping noise as if swallowing acid indigestion.

An ulcer can't be that far away.

'Well you are,' said Harvey. 'And Friday afternoon, two o'clock sharp, I want you in Inspector Foxwood's office to answer questions regarding the death of Alderman Fetherton.'

Barlow said, 'You will inform the Federation of the meeting?'

'It's already done.'

Barlow glanced over at Foxwood who nodded. He turned back to Harvey. 'Anything else, sir? I wouldn't want to keep a busy man like you back.' *From using police cars and police time to shag your girlfriend in Belfast.*

'Yes.' Harvey threw a piece of paper onto the bed. 'A policeman, especially a Station Sergeant, suspended from duty on suspicion of murder reflects badly on the Force.'

And you personally as his superior.

'The Police Doctor, after a careful review of your condition and after consultation with the hospital, has placed you on the Sick List for the period of one month.'

'I don't remember the doctor being in. He must have checked me over when I was still unconscious,' said Barlow.

'Friday, two o'clock, and don't be late.'

Harvey pointedly said his farewells to Denton and left. Foxwood nodded to Barlow and followed him out. Barlow felt sick with exhaustion and was glad to see them go, especially when Denton made ready to leave as well.

On his way out the door Denton stopped and looked back. ‘I’ll have to lay men off, old soldiers.’

Barlow said, ‘I’m glad you called to cheer me up.’

Chapter 36

Friday was always going to be an odd day. Barlow was being discharged from hospital, much to the Pathologist's disappointment. 'I'd this lovely cold slab picked out for you.' He was going back to an empty house because Vera was in Donaghadee, being bridesmaid at her Aunt Daisy's wedding.

Barlow had dreamed of Louise driving him home and of them making love. Instead he found himself feeling light-headed and uncertain, and glad to sit in his chair in the kitchen while she made him a cup of tea. Vera, pointedly, had stocked the larder and fridge with fresh bread and milk and precooked meals. No way did she want Louise to feel needed in *her* home.

Louise sat beside Barlow, tea in hand, and dabbed cold sweat off his brow. 'You should be in bed.'

He tried to sound suggestive. 'So should you.'

His voice sounded weak and shaky even to him.

In the end she left him because Friday up until four o'clock was a 'golf day' for the ladies. Over the weekend the men saturated the course with their testosterone and ladies were, pointedly, not wanted. Louise, Barlow thought, was also subtly making the point that a Mary Jo Cosgrave in his life would not be tolerated. He didn't know where to start explaining Mary Jo to Louise. He didn't know what there was to explain. Or even if he should.

At two o'clock on the dot, Johnny Scullion and his taxi dropped Barlow off at the police station. Barlow pointedly ignored Sergeant Pierson's face at the window looking out for him. He splashed across the pavement and ran up the steps to get out of the still pouring rain. Pierson was off duty but had come in especially to escort Barlow to Foxwood's office.

'That's very thoughtful of you,' said Barlow.

'My pleasure,' said Pierson.

This time he pushed on ahead of Barlow and announced him into Foxwood's office with obvious enjoyment. Foxwood and the Federation Representative had cups of tea in front of them and obviously got on well together.

The first thing Barlow noted was that the wall posters about drugs had been replaced by Duty Schedules. Foxwood never bothered with that particular job when Barlow was about. Pierson, as Barlow knew of old, was too busy posturing and being Harvey's blue-eyed boy to be dependable.

Barlow was offered a chair but not the tea.

Foxwood said, 'To start with, Barlow,' Foxwood looked in the direction of the Representative for confirmation. 'It has been suggested that meetings between yourself and Mr. Harvey tend to become clouded with personal issues. Therefore I am handling this enquiry. Any decisions taken will be mine and mine alone. Do you understand?'

Barlow nodded in reply. He understood all right. Harvey hoped he'd be charged with murder and no one liked a policeman who got another policeman into trouble, no matter how guilty. It would be Foxwood's name on the Charge Sheet as the Arresting Officer and Foxwood's name tarnished for future promotions.

'In fact,' continued Foxwood. 'To show his even-handedness in this case, Mr. Harvey has taken his wife to London for the weekend.'

'I'm sure he'll pick a nice hotel,' muttered Barlow, meaning one that Harvey hadn't already taken a girlfriend to.

Foxwood got the sarcasm in the words and coughed a warning for him to behave. 'Barlow, I don't want to make this meeting official by giving you a formal caution, but anything you say will be noted. Is that understood?'

'Yes, sir.'

He understood all right. Foxwood was as windy of risking future promotions as Harvey. No one outside the room would ever know what had been said.

'Right, Barlow, I want an account of your movements from

lunchtime on Friday the ninth until the Sunday morning when you reported for duty.'

Barlow looked at the Federation Representative who said, 'Sergeant, there is no need to answer that question.'

'I've no intention of answering it, sir.' He looked over at Foxwood. 'Unless, of course, you are willing to tell me Fetherton's time of death?'

Foxwood's fingers tapped the desktop impatiently. 'Barlow…'

'PTQ, sir.'

He didn't know where that came from but it sounded good. PTQ was the title of the yearly magazine produced by the young bucks at Queens University, Belfast. It stood for Pro something or other and meant like-for-like.

'Fair enough,' said the Representative.

Foxwood said, 'On the Saturday night you were seen in Ballymoney, dining with a lady at the Manor House Hotel.'

'Was I now?' said Barlow. *How the hell did he find that out?*

'After which the lady drove you home in her car.'

Barlow said nothing, his mind buzzing with possibilities of people who might have seen and recognized him.

One thing in his favor. Foxwood didn't know who the lady was or he would have mentioned Louise's name.

Chapter 37

***The meal finished and the plates taken away**, Barlow and Louise refused dessert and sat over their coffees. A faint yellow glow was all that remained of daylight. He knew that Louise could drink too much when under pressure, had seen her at it. Her drinking that night was moderate and he didn't sense any quivering need in her for more.*

Early days, mind you.

'We should go,' she said, checking her watch, and he realized that he'd been staring at her, not saying a word, for a long time.

'I'm spoiling the evening for you,' he said angry with himself.

She went to the bathroom while he settled the bill, which was less than he feared. When she came back she took his arm.

All his doubts faded. He said, 'You look good enough to eat.'

'Dessert's in the car,' she said and he was trying to figure what she meant by that when she added, 'The box of chocolates.'

'Oh.'

At the car she said, 'I'll drive this time.'

He got into the passenger seat and they drove off. When they had turned the bend at the Presbyterian Church he risked a hand on her knee. It was almost totally dark by then but a full moon shone from a cloudless sky, enabling him to see her turn his way and smile.

She'd wanted him to make a pass. After that it was up to the lady how the evening went. In a way he wanted her. In another way he was enjoying the undemanding evening in her company.

He let his hand drift up her leg, bit by bit, until she pressed his hand still , again accompanied by a look and a smile. He thought that her panic line, where wandering hands had to stop climbing, was moderate. He'd have expected no less of her. Mostly they sat silent just enjoying the dregs of the evening.

Nearing Ballymena she detoured onto the Old Ballymoney Road. He couldn't stop himself tensing with hope, especially when they turned off onto a "B" class road that doubled as a flood barrier along that part of the river. Their speed slowed. She appeared to be looking for somewhere or something.

She said, 'The last time I was here I was a married woman.'

That was telling him something, but what he wasn't sure. Having spent all her inheritance, her husband had dumped her and run. That was ten years back. The divorce had gone through just in time for the husband to be killed in Korea and for her to lose out on a War Widows Pension.

A layby came up. She gave a sigh of relief and pulled in, switched off the engine and the lights. Surrounding trees diffused the moonlight.

What if anyone came along, he wondered, but it's what the lady wants.

He turned in his seat. She caught his fingers as they reached to caress her neck and jaw. Brought his hand to her lips and kissed the palm. Then she said, 'Come on,' and got out of the car.

He followed her, puzzled, but trusting her. He knew the area in a general way. Give him a minute and he'd be able to name the townlands and the names of the local farmers. They weren't that far out of the Ballymena town boundary, maybe a couple of miles. Good land, if he remembered, mostly in grain: wheat and barley and owned by.... He could remember an ageing farmer living on his own. Somerton, that was it, Arthur Somerton.

They went through an old farmstead that had been abandoned generations back. There was no sense of animals moving restlessly in the old buildings though the roofs had been tined over for winter housing.

She led him diagonally across the stubby farmyard and through the remains of a vegetable patch. He used to grub there for potatoes and root vegetables when he was a child on the run from the Workhouse Beatle and the police. He was sure that somewhere in the archives at the station was a file on a missing twelve-year old John Barlow. No policeman could collar the young John Barlow though there was many a good chase and many a curse followed his rapidly disappearing back. Then, gradually, the chasing eased into eyes that never registered his presence, maybe even granted him a nod of vague recognition.

The police knew that young John Barlow was no trouble, hadn't turned into a sneak thief or worse. Was making his living as best he could by running errands for stallholders or driving cattle at the Wednesday and Saturday marts, mucking out or tidying, doing whatever dirty job was going. The one thing the young Barlow had learned was always to be clean and presentable. People were more likely to hire you, or at least not assume you were up to no good.

Beyond the farmyard and the vegetable patch was a gate that hung crooked on its hinges. And beyond that, instead of the patchwork of little fields Barlow saw one huge field, two hundred acres of rippling wheat ready for harvesting. He stopped in surprise.

Thinking he was unsure of his way, Louise slipped her hand into his. He realized that they hadn't spoken since the car, had moved independently across the farmyard, both of them busy with memories. His at least best forgotten.

Her hand was warm and soft in his. He held it lightly yet with tension, as if holding a little child's and on guard in case the little hand slipped from his and ran into all sorts of dangers.

Once through the gateway, on the strip of land between the hedge and the wheat she turned and kissed him with puckered lips. He got the message. This wasn't their final destination. Their final destination had to be the hill ahead.

Really not much more than an erratic rise in a land full of little lumps of matter left over when the ice retreated all those millennia ago. This one was slightly larger than most and probably surrounded by a Norman palisade in less safer days. A palisade now marked by a circle of trees. Oak, he thought, from their venerable girths. The trees and a galvanized shed in their center gave cattle shelter in rough weather.

A small stream, hardly more than a good stride wide ran round the base of the hill. Louise's hand tightened against his as she stepped onto a narrow footbridge with no safety railings. He saw her safely over then followed.

Nearing the crest she kissed him again, lips warm and soft against his but refusing to yield to his tongue. Her lips tasted spicy from the red wine. Something bumped his side. The box of Milk Tray. They'd forgotten about the promised dessert in the car. At least he had, and she'd brought it with her.

She took his hand again. He let himself be led, loving for once not to be the one in charge. At the crest of the rise, at the edge of the stand of trees she settled herself on the dry ground, her back against a windfall oak tree.

He joined her and stared out over the field of wheat, watching a vagrant wind moving the heads in an elegant swathe, this way then that. The wheat was like a lake of yellow in a dark green landscape of grass that occasionally sprouted stacks of hay saved for the coming winter. Wisps of cloud appeared in the sky, making the moonlight flicker uncertainly.

At the far end of the field figures straggled into vague sight. After a time the figures separated, some moving further into the field. Lights appeared.

Barlow jumped to his feet. 'They're trying to burn the man's crop.

Chapter 38

Foxwood raised an eyebrow in an interrogative smirk. Barlow stared hard at the rub-outs and penciled in changes to the Duty Rooster, *that useless plonker, Pierson,* rather than let himself blush.

Foxwood asked, 'What was the lady's name? We need to talk to her.'

'I'm surprised you can't tell me. You know everything else,' said Barlow.

'The name?'

'Who says I was in Ballymoney in the first place?'

Them knowing about Louise even if they didn't have her name, had him unsettled. Foxwood recognized this and was plainly enjoying himself. He hadn't forgotten that Barlow had conned him into summonsing local councilors and leading business men for having ragweed in their fields. Harvey had cancelled the summonses but Inspector and Mrs. Foxwood still weren't welcome in certain households.

'Milk Tray,' said Foxwood in a thoughtful voice. 'I'd have bought something more upmarket.'

And so Barlow would have, but that would have meant a trip to Fountain Arcade in Belfast. He looked over at the Representative who worked at maintaining a studiously bland expression. 'I'm guessing you're a Black Magic man, sir?'

'Perhaps we are somewhat deviating from the point,' said the Representative.

Foxwood nodded. He reached down the side of his chair and produced a one-gallon petrol can. A can so old that the original "Castrol Motor Oil" logo had virtually disappeared. Yet the can gleamed clean.

'Do you recognize this, Barlow?'

'No?'

‘We found it hidden in your shed?’

‘What do you mean “found” and why “hidden”?’

Foxwood ignored his questions and continued. ‘A petrol can so old you’d expect it to be layered with generations of dirt and fingerprints, yet there wasn’t one, Barlow. Not one fingerprint could Leary find anywhere on this can.’

Barlow stared hard at the Duty Rooster. He had expected a difficult interview but this was a straight-forward bludgeoning. Already quivering with weariness from the long stay in hospital, his body threatened to curl up on him, for his mind to stop working.

The Representative bought him time to get over the shock. ‘Inspector, please answer Sergeant Barlow’s questions. Why “found” and why “hidden”.’

Foxwood left the petrol can sitting on the desk and did Harvey’s trick of opening a file. He handed a form to the Representative. ‘A Search Warrant properly drawn up and attested by Judge Donaldson allowing us to search Barlow’s home and outbuildings.’

‘We?’ asked Barlow.

If Pierson ever hinted let alone gloated that he’d been one of the search party, he’d sort that bastarding man out some dark night.

All this silent cursing isn’t me. He knew he couldn’t take much more of this pressure.

‘Myself, DS Leary and Acting Sergeant Gillespie,’ said Foxwood.

If they had to go through his things, then those were the three men he minded least.

‘Thank you for that, sir.’ Another thought occurred to him, delayed he guessed due to his weariness. ‘Was Vera there? I mean…’

‘We let ourselves in. Vera had already left for a wedding in Donaghadee. Her aunt’s, I believe.’

He blessed Foxwood and especially Gillespie for that

consideration. Having the house searched would have shattered Vera. Still he found it hard to get his head around strangers poking through his things.

'Only a Yale lock on the front door, Barlow,' said Foxwood, disapprovingly. 'A child could open it with a piece of plastic. In fact we did.'

'Aye.' That was one of the things he hadn't got round to sorting.

Maybe with a month off on the sick he could. *If I'm not in jail.*

Foxwood continued. 'A petrol can hidden behind a load of junk. A petrol can that once held petrol but is now empty. A petrol can that hasn't one fingerprint on it.' He leaned forward accusingly. 'A petrol can when you have no car, never had a car and have only a manual mower to cut the grass.'

The Federation Representative said, 'Barlow, perhaps at this point I should remind you that withholding information about an ongoing enquiry, could cause you your job.'

Foxwood leaned even closer. No longer the reluctant and over-burdened administrator but a policeman who had earned his rank through ability and hard work. 'The problem is, Barlow, we have no clear proof that you killed Alderman Fetherton and no known compelling reason for you to want to kill him. But things keep stacking up against you.'

Chapter 39

One hour of bludgeoning questions later Inspector Foxwood told Barlow that he could go.

'Yes, sir,' said Barlow.

That was the first direct reply he'd given Foxwood in all that time. When he wasn't prevaricating he was obeying the Federation Representative's instruction. 'You are not obliged to answer that question.'

Barlow marched out of Foxwood's office, ramrod straight. A ramrod held together by less than set jelly. It was all he could do not to stagger into the kitchen and crash into a chair.

Three people were there already. Wilson, Gillespie and WPC Day. They sat grouped around the old deal table, their heads bowed over manuals and writing pads.

'Papa Bear, are you all right?' asked WPC Day.

'Aye, fine.'

'You look like death warned up,' said Gillespie.

Barlow glared in reply, sat straight and squared off his shoulders.

Wilson got up and poured him a cup of tea that was just off the boil. Every sip helped turned his near-jelly back into rigid spine and solid determination. Things were going on around him, things he didn't understand. Someone or a group of someones were out to get him into trouble, *serious trouble*, and for once it wasn't Harvey orchestrating from the rear.

Not the Dunlops. Geordie and his son would happily kick his head in given half a chance, but they'd do it to his face. There'd been other serious threats over the years from disgruntled offenders, *a lot of them,* but people had calmed down or knew better than to try anything. Anyway, all those possible enemies were low-lives and these attacks were sophisticated.

Barlow had served almost continuously in Ballymena from

11th December, 1936. He knew the date well. It was the day that he and his old District Inspector and King George VI had all taken up their posts. In early 1939 he'd had a run-in with Edward's older sister, Grace that resulted in him being posted to Donaghadee. *Where, for my sins, I met and married Maggie.* From there he went straight into the army and wasn't back in Ballymena again until Christmas 1945.

It seemed impossible, but had anything gone on in Ballymena during the years when he had been elsewhere? Something that could be laid at his door? Could someone have harbored a resentment against him for all these years? He tried not to think of the devil worshippers or their master.

The level of tea in the mug had dropped in proportion to the build of determination in his mind to find out who had a pick against him and to sort them.

He drained the mug and thumped it down on the table. The group's worrying glances at his obvious exhaustion changed instantly to wariness. *They know me too well.* 'Wilson, I want you to go through the Incident Books and Station Diaries for the period January 1939 to December, 1945.'

'Yes, sergeant.'

Wilson looked both puzzled and dismayed. It was a big favor he was being asked to do. Pierson wouldn't let him go through the books during his shift so it would have to be unofficial overtime. It would also seriously impact on his study time for the impending examinations.

Still the young officer had said "yes" and he meant it. In a few short months since Wilson's posting to Ballymena, Barlow had taken a chip off his shoulder and given him back both his career and the trust of fellow officers. Wilson had done the one thing Foxwood feared to do, Wilson's testimony in court had resulted in fellow officers being jailed. In their case justifiably for torturing a prisoner. Even so nobody wanted Wilson in their station or trusted him, until he came under Barlow's wing.

Gillespie had walked off without saying another word,

which always meant he didn't want to be held accountable for his actions.

WPC Day looked back from the cooker where she was making Barlow cheese on toast. 'Other than that Papa Bear?', 'What are we supposed to be looking for?'

'Promotion,' he growled. He'd been at Gillespie and WPC Day often enough to go for their stripes. Now they were willing to risk that chance to help him.

'Anything, no matter how trivial, that relates to ongoing cases.' He couldn't put it more clearly than that because he was only going on an itch of annoyance that things had happened in Ballymena when he was in Donaghadee or in the army that he didn't know about.

Gillespie came back and dumped a small grip at Barlow's feet. 'With the greatest respect, Sarge, would you take your smelly socks home and wash them.'

Barlow said, 'I've always pitied your poor wife having to deal with yours.'

He hefted the bag, feeling its weight. It weighed more than it should, about the weight of a Webley pistol. Even the very presence of the pistol in the bag gave him a greater feeling of security. There was an inner bolt on the front door. He'd ram that home at night as well.

He ate his cheese and toast, noting how the other officers managed to keep a conversation going in spite of them dying to know how he'd got on with Foxwood. The fact that he was still free and not detained told them a lot.

That freedom also gave him a chance to fight back against his enemy or enemies. That meant a lot of toing and froing around the town and out in the country. Even the thought of walking home put him in a cold sweat.

The cheese and toast safely deposited in his stomach along with a second mug of tea, he looked Wilson straight in the eye. 'Son, your car, could I borrow it for today?'

'Sure, Sarge.' Not even a hesitation, but a pause. 'Other

than tomorrow evening you could hold onto it for a few days.'

WPC Day touched Wilson's arm. 'We... You could get the train.'

She blushed prettily.

Barlow didn't even let his eyebrows flicker. The young officers were in the position of himself and Louise. Early in a relationship, unsure of where it was going but hoping for the best.

Wilson handed over the keys. 'Hold onto them if you want, Sarge. I've got a spare set.

Barlow said, 'You'll have it back tomorrow lunchtime at the latest.'

Now he had wheels and a gun, someone somewhere was going to find out the meaning of real revenge.

Chapter 40

The wipers on Wilson's car could hardly cope with the rain beating down. Even getting to the car in the first place had Barlow wishing he could walk on water. The little stream forming the boundary of the station's back yard had overflowed and had already crept past the car's wheels.

It was late Friday afternoon and every doctor in the town was off duty. Except for Dr. Ingram. Luckily, Barlow was able to park outside the surgery. He pulled his jacket over his head and ran into the vestibule. He looked back. Water was pumping out of the storm drains and flowing away to form linked ponds the length of the street.

He pushed on into the Waiting Room where five old ladies gathered in two groups, chatting. Keith Ingram sat on his own, his feet stretched out towards a weak gas fire, his nose in a magazine. The talk stopped as Barlow entered. He sensed friction in the air, of people not talking to people. He nodded to the ladies and sat down. The silence continued until one lady tried to whisper something and was shushed down by her companion. Covert glances came his way, more wary than gloating.

What do they know that I don't?

The surgery door opened and Dr. Ingram ushered out a patient. He looked around the room and spotted Barlow. 'Come on in Young Barlow.'

'I'm not next, Doctor.'

Dr. Ingram laughed. 'Don't worry about the social club.'

All the same, Dr. Ingram looked back with a frown as he closed the surgery door. He ran Barlow through the usual tests and then tapped his folder. 'The paperwork is growing but I can confirm that you're still alive.'

'I'm as weak as water, Doctor. That's why I'm here.'

Dr. Ingram looked at him over his glasses. 'You could

always rest.'

'There's things going on.' He stopped, not knowing how to put it better.

'You're lucky to be alive.' The Doctor pointed at Barlow's stomach. 'That belt of yours is pulled in two notches and you're just out of hospital. What do you want, miracles?'

'Something to keep me on my feet if I need to.'

He could only wait and hope while Dr. Ingram thought over his request. After a pause the Doctor searched in a drawer and produced a small bottle of Benzedrine. 'You've taken these before?'

'Yes, during the war when we had to stay alert.'

'Only if you're desperate and even then you stick to the recommended dose. If you don't, in your condition you could damage your heart.'

The doctor opened the bottle and shook a tablet into Barlow's hand. Fetched him a glass of water so he could swallow it easily.

He held the bottle of tablets enticingly close to Barlow. 'You're getting these on two – no three conditions. You eat properly, you take a bottle of Guinness a day for the iron and you get plenty of rest.'

'Done,' said Barlow though he wasn't so sure of the "rest" bit.

When he went back into the Waiting Room, Keith Ingram had gone. Again he got the impression that he had interrupted a heated discussion between the ladies. Dr. Ingram's problem, he decided, and made a hasty departure.

On his drive through the town he began to wonder if he was in a car or a speedboat from the spray thrown up by the wheels. Driving down Bridge Street was like being caught up in a miniature torrent. Approaching the tin bridge he could see that the river was high. Even so he thought the bridge well above river level and shouldn't flood.

The tin bridge got its name from the metal bolted onto it to hold it secure. The multi-arched stone bridge, built in the time of stagecoaches and lumbering dray horses, had never been designed to cope with the weight of American Sherman tanks practicing for the invasion in 1944.

Once over the bridge he turned right into the industrial center. He parked in a visitors' bay at the Ballymena Brewing Company and trudged up the stairs to the General Office.

The General Office was a long room with lines of filing cabinets and desks overflowing with invoices. It had the air of people winding down at the end of the working week. Edward sat at a desk beside the door leading into Denton's private office. Denton was out, Barlow noted with relief, as he took a chair across from Edward.

Edward's desk was clear of everything except one sheet of foolscap paper. Barlow could see a list on names on the page. When he saw the pain in Edward's eyes he knew what the list was for. The names of people Denton would have to let go to save money and perhaps the firm.

'My dear chap,' said Edward, turning the page over before Barlow could make out any of the names.

Barlow had been off ill so long that he hadn't a clue what was going on in the case, so he asked, 'I suppose there's no news of the missing drink?'

'Captain Denton remains in contact with Mr. Harvey on a daily basis. One regrets that to date…' Edward made a gesture of helplessness.

Barlow almost felt sympathy for Harvey because Denton was difficult to deal with at the best of times. Even so he couldn't see how there could be any leads. One bottle of Denton's whiskey looked exactly like another.

He said something to that effect to Edward who raised his eyebrows in surprise. 'In fact, Mr. Barlow, it's the easiest thing in the world. Miniscule nicks at the side of each label tells when a whiskey was laid down and when it was bottled.

'I only drink the stuff,' said Barlow, nettled at his lack of knowledge of something so obvious. He covered quickly. 'I bet that Denton's travelers have to check every bottle of whiskey they come across in case it belongs to the missing batch.'

'And every other drinks traveler in the Province. Among the wholesalers there is a surprising esprit de corps in adversity.'

Barlow checked his watch, and not for effect. Time was moving on and he needed to get down to the real reason for his visit.

'Major.' Barlow paused, surprised at himself. He'd called Edward Adair "Edward" for fifteen years. Edward had insisted on that the day they'd been discharged from the wartime army and were making their torturous way home by train, boat and finally bus. Somehow, in the office setting, Edward was no longer the town drunk and "Major" was more appropriate. 'If you remember, I asked you to add names to that list of dev… Lug worshippers.'

'Unfortunately, Sergeant Major, not surprisingly people are somewhat reticent about admitting to any involvement in pagan rites.' He smiled reassuringly. 'But one will prevail in the end.'

'Thank you, sir.'

Again the "sir" seemed right.

Barlow added. 'If you're in the Bridge Bar later, perhaps I could buy you a drink?'

He made it sound like a one-off, but he bought Edward a pint and chaser every week to help fund his drinking. Only recently had Edward enough money to buy him a drink back.

'Sergeant Major, you'd oblige me better by attending tomorrow morning's parade.'

'With pleasure, sir.'

Normally Barlow led the "Black Mans" parade through the town. It would be interesting for once to watch it. Especially Harvey's reaction as the parade passed the podium.

Chapter 41

The rain had eased by the time Barlow left the building with a complimentary bottle of Guinness in every pocket. He wound his way around puddles back to his car. There was a dozen things he wanted to do, needed to do, like seeing Geordie Dunlop when he was at that end of town.

Right then home and his feet up seemed more pressing. Even at home he couldn't rest straight away because he had things to do in the garden. On the way past, he slung the grip into the sitting room, and went on into the scullery where he put one of Vera's pre-prepared meals, a shepherd's pie, in the oven to heat

An electric oven, what will they come up with next?

Even the coal fired range with a double oven in his old house seemed a miracle to a man who had started life cooking on a salvaged primus stove.

Before he left the house he put on an overcoat and cap against the rain. Louise had checked the whole garden for dangerous plants but he had to do it for himself. On the way out the door he thought to pull on his police gloves. *Once bitten.*

The place where the blue flower had been was a waterlogged hole. Search as he might he didn't come across any other blue flowers or evidence of anything recently dug into his weed choked flowerbeds. Someone had cut the back lawn for him, Gillespie he supposed. When he tried to walk on it his boots left deep imprints in the grass. He stepped back onto the path.

By then he reckoned his meal would be ready and went back indoor. He drank a bottle of Guinness and ate nearly half of the shepherd's pie before exhaustion took over. He left the dirty dishes, kicked off his boots and went into the sitting room. He lay down on the settee and put a cushion on his chest for warmth. *An hour and I'll be myself again.*

When he woke up the room was dark and closing time at

the pub had come and gone. He took the tablets the hospital consultant had given him and creaked stiff muscles down the corridor, undressed and crawled into bed. He lay on his side and thought of that awful day when Louise had run him home and shared his bed.

He missed her nearness and the comfort of her arms.

Chapter 42

Louise caught hold of Barlow's trouser leg, *not that he was about to leave her. Not with those devil worshippers loose in the countryside.*

'Wait and watch,' she said.

He looked back at her, puzzled by her calmness. If he ran off now to raise the alarm he'd have to drag her with him. And something else. Those flames weren't being spread haphazardly, they were being placed to form a large circle. "Wait and watch" she'd said, so she had to know what was going on.

He asked, 'Would you mind letting me in on the secret?'

'Only if you sit down.'

He sat down again, still wary. Ready to run and sound the alarm and save Arthur Somerton's crop. He felt her fingers ease between his shirt buttons, and relaxed because he trusted her. The fact that he trusted her didn't surprise him. The degree of trust he had for a woman he hardly knew, had him startled.

She said, 'They're using lanterns or safety lights. They've never burned a crop yet.'

'Yet?'

'Yet,' she said, 'Now watch.'

He did as he was told and watched as the group of people gathered in the circle of light and held hands to form an inner circle.

Barlow asked because he had to be sure. 'Are they buck naked, all of them?'

'Yes.'

'Men and women?'

'Yes.'

In a way she was laughing at his innocence.

'They're tramping down that wheat,' he said, using his policeman's training to make sense of things. Trespass, willful destruction. *He tried to count the number of people involved but*

with the distance and the poor light he couldn't be sure. More than half a dozen anyway.

The circle of people began to revolve anti-clockwise in a slow dance. Some sort of chant reached him, melodious and yet with an edge of threat.

He pointed. 'That's them devil worshipers you hear about in the papers.'

'Hardly,' she said.

Her thumb undid a shirt button and her hand slid in further. Her nails ticked his skin and his heartbeat became more pronounced.

'They're not naked, they're Skyclad,' she said.

'That's a new word for it.'

She obviously knows about this sort of goings on.

Most of his professional curiosity disappeared when her fingers played along the top of his trousers. Handcuffs couldn't have held him back more securely, and she knew it.

'Is there any little service I can perform for my lady?' he asked.

'Not yet, John.'

He liked the "yet" and wondered what she would want unbuttoned when the time came. Maybe even Skyclad? It seemed like a word people had invented so they could pretend they weren't actually starkers.

She dunted his jacket sideways with her head until he dared slide if off. He bundled it where she could rest her head when the time came. He partly turned into her and slid a hand down her nyloned leg then upwards towards her panic line. This time under the dress. Her hand stilled his much lower down.

'You're a desperate man,' she said.

How does she know I say that?

Meanwhile the dancers had sat down, still in their circle form. They held hands and continued the chant. Occasionally an individual voice would rise in cadence.

'They're praying to the bugger,' he said.

'What "bugger"?'

'The devil.'

Another shirt button gave way under her thumb. Now she furrowed the hairs on his chest. He wanted to possess this woman, to Skyclad her and pour his manhood into her. He eased himself lower against the log so that she could lie into him more comfortably.

'It's not the devil they're praying to,' she said and came lower with him.

'What then?'

Not that he cared right then but it stopped him from reaching for her when she wasn't ready. He slid his hand past the original panic line and she didn't stop him.

She said, 'It's Saturday night. Last Saturday was wet if you remember.'

'What's that got to do with it?'

'And the first Monday of the month was the feast of Lughnasa.'

'Come again?'

'Lughnasa, it marks the start of the harvest season,'

She was laughing at him again.

It was his turn to still her hand on his chest. 'Tell me or I'll march you back to the station and take a rubber truncheon to you.'

She laughed on. He loved that laugh, thought it clean and clear as a mountain stream.

I'll be reciting poetry next.

She freed her trapped hand and brushed his hair tidy. Allowed him a second puckered kiss before she explained that Lughnasa was the feast of Lug, the Celtic god of the harvest. On the feast of Lug or at the next full moon, certainly before the harvest was taken in, the followers of Lug held a service in his honor.

'More like a bit of how's-your-father,' muttered Barlow.

'Certain people will always find an excuse for excessive behavior,' Louise said in a cold voice.

Barlow remembered the remark about her not being in this area since her married days. He gave her a kiss to indicate that he knew and understood how a young bride might sacrifice her pride in an attempt to save her marriage. She responded by caressing his lips with her tongue.

Chapter 43

Barlow woke early and lay and listened to the day starting up in the road outside. Fell asleep again just before he'd intended to get up. When he finally did waken he shot out of bed knowing that he was already well behind in the things he intended to do.

There was no time for the emersion to heat the hot tank so he ducked in and out of a cold shower and danced a jig on the equally cold linoleum while he toweled himself dry. By the time he had dressed in his best suit and headed downstairs the feeling of ice on his skin had changed to a glow of warmth. A mug of tea, a round of toast and two boiled eggs filled the inner man. With the last mouthfuls, energy shot into his system and he blessed Dr. Ingram and his instructions about sensible eating. Barlow felt more like his old self, 'Carnaptious and cantankerous,' was the way he put it as he headed out the door.

The rain had stopped though dark clouds still loomed over the town. He checked his watch as he got into Wilson's car. If he hurried he still had time to make the Post Office before the parade started. At that time of the morning the town, like himself, was only starting its day and he had no trouble parking in Wellington Street.

He started the telegram with "Mr. and Mrs. Gardiner" and the name and address of the hotel where the reception was being held. "Sorry I can't be with you" came easy. He chewed a pen while he thought of what to say next. "May all your troubles be little ones" wouldn't do. Mr. Gardiner had grandchildren and Daisy was past child-bearing age. Finally he wrote "May the light of your love be like the light from a good fire".

That, he knew, would bring a blush to Daisy's cheeks. They had made love while the flames from the fire played along the living room ceiling.

Pleased with what he'd written he walked across to the

counter. The terrazzo floor was already marked from the feet of that days customers, though there was no one else in at that time.

It's Saturday after all and pension day is....

'God Almighty!'

The clerk already had her hand out for the telegram. She looked shocked at his outburst.

'Sorry, love, not you.'

He handed over the telegram and waited while she counted the words and worked out the charge. It gave him time to think and to berate himself. Another murder on the same day or not, there was no excuse for missing the obvious. During the search of the house they'd never come across Mrs. Cosgrave's pension book nor a savings book. Old people like her always had enough put by to pay for their funeral, and there was no record in the documents Leary had given him of finding money.

He paid for the telegram and waited patiently for the clerk to send it on its way. Then he leaned his arms on the oak counter and asked, 'Mrs. Cosgrave, the lady from Balmoral Avenue who died recently, do you remember her being in?'

The lady clerk had been a long time in the job. She was one of the unlucky ones. At the right age for marriage when the eligible men were off at war, and no longer young and fresh-faced when they returned. A life of routine had made her sharp without being resentful.

She said, 'I'm afraid I can't discuss…'

Barlow interrupted her. 'You know who I am. I might be in mufti but this is an official enquiry.'

He was surprised at himself for saying "mufti", the army term for civilian clothes. It had to be the thought of the coming parade that put the word into his head.

The clerk's words came out slowly at first. 'She was in every Thursday to collect her pension, first thing in fact.'

'Did she take it all in cash or would she have put some into a savings account?'

'An Investment Account.'

Barlow deliberately looked surprised. You could only open an Investment Account if you had at least one-hundred pounds in an Ordinary Account. A hundred pounds was a lot more than most people could save in a lifetime.

The clerk said in a puzzled voice, as if the unusualness of it had only occurred to her. 'Every week she put all of her pension into the Investment Account.'

Now Barlow's surprise was real. He knew old people tended to be tight, but to lodge every penny of her pension into a savings account? Mrs. Cosgrove's late husband had been a casual laborer, when he bothered to work, so there was no pension coming from there. *She couldn't have lived on fresh air.*

He began to wonder if Mrs. Cosgrave had drawn out a lump sum every so often and lodged the money to a check account to meet her bills. A check account in a real bank seemed awful grand for someone from Balmoral Avenue.

There again, the Cosgrave's always thought themselves a cut above buttermilk.

'What about withdrawals?' he asked.

'They'd have to be done through headquarters in Glasgow.'

He sensed evasion and tried a bit of buttering up. 'You're a smart lassie, I'm sure you notice things.'

'We…ll.'

'Go on.'

She looked like she'd been caught fiddling the petty cash and glanced sideways to see if the clerk at the next position was listening in. Fortunately the other clerk was dealing with a girl from a solicitor's office purchasing a complicated mix of National Insurance Stamps.

'You see, when you make an entry in the book… you've got to use the next free line and it's impossible… You see things that aren't your business… It's not that you want to, but you can't help it.'

She'd said "an entry" not "entries" and that seemed important. Barlow leaned closer and cocked an ear, encouraging the confidence.

'There was this entry, thousands…'

He managed to stop his mouth falling open in surprise. Not a thousand but "thousands." Two thousand would buy a good semi-detached house. Would nearly buy his bungalow on the Ballymoney Road outright.

He had this gut feeling that whatever the late Mrs. Cosgrave had been up to, to earn that sort of money, it had nearly cost him his life.

Chapter 44

The muster for the Royal Black Preceptory's parade was set for a ten-thirty departure. By the time Barlow finished at the Post Office it was approaching ten. Still time for him to detour round by the Orange Hall and inspect the turnout of the parade before it set off. Sergeant Pierson was in command of the parade. However he had never served in the army and it showed in his personal appearance and in the standard of dress he expected from those under his command.

When the previous District Inspector was in charge, the constables escorting the marchers reported to the station where they were inspected and given their orders for the day. After that they made their own way to their respective posts throughout the town. On taking over, District Inspector Harvey had insisted on parading his officers in front of the Orange Hall. Harvey wanted to demonstrate to the bosses of the town that he was now the senior officer and worthy of greater things. Instead it came over as "This is us and we are one with the bosses". Not on my watch, was Barlow's opinion. *Though try proving that to some of the hotheads when they've drink taken.*

Harvey had mustered over twenty men to guard the parade: mostly regulars but some men from the B Special Reserves. He saw Barlow arrive and rushed over. 'What are you doing here?'

Barlow looked puzzled. 'Why call up the "B" Specials?'

'Because they're trained to take control in situations where there is civil disorder.'

'I'll agree with that, sir, but they're never available when Linfield is playing Ballymena United at home.'

Harvey flushed. 'Are you questioning my judgment?'

Barlow said, 'Last year there was only me, and a couple of constables for show.'

'A totally insufficient number if trouble had erupted.'

Harvey went rigid with indignation. 'Barlow, I have nothing against you personally, but you leading the parade? Really!'

Barlow said, 'They may be Protestant to a man but they're mostly old soldiers like me. They like a bit of swank so I call the time and so on.' His eyes drifted to Harvey's civilian medal ribbons.

Harvey bristled at the implied insult. 'Either way, it's got nothing to do with you this year so go on about your business.'

'Very good, sir.'

Barlow nodded to Harvey as if they'd been having a friendly conversation and walked off. His route took him past the lines of marchers. Gillespie stood in the front row beside Charles Denton. Like the rest of the "Black Men" they wore a pinstripe suit and bowler hat and carried a black umbrella neatly furled.

Barlow checked the marchers themselves. *A nearly perfect turnout,* was his opinion as he adjusted a chestful of medals to hang correctly. Latecomers were still arriving but the man he was looking for was a "no show". *He'd be here by now if he was coming.*

He stopped opposite Gillespie. 'If that bad chest of yours doesn't carry you off for walking in the rain, I'm cancelling your chit for flat feet. You'll be on foot patrol the day I'm back.'

'You do that every year. It's victimization because you're a Catholic and you're against us,' said Gillespie.

Barlow touched Gillespie's shoulder where an inspector's bars would sit.' You know what to do.'

Gillespie smiled at the thought of ordering Barlow around. 'Okay then, you're not a bigot. Just a pain is the ass.'

'You pass that exam or I'll make your life hell.'

Only being on parade stopped Charles Denton from laughing out loud. 'There'll be a blue moon the day you two agree on anything.'

Chapter 45

Barlow walked back to his car, keeping the pace down. It was going to be a long morning and he still wasn't feeling one hundred percent. He thought he'd bested Harvey in that minor confrontation, and that did him better than the tablet the doctor had given him. At the top of the town he parked his car in Warden Street and joined Edward at the junction of the Cushendall Road and the Broughshane Road.

Out of respect for the old soldiers on parade Edward wore his best suit and regimental tie. Pinned to his jacket was an impressive array of medals, starting with the George Cross and the Military Cross.

He gave Barlow a formal handshake. 'Good morning, Sergeant Major, I appreciate your attendance as my ADC on this auspicious occasion.'

'My pleasure, Major,' said Barlow as he attached his less impressive clip of medals to his jacket. He knew Vera would be annoyed when she spotted the two holes in the new material. He took position one step behind and to the side of Edward.

They waited for the parade to appear. The pause gave Barlow time to register a difference in Edward. This year there was no smell of alcohol off his breath. At the same time there was a hint of nervousness in Edward's stance that had nothing to do with withdrawal symptoms,

It puzzled him enough to do a bit of nosing. 'I didn't see you in the bar last night?'

In a way it was the truth, he hadn't been there himself.

Edward said, 'One was otherwise engaged.'

He knew Edward well enough to sense evasion. For years, Friday nights and other men's paydays, had always been reserved by Edward for serious drinking. Many a Hibernian parade or "Black Man's" day had been acknowledged by a man still the worse for wear from the night before.

'You'll be in tonight as usual?' Barlow asked.

'I'm afraid not, my dear chap. I've a little something special laid on for my dear lady.'

During the working week Edward remained sober. At weekends Edward's lover, Mrs. Anderson, allowed him to drink as much as he could hold. Yet here he was making excuses for remaining stone cold sober.

During the war Edward and Barlow had served together as bomb disposal officers. All through those years Edward had never touched a drop of alcohol and never took a day's leave. He wanted to be available and fit to deal with any bomb that the men under his command found difficult. Edward staying sober again could only mean that he was gearing himself up for something dangerous.

What that was had Barlow puzzled and it made him thoroughly uneasy. *I should have a word with Mrs. Anderson. See what she thinks.*

Right then a police van pulled into Warden Street and disgorged a squad of officers, including Harvey. Barlow thought that Harvey could never surprise him but he was stunned as Harvey detailed men to guard every road and kept a phalanx in reserve to bolster any group under pressure. In the distance the off-notes of the silver band accompanying the approaching marchers died away.

Edward called over to Harvey, 'My dear chap, may one enquire what one is about?'

Harvey didn't dare ignore Edward because Edward had the ear of Captain Denton. 'This is a potentially dangerous area,' he said. 'I'm ensuring that the parade passes through unmolested.'

The potential molesters were a handful of children swinging off the church rails while they waited for the excitement of the parade. Mothers bustled past carrying shopping bags.

Edward said, 'One hardly sees the point of such a show of force.'

Barlow muttered in his ear. 'All the potential troublemakers are at work.'

'And a final point,' said Edward. 'Why does the parade always choose to come in this direction when the railway station and the waiting train is at the other end of the town?'

Harvey pretended not to hear that question. Instead he took up position as the parade came into view. The morning air was filled with the sound of a single kettledrum and the tramp of marching feet.

Barlow said loud enough for Harvey to hear. 'Major, they do it to keep the workingman down. It reminds him of his dependency on their goodwill for a job.'

After that he concentrated on the approaching formation. The band he ignored. His attention was on the "Black Men" and their accompanying policemen. Pierson was in the lead followed by Denton carrying the silver sword of office. The men were trying to march in step but the long distance from the Orange Hall and the years that had passed since their army training had taken its toll. Their step was ragged. Denton was puce with annoyance at Pierson's inability to call time.

Barlow bellowed the beat. The whole parade snapped alert and boots crunched the tarmac as one. The parade reached the roundabout at the five-road junction. Edward stiffened to attention and put his hand over his heart as the band swung around the roundabout and headed back the way they had come and on to the railway station.

When the "Black Men" came level with Edward and the Catholic Church, Barlow roared the order for a general salute, 'Parade. Eyes… left.'

Chapter 46

Fortunately for Barlow the "Black Mans" parade was followed by rag-tag group of children and idle men. It gave him the chance to say a quick, 'See you around, Edward,' and head briskly for Warden Street and his car before Harvey could get to him. Two right-hand turns and he was back on Broughshane Street and ahead of the marchers. Church Street, Bridge Street and he was splashing across the tin bridge heading to the lower half of the town. That half of the town, better known as Harryville, housed much of the industry of the area – and some of the worse housing for the workers.

Barlow's destination lay in an estate of wartime prefab houses. The houses had small gardens and the occupants little hope of getting anything better from the council. Geordie Dunlop's house was better kept than most. What Connie Dunlop couldn't clean or fix, she stood over Geordie and the sons until it was done. Her garden had an immaculate little lawn squared off by seasonal flowers bought at the Saturday market.

She opened the door to Barlow's knock and immediately took in the dark suit. 'I take it it's the Sergeant Major that's calling and not that bastarding policeman?'

'Make me a cuppa, Connie, I'm gasping.'

Usually she'd stand back and let Barlow go first. This time she blocked his way to the kitchen, calling out, 'Geordie, it's Mr. Barlow to see you.'

Barlow heard a chair scrape back, glass rattle against glass and a cupboard door slam shut. Nothing unusual in that, he thought. Geordie had a bad conscience even when he had nothing to hide.

By the time Connie had struggled open an apparently stiff kitchen door Geordie was back at the table, deep in that day's paper.

Barlow sat across from him in the narrow wee kitchen, shocked at the difference in the man. Geordie had put on weight, not a good weight. He was bloated and his cheeks had gone through deep red to showing a tinge of purple.

'Whiskey always had that effect on you,' said Barlow.

'Never touch the stuff.'

Geordie burped. A puff of drink-laden air wafted over Barlow.

'It'll kill you, and serve you right. A lot of good men are losing their jobs because of you.'

'It wasn't me. I didn't go near the brewery. I got witnesses.' He gestured impatiently for Connie to leave the tea-making and join them. 'You tell him, Connie. Where was I that night?'

Connie called over. 'We were at The Thatch in Broughshane. Yon fat detective, Leary isn't it, checked with the owner for himself.'

'Did he now?'

Geordie couldn't have been in custody for more than an hour or two, so his story had held up. The son, Young Geordie, had been held longer but finally released for lack of evidence.

'It's a bad do, isn't it Mr. Barlow,' said Connie bringing his tea over. She pushed aside a pot holding a cascading plant to give him some elbowroom.

Barlow didn't know what to make of that days "cuppa". Normally he got the sharp edge of her tongue or a mug of tea in his hand. This time the tea came in a china cup with matching saucer and plate. The plate held apple tart straight out of the oven.

'Connie, love, if we were both free I'd marry you myself.'

'I soon will be the way certain people are going.'

A tear glistened at the edge of her eye.

She sat down between them. 'Tell me, Mr. Barlow, if you get the men responsible will it be a jail job?'

A tear glistened now in the other eye.

'It will, Connie, it was a bad steal. A lot of good people are suffering because of it.'

Grateful for the chance to rest his feet and for a bit to eat he took his time over the tea and apple tart. A mouthful of tea helped him gulp down one of Dr. Ingram's pep pills. Connie asked what he'd taken.

'A vitamin supplement.' He nodded at Geordie, 'Dealing with men like him, a packet of headache pills would come in handy.'

When he was ready to leave he stared hard at Geordie. 'So there's nothing you can tell me about it?'

Geordie shook his head.

Connie stood to show him out.

In the kitchen doorway Barlow looked back at Geordie. 'What about a Saab with a Belfast Registration?'

'I'm no grass,' said Geordie.

'Merely an idiot,' said Barlow and went on.

Chapter 47

***A right pack of idiots**, Barlow thought of the devil worshippers in the field below him.*

And devil take the Skyclad. That's only a fancy word for buck-naked and up for a bit of how's-your-father.

'So?' he asked Louise, the policeman in him needing to know about goings-on in the wheat field that Barlow the man currently didn't want to hear.

Louise settled against his chest, content that he now knew of her past life and hadn't reacted in disgust at her wantonness.

She said, 'Lug is the Celtic god of the sun. The rays from his radiance run in veins through the earth bringing warmth and light to the world. It also works with the other elements: water, air and the earth itself to provide all creatures with the sustenance of life - they make things grow.'

'And?' He didn't need to interrupt her with a question, he knew she would continue anyway, but first he wanted to run that word "sustenance" around his mind. He knew what it meant, could pronounce it in his head but never before had he heard it spoken. Times like this he regretted his lack of a formal education.

Down below the chanting had stopped. The worshippers - if that's the right word - *were sitting on the ground passing items one to the other. A gleam of light and a head tilted back had to be drink taken straight from the bottle. A glow-worm passed from hand to hand.*

I hope they watch those cigarettes.

Instead of talking on, Louise made herself busy tearing the crinkly paper off the Milk Tray. She scrunched it noisily into a ball and slid it into the folds of his jacket. He liked that, her wanting to take their rubbish with them instead of leaving it for some stupid cow to choke on. She opened the box but instead of giving him first choice she held the box up to the moon and selected two sweets. These she placed on the trunk of the fallen tree.

He asked, 'You're not going to eat those now?'

'It's an offering to Lug.'

It seemed daft, her more-or-less throwing good food away. 'So the tree gets first dibs?'

She selected a third sweet and pressed it into his mouth. He knew the taste, it was the sweet with the pink creamy filling. One of his favorites.

She said, 'Lug got the Turkish delight. I can't bear even the thought of it in my mouth.'

He agreed with her there.

She balanced the box on their thighs and they shared the chocolates while they watched the revelers below. Every time her hand delved into the box the contact transmitted itself to his body and made him tingle in contentment. Especially when she took her time selecting the chocolate she wanted. He made a point of only selecting a chocolate from the side of the box balanced on her thigh. Her smile and the way her body leaned into his let him know that his attentions were welcome.

Finally the harvest celebration involving the drinking and the smoking ended. The group stood up and clustered together, seemed to grow smaller. Then two of the men reappeared dragging an equally naked woman between them. She struggled to get away but the crowd pulled the feet from under her and lowered her to the ground.

He spat a chocolate out of his mouth. 'What the hell!'

He was half on his feet again, the chocolates spilling out of the box onto her lap.

She made a grab for him but missed. 'Wait!' she called before he could start running towards the group.

He pointed. 'Can't you see what they're going to do?'

'Yes, rape a virgin.'

He found himself standing poised to run, hand pointing: mouth open, angry at her lack of concern for the woman.

She said, 'It's been a long time since any of those women were virgins, or the men virile gods.'

Right enough, when he thought about it those weren't children or young adults down there. Sideways on, most of the group hung heavy with years of self-indulgence.

He sat down again and watched as one of the men went down on the woman. The rest circled them in a slow dance. He couldn't make out the words but the voices were definitely encouraging the couple on. When the man stood up again another man took his place.

'The dirty, filthy...'

This time instead of staying to watch, the group split up. Some women took a man by the hand and slipped out of the circle of lights. Others disappeared into the night hotly pursued by the men. One naked woman sneaked through the far hedge. In the end only the copulating couple remained on the ground while another man waited his turn.

Barlow didn't know what to think. There had to be a law against that sort of thing, lewdness in public. Maybe he should make a point of having a word with those devil worshippers in their homes and at their businesses. Panic them into putting an end to their little games.

Louise rolled into him until her breasts and stomach touched his. She kissed him open mouthed. He tasted chocolate, felt the granules of sweetener on her lips.

'Are you going anywhere, John?'

'Nowhere in a hurry.'

Chapter 48

The pep tablet began to take effect but Barlow knew he was pushing his energy levels dangerously low. Even so he had two more people to see and it would be unfair to keep Wilson's car beyond his lunch break. On his way out the Ballymoney Road he pulled into a garage and filled the petrol tank. He felt it was the least he could do for the young officer for being so generous with his beloved car, an old Austin A5.

Arthur Somerton was in his kitchen when Barlow drove into the farmyard. The rain, which had been fairly light until then, suddenly hammered down. Barlow parked as close to the back door as he could and ran the rest of the way. Arthur hadn't come to the door to greet him but remained in his chair by a roaring fire and shouted for him to come in. Barlow walked into the kitchen, shaking himself like a dog.

He started with. 'You didn't go to the parade today?'

'I'm getting on a bit. It's time I stopped that nonsense.'

Barlow sat in the chair opposite Arthur and pushed it well back from the fire. His legs were toasting in seconds yet Arthur wore an old cardigan. Arthur coughed on and off, occasionally he spat sputum into the fire.

Thanks to Louise's remark "the last time I was here I was still a married woman" Barlow knew he was on solid ground when he asked. 'The hanky-panky going on the night Fetherton was killed, it wasn't the first time, was it?'

'I wouldn't know,' said Arthur.

'Ah you would.'

'I'm a grand sleeper.'

'Arthur, with that cough?'

Arthur's smile was of embarrassment at old exploits being discovered. 'People would think I'm a dirty old man.'

'Well you are, but I bet you weren't the first time you saw

them.'

Arthur laughed himself into a fit of coughing. 'By God, Barlow, you've got it in one there. The very first time I got lucky. She came at me so hard I'd lost my virginity before I even knew it was at risk.' He sat back and sighed. 'There was a quick wedding soon after. I often wondered….'

An air of wistfulness came over Arthur.

'Why you didn't get lucky every time,' prodded Barlow, determined to keep the story going.

'They're not out there every year, it depends on the weather,' said Arthur knowing he was caught and deciding to come clean.

'So you pray for a dry Lughnasa?'

'None harder.' Arthur fought down the laugh and the cough that threatened to come with it. 'They never do any damage and often enough I got my bit of fun.'

Arthur's cough threatened to get the better of him. He nodded to the sideboard where a bottle of Bush sat among the bottles of tablets. Barlow got up and poured them both a decent glass.

Arthur drank and the cough settled. 'I was fine, Sergeant, until you came stirring old memories.'

'That hay cough?'

'It's been bothering me lately.'

Barlow was more a Jameson man but he liked the rawness of the Bush in his mouth. 'So you've watched them come and go all these years?'

'From girl to woman to old crone.' He thumped his chest. 'I'm not even fit to watch now, and that weather has put an ache in my bones.'

Barlow watched the flames dance in the fire as he sipped at his whiskey. He fetched Arthur a refill but only threatened his own glass. Settled back in his chair and watched the flames dance through the logs, letting silence work on Arthur's mind.

After a long pause Barlow said in a voice more in wonder

of youth at play than anything else. 'You'd have been telling Willie? I can see you two young bucks heading out there every Lughnasa seeing who you could pull.'

'Never,' said Arthur with force. 'Willie was better reared than me. Besides his old mother… May she rest in peace because she never gave peace to herself or anyone else in this life.'

Barlow remembered a crone of a woman with a sour look about her. 'A bit of a targer then?'

'You could say.'

'With Willie under her thumb?'

'Until the day she died.'

He could see it. An only son and an only child, a widowed mother and a farm to work. Willie on the go from dawn to dusk, because the old woman begrudged paying for something that could be done for nothing. The years had started to run together in his head but he thought Willie had been in his late thirties when the old woman died.

Barlow asked, 'You might have mentioned the goings-on after the old woman passed on?'

'No.'

That was a definite denial.

'And why not? You and Willie have been like brothers since way back.'

'Didn't Willie have a notion of Anna and didn't Anna have a notion of Willie?'

'So they were walking out together?'

Arthur spat a phlegm, more of disgust than content. 'If only.'

Barlow did a bit of calculating in his head. Arthur and Anna were sixty, give or take. Her twins were fifteen or sixteen, so she'd married in her early forties. Going by Arthur's "if only" that left a lot of years of non-courting. Barely enough time to start a family before it was too late.

He didn't know why he was bothering counting the years, but there was so much unknown about all these deaths that something, somewhere had to fall into place.

He said, 'Could you not have brought them to the mark sooner?'

Arthur said, 'They were shyer than me and look at the success I had in that department.' He indicated his house empty of a wife.

Instead of looking bitter or sad, a faint smile of memory played on Arthur's lips.

Barlow picked up on it. 'How did you manage it in the end?'

The smile became broader. 'I waited until a night of the Lughnasa, then I rang Willie and told him to come by the back road instead of his usual shortcut across the fields.'

'And?'

Arthur drained his glass in celebration of a personal victory. 'Wasn't I worried about strangers cavorting on our land? I insisted that the three of us go out to investigate. Disgusting it was all those naked people throwing themselves at each other.' He laughed until he choked. 'Didn't the night air get to my pains. I asked the two of them to stay on and make sure the wheat didn't go up in flames, while I went back to the house.'

'And it worked?'

'Aye, she came back with a look in her eye you'd see in a young heifer that's been well bulled.' He indicated a photograph of two teenagers. 'They popped out nine months later.' He leaned forward anxiously. 'That's between us, Mr. Barlow. I wouldn't want you writing that down anywhere.'

Barlow held up hands empty of anything other than his whiskey glass.

Chapter 49

Time was pressing and two o'clock and the promised return of Wilson's car getting close. Even so Barlow thought he should pay a courtesy call with Willie and Anna. Speaking to every witness was good police procedure and it didn't hurt to have Arthur's statement about the death of Fetherton checked out.

Willie and Anna's house was a modern bungalow set well away from the farmyard and its smells. The old house that his mother dominated in life had been turned into a piggery. *A bit of revenge there.*

Willie met him at the door. Willie was a moderately tall man with a bloom of health in his cheeks. From the way he brushed at a streak of grey in his hair it had to be recent. Willie's work clothes had been ironed and the house gleamed. God and love showed in every shining surface. At least that was the only way Barlow could explain it to himself, especially when he met Anna.

The only thing he saw of the children was their curious faces peering round the kitchen door. Anna shooed them back in and stood before the door as if on guard until Willie motioned for her to come and greet their visitor.

Shy and worn thin with nerves, was Barlow's quick assessment. Maybe more jittery than he'd expected of her, but people always felt uneasy when a policeman called unannounced. Her thumb constantly played with her wedding ring.

Barlow made sure he was smiling when he said, 'This is a courtesy call, just to see if Willie can add anything to his original statement.' He shrugged. 'It's funny the things people remember afterwards that could be helpful.'

He was escorted into a sitting room of deep pile carpet and plush chairs. Willie's old mother might have scrimped and saved, but obviously Willie thought only the best good enough for his

Anna. Good money had been spent on the furnishings and yet Barlow sensed an unease of style about the room, about the house itself. *Now what would I be knowing about these things.*

He refused the offer of a cup of tea. That was almost an insult when calling at a farmhouse but he was conscious of the time. He took a seat. Anna tried to slip away but Willie quietly pressed her to stay. They sat side by side on the settee. She leaned into him and he had an arm around her waist.

Arthur had said that recently Anna's nerves had got the better of her. Barlow envied Willie. His own wife's nerves were never as good as that at any time.

Willie hadn't seen or heard anything going on the night the devil worshippers were in the field: no noise, no cars and no fires. The first thing they knew of it was when Arthur rang and said for Willie to come, a rick was on fire. Finding the body was awful. Even now, a couple of weeks on, Willie looked upset at the memory. Anna confirmed all this with a nod or a shake of her head.

The timing of the fire puzzled Barlow. Presumably Fetherton had been killed during the devil worshipping. Why had someone, presumably the killer, waited until near dawn to set the rick on fire?

With no answers to be got from Willie and Anna, Barlow took his leave and headed into town by the back road. His way lay along the river. Normally it was little better than a stream. That day it had swollen with rain until it licked along the embankment. The low-lying meadows on the other side of the river were already under water. *There'll be trouble yet.*

That opinion was confirmed when he came across Water Board Lorries parked up. An engineer was looking up and down the length of the embankment, scratching his head.

Barlow stopped opposite him. 'Bad is it?'

'Nowhere near flood level, but that's not the point,' said the engineer.

'So what's the problem?'

'It's the embankment itself,' explained the engineer. 'It's high enough, as I say, but the rain we're getting this year has soaked through to the lower strata. Much more of this and it's likely to give way.'

'Send for a load of Dutch boys,' said Barlow and drove on.

The backyard at the police station was little better. Flood water from the little stream now seeped well up the yard. Barlow parked Wilson's car in a dry spot and slipped into the building by the backdoor. That way he avoided running into Harvey. He was sure something would be said about ordering a general salute when the "Black Men" were opposite the Catholic Church. *They didn't have to do it, they've got minds of their own.*

He found Wilson in the kitchen, the table ladened down with old ledgers and dusty files. He had never seen the boy look so content.

'With the greatest respect, son, you should be studying.'

Wilson burrowed his mind out of the papers in front of him. 'Sarge, I'm sick of exams, I've been doing them since I was at primary school. Whereas this…' He waved vaguely at the table in front of him.

This was the boy who had come to Barlow, angry and frustrated and determined to "show" everyone by getting promotion. 'You'll be glad of those exams someday.'

'Maybe, but right now the last thing I want to do is to figure out Shift Schedules and Personnel Reports.'

Rather than argue, Barlow thought he'd have a word with WPC Day. Her lips might be more persuasive than anything he could say. The Force needed people like Wilson at the top to sort out time wasters like Sergeant Pierson.

'Well seeing you're not revising for the exam, what have you got for me?'

Wilson handed over a thick bundle of papers. 'Every sighting of a Dunlop over the past two weeks: where they were seen, where they came from and where they went to.'

The reports of the sightings were heavy enough for Barlow

to feel their weight. 'Have they been running around the town like ferrets?'

'More or less.' Wilson indicated the old ledgers in front of him. 'They turn up in every page of these as well.'

Barlow blamed it on being ill, on not feeling the best. Better that than putting it down to stupidity on his own part. He'd told the boy to go through the old books and to pick out names in the early forties relevant to current cases.

He said, 'My fault, forget the Dunlops. Back then Geordie was in the army and the rest were of no account.'

Wilson said, 'I've got a sore hand from writing about them: Drunk and Disorderly, Causing an Affray, burglary, petty theft. You name it.'

He claimed that he was ready for a break and offered to run Barlow home. Barlow was glad to accept. It was either that or take another of Dr. Ingram's pills.

Chapter 50

The phone started ringing as the exhausted Barlow staggered in the front door.

He dumped Wilson's reports on the Dunlops onto the floor and grabbed the receiver.

Louise's voice came down the line. 'Where have you been?'

She sounded sharp, irritated. Standing while he took the call seemed too much effort. He slid down the wall and eased himself comfortable on the hall mat.

'Here and there,' he said.

'Here and there since early this morning? It's not good enough John, you're supposed to be resting.'

'I'm in for the night now.'

It sounded weak even to him.

'I should hope so.'

'How did the golf go?' he asked remembering her excuse for leaving him when he was just back from hospital.

'Don't try to change the subject.'

He took a berating about how ill he'd been. Lied a little about what he'd eaten for lunch – actually a bar of chocolate out of a shop near the petrol pumps where he'd filled Wilson's car. He loved listening to her voice and knowing that she was concerned for him. *This is what married life is supposed to be about.*

When she started to repeat herself, he asked in as contrite a voice as he could manage, 'Did you only ring to give me a bollocking or was there something else?'

She started to laugh down the phone. 'Don't try that little-boy-lost voice on me, John Barlow. It won't work.'

The reason for the phone call was simple and started with a question.

'Did you read that book I left you on the Wicca?'

'I did, it wasn't what I expected.'

'No goblins and evil spells?'

He couldn't resist saying, 'I see that modern witches are out of beaked noses and into sharp tongues.'

'Only when well deserved. You need a keeper.'

Is she considering taking on the job?

He kept that though in his head while she explained that she and other, unspecified, people were meeting in her house the next morning, Sunday. She thought that attending a service and being able to ask questions off her friends might help him with his enquiries.

His attendance wasn't an offer or request. It was a downright order and he couldn't believe that he didn't even dare argue. *Me, Station Sergeant Barlow? Even the Chief Constable is wary of crossing me.*

That day he wasn't fit to argue back. He could see years of verbal battles and standoffs stretching ahead of him, and loved the thought.

One thing he had to query.

'These Wicca services. You've this Skyclad thing where everyone takes off their kit and stands around.'

'And?'

'Well… I mean… I…'

'Eleven o'clock sharp. And make sure your underwear is clean.'

She hung up on him.

Chapter 51

When Barlow woke up it was dark and he was cold. He had fallen asleep on the hard tiled floor of his hallway, with Wilson's reports lying scattered around him. Barlow had gleamed one thing from the reports, something that the over-keen young constables had missed. Once the Dunlops realized that their movements were of *interest* to the police the extended family had led them in aimless circles around the town.

At that point Barlow had gone to sleep and now he was paying for it with cramped legs and an aching neck. The house was empty with Vera away at the wedding, so he could groan himself to his feet and hang over the hallstand until he got his back straightened.

He put on the light. The face that stared out at him from the hall mirror was drawn and haggard but he could sense strength coming back at last. He took one of Vera's pre-cooked meals out of the fridge and heated it until it was no longer chill.

While he ate he separated the reports into two piles. Those that mentioned Geordie or Young Geordie and those that didn't. The ones that didn't concern Geordie and his son he pushed aside. Most of the names in them were of young tykes who couldn't hold their water let alone keep a secret. If every brewery traveler in the country was on the lookout for the missing whiskey then no retail outlet dare buy it. If the Dunlops couldn't sell the stuff then they had to have it hidden, and somewhere handy going by the amount of whiskey Geordie was pouring down his neck.

The meal finished Barlow went to change out of his good clothes. The bed looked inviting so he thought he'd lie down for an hour.

He woke at four in the morning panicking about being at a Wicca service and having to strip naked in front of a lot of people. He quickly nodded off again but it was a disturbed sleep, with the same people scrubbing his body with spikey witches' brooms. He was almost glad when it was time to get up and switch on the emersion heater. No quick shower for him today. This needed a long hot bath and every inch of skin scrubbed clean at least twenty times.

He ate what should have been an enjoyable breakfast of porridge and toast. The thought of what lay ahead and the embarrassment that went with it twisted his stomach. He read through the reports again. Not that he held out much hope of finding anything useful but it diverted his mind. The town had plenty of rat-runs and hidden ways for the Dunlops to use when they wanted to avoid the police.

At eleven o'clock on the dot he presented himself at Louise's door. People were already there because the driveway was filled with cars. *Expensive ones too.* That didn't help.

Louise opened the door and took in his freshly pressed suit and shirt, and gleaming shoes.

'Underwear?' she asked.

'Brand new.' In his head he added, *Bitch*

She was wearing a blouse and skirt. *Easy to step out of.*

'Are you coming in or not?' she asked because he stood frozen on the top step.

'Aye, and why not?'

He stepped into the hallway and heard muted voices coming from the sitting room. She even had the sitting room door closed to drag out his worry about who he was going to meet, *and what they're not wearing.*

'Shoes,' she said and he took them off. Left them among a clutter of shoes, mostly women's, behind the door.

The people in the sitting room were all properly dressed, that was the first thing he noted. Ten of them, and he knew them all: three married couples, a widow, a widower and two old sisters. Decent too the pack of them, he thought, surprised that they were into this sort of thing. The room itself was large. The cream wallpaper and carpet gave it a sense of airiness. Red roses with entwined stems formed a large circle on the carpet.

Louise said, ‘I think you know everybody?’

‘I do,’ he said.

Just to show that he wouldn’t be intimidated he went round the room shaking hands with everyone there. Anyone who called him “Sergeant” he said “John” and that surprised him too, because anyone calling him “John” made them a friend.

An important government official, who worked in Stormont in Belfast and who rated a salute when passing him in the street, was now “Anthony.” *Eat your heart out Mr. Harvey.*

Anthony said, ‘John we don’t have a leader in our Chapter.’

‘I thought they were called covens?’

‘We prefer Chapter, like the Hell’s Angels.’

Anthony had made a joke of the interruption but Barlow knew he’d been rude.

He held up his hands in submission. ‘Sorry, professional bad habit.’

Anthony continued. ‘We meet more or less monthly in someone’s house. Our host will usually chair, guide, facilitate the service - call it what you will. However Louise thought it best that I take the lead today.’

Barlow sensed people taking up position when Anthony added, ‘Perhaps the best way to explain Wicca is for you to join us in a short service.’

‘I’d be honored to,’ said Barlow, his eyes busy going from left to right and back again.

Louise was busy putting a tray holding colored candles and a stick in the center of the carpet. The stick he recognized as a swagger stick, presumably her father’s from his army days. Beside the tray she placed four miniature cushions, all of different colors. The other members of the Chapter clustered together at the fireplace.

When Louise had finished making things tidy she took Barlow’s arm and guided him into the group. He was greeted by smiles and a squeeze of welcome from the old ladies. He noted with relief that nobody was unbuttoning anything or taking anything off. The men's jackets were already draped over chairs at the back of the room.

Anthony said, 'John, if you like you can remove your jacket. Once we start, the circle must not be broken otherwise bad forces may disrupt the forces of good and bring evil to our souls.'

Even slipping off his jacket seemed like the start of something dangerous. Louise took it off him, but first stood close to him, her hands and his entangled together in the material.

Her lips mouthed, 'I.'

His lips finished it for her, 'Love you.'

She stepped away from him and put his jacket with the rest. Joined him again and stood with the back of her hand touching his.

When they were all gathered together Anthony walked into the center of the roses and picked up the swagger stick. He swung it chest high in a slow circle saying, 'I call on those who enter the circle do so in perfect love and trust.'

Then he picked up the green cushion and placed it on the settee, saying, 'I call on the north and the earth to watch over the rights and wishes of all those present today.'

A yellow cushion was placed at the feet of those waiting to enter the circle. There Anthony invoked the air and the east. A red cushion was placed near the window, representing the south and fire, and a blue cushion near the door, representing the west and water.

Louise whispered, 'Normally we use lighted candles, but not on my good carpet.'

Finally Anthony stood at the yellow cushion and took the hands of the old ladies. 'Enter the circle with love and peace.' He escorted them to the settee where they sat down with obvious relief.

Each couple in turn received the same greeting. Barlow was brought in with Louise and made sit cross-legged on the arc of roses nearest the door. *And a quick flight.*

They all took the hand of their neighbors. Louise's hand was soft and warm in his, her smile encouraging.

He wondered when he should start worrying about clean underwear.

Chapter 52

Having closed the Wicca Circle and delineated the points of the compass, Anthony sat down and took the hands of the people on either side of him. He called out. 'The circle is complete. We will now enjoy a few minutes of Soul Flight.' He looked across at Barlow. 'Meditation. It brings stillness to our souls.'

Louise and the woman who held Barlow's other hand disentangled theirs from his and folded them on their laps. Bowed their heads. He did the same though he wasn't sure what he should do with all this stillness. *Maybe pray that no more kit has to come off?*

Without moving his head he eyed the people in turn: who they were and what they did. The problems they had to deal with. The single woman and man were long time widow and widower, both with grown children. They sat together, hips touching. That didn't surprise him. Once a year the man rang the station to say he'd be away for a week and would the police please keep an eye on the house. The woman always rang a day or two later to say she'd be away the same week.

Whatever stopped them from living openly together, Barlow hoped it would go away. *Is that what stillness is about, having time to think of others instead of yourself?* He thought of his sister in law, Daisy, just starting married life, of Vera and of his wife, Maggie. *Poor Maggie.* Even if Maggie wanted to come back, the family home she knew was no more and the wedding ring she had abandoned, destroyed.

He didn't know if he should say a Christian prayer or not. Maybe not a formal prayer but he could talk to God direct about things. *No harm in that.*

Anthony began to pray out loud. 'Brothers and sisters in The Secret, we are gathered here this day on the eve of a full moon. As the new moon waxes to its zenith let us gather our strengths into a combined whole. By faith we can improve our own selves. By faith we can help others achieve their needs.' He looked at Barlow. 'We cannot help those who do not wish for help.'

It was a warning. Whoever was using the powers of Wicca against him could not be stopped by prayer alone. *Who and why?*

Anthony motioned for everyone to join hands again and continued the prayer. 'We acknowledge the moon, the sun and the stars as the representatives of the Goddess in all her three forms: the maiden, the mother and the crone.' Again he seemed to speak mainly to Barlow. 'It is through the power of the Goddess that all things come in threes, even to those who don't believe.'

Threes! He had those all right, *in a triple dose*. Fetherton, Granny Cosgrave and Mary Jo; Vera, Louise and Maggie; Edward, Geordie and Harvey.

Somehow those combinations didn't seem right.

Wicca curses had been used against him: the Wolfsbane and the broken heart. That made two. *Things come in threes.*

At least it wasn't a long prayer. Anthony was winding up.

'What we give in faith we receive back threefold. What we give in bad faith comes back a hundredfold.'

Then to Barlow's surprise he produced a bible. Instead of tearing it up or burning it or impaling it with a sharp blade, he opened it at a marked page and began to read: "Matthew 17: 20. If ye have faith as a grain of mustard seed…"

The reading finished there was a short Soul Flight then Anthony walked to the center of the circle and knelt before the tray containing the colored candles: one black, one orange and one white.

He addressed the whole Chapter while speaking directly to Barlow. 'John Barlow, all here know you to be a man of integrity who has served this town faithfully and well over many years. We know that over the years you have had more than your share of troubles and are currently beset with new problems.'

He struck a match and lit the black candle. 'By this light

may your troubles be brought to the fore.'

He lit the orange candle from the black candle. 'By this light may those troubles be drawn out.'

Finally he lit the white candle from the orange one. 'And may you live in peace.'

The ceremony was over. Everyone stood and walked in single file out of the circle. As they stepped out they said, 'For the good of all and the harm of none.'

Barlow helped Louise to put the furniture back in place and then joined the rest in the kitchen where tea and coffee were being poured. A plate of biscuits was doing the rounds.

Anthony took Barlow aside. 'Not quite what you were expecting?'

'To be honest, Louise had me a bit wound up about…'

Anthony raised an eyebrow. 'Being Skyclad, like our friends in Somerton's wheat field?'

'Well yes.'

He got a sympathetic nod. 'Some people use the Wicca Way for unsavory rituals. Others, like the Gardnerians genuinely find nakedness the way of enlightenment.'

More like titillation or worse, in Barlow's opinion, but he didn't say it.

Louise was watching them from across the room. If she'd been close enough Barlow would have wrung her neck for the worry she had caused him about having to strip off in public.

'So this Chapter doesn't do it then, the Skyclad thing?'

Anthony had caught the look between him and Louise and was highly amused. 'Oh we do the "Skyclad thing", but only on two specific occasions. When a new member is initiated and every Beltane – Mayday to you – when we renew our marriage vows by a Handfasting Ceremony.'

'But buck naked? What's the point?'

'That, John, is something you have to experience to understand.'

Chapter 53

The tea drunk and the biscuits eaten people began to leave. One of the elderly sisters wanted to stay and wash the dishes. "We always do,' Barlow heard her say. He also saw the nudge-nudge, wink-wink, between the other members of the Chapter. To them at least he and Louise were in a relationship, and they approved. That gave him a warm feeling. Especially when he saw the heightened color in her cheeks and the extra bounce in her step.

He stayed in the kitchen stacking dirty dishes while the final goodbyes were said, the last car driven off. Louise came back into the kitchen. It seemed right for them to come into each other's arms. He enjoyed her scent, the feel of her hair on his cheek. Enjoyed the sensation of his hand on the zip of her skirt and knowing she wouldn't object if he pushed the zip down and undid the hook and let the skirt fall.

When putting the milk back in the fridge he'd seen a bowl of potato salad big enough for two people and two lamb steaks. No dessert, they'd find that in bed together.

Instead he pulled back from her embrace. 'I've got to go.'

'What?'

He hated the thought of leaving, but if he didn't go now he'd never surface from her body until it was too late.

'Sorry, there's someone I have to see.'

'Couldn't you put it off? I've everything ready… I thought you'd be staying.'

He could sense it, the pain for the number of men who had come and used her body and gone callously back to their own lives. He hated hurting her. If even one tear appeared he'd be lost.

'What you could do for me,' he said praying for his voice to stay firm, 'is to meet me in forty-five minutes outside McCann's pub.'

'You're not going drinking?'

'It's Sunday, the pubs are shut.'

'See yourself out.'

She marched over to the sink and started to wash the dishes in a froth of water and soap suds.

He made himself walk to the kitchen door and open it. 'You'll be there, McCann's, in forty-five minutes?'

'I've got things to do as well.'

'Please.'

Her "okay" hit him like a whiplash. Delicate china plates and cups were swirling around in the water, stirred by her furious hands. He left because there was nothing else he could do.

His route took him onto the Galgorm Road and up Princes Street to Balmoral Avenue. He supposed he should be grateful that the rain had eased to a mizzle. It saved him arriving at the Cosgrave house looking like a drowned rat.

Some of the neighbors had taken the opportunity of the break in the weather to catch a breath of fresh air at their doorways. Barlow slowed his pace to a leisurely stroll.

'It's a grand day,' he told one old man who stood in his shirtsleeves, braces hanging down the back of his legs.

'If you're a duck,' came the reply.

Barlow pulled out a new packet of cigarettes, opened the pack and put one in his mouth. He offered one to the old man who accepted with a nod of thanks. They lit up. Barlow inhaled carefully. He hadn't had a cigarette since being ill and was afraid it would make him dizzy.

'It's quiet around here,' he said.

Not a car or person moved in the street though he could hear traffic on the now distant Galgorm Road.

'It's good practice for the grave,' said the old man.

'And even quieter since Mrs. Cosgrave passed on.'

The old man said nothing, drew pointedly on his cigarette.

'A lot less cars about, that makes it safer for your grandchildren when they go out to play,' Barlow said.

'If they ever visit.'

Barlow took that bitter remark as confirmation of fewer cars coming into Balmoral Avenue. He had a couple more puffs for forms sake then ground out the cigarette on the pavement and walked on.

Chapter 54

Mary Jo Cosgrave had seen Barlow enter Balmoral Avenue. She had rearranged the furniture in the small sitting room so that she could sit and look out the front window.

'Better that than staring at the fireplace where Granny died,' she explained as she ushered Barlow into the sitting room. She looked pleased to see him.

'I can understand that,' he said.

He took Granny's chair near the fire. Mary Jo sat down and adjusted her skirt until a bit of knee showed. The skirt was the one she'd worn on the day they first met. Which reminded him to check out the cut under her chin. It now an angry little mark that was quickly fading.

Barlow said, 'I'm not here for any particular reason.' He waved his hands about to show uncertainty. 'Well… I wanted to thank you for coming to see me in the hospital.' He ignored Mary Jo's dismissive gesture. 'I appreciate you thinking of me when you had your own problems.'

'It was a pleasure.' She seemed to mean it.

He said, 'I was wondering about something you said when you visited. Funerals cost money. Was there enough money to pay the bills? I know we didn't find any Savings books and I was worried, wondered really how you were going to cope.' He paused, seeking for the right words. 'Call it a professional courtesy thing.'

Mary Jo beamed. 'You're absolutely charming, Mr. Barlow, a real friend.' Now he could look embarrassed while she added. 'Yes I found the passbook, it was caught in among a lot of papers.'

'That's great. And everything's okay?'

'There's enough there to pay the bills and leave a few bob over.'

'That's great.' He repeated and checked his watch. The second hand seemed to be blurring round. 'Why don't I take you to the Castle Arms for a drink to celebrate?'

'It's Sunday,' she reminded him. 'No bars are open.'

He looked at her from under his eyebrows.

She laughed. 'It's the same in England. I'll get my coat.'

She bounced out of the room, her footsteps pounded up the stairs. He got up and stood by her chair at the window. From there he could see up Balmoral Avenue to the turn onto Princes Street.

Mary Jo popped her head around the door. 'I'm forgetting my manners. I never offered you a cup of tea.'

He hadn't heard her slip down the stairs.

He said, 'You can buy the first round.'

'Deal.'

She disappeared again. This time he heard her footsteps on the bedroom floor. That, he reckoned, gave him thirty seconds at most. He tiptoed across to the sideboard and opened the drawer where Wilson had found the book on witchcraft. Searched through the envelopes and even looked in them, but the book had gone. He closed the drawer and was back at the window before Mary Jo's footsteps sounded coming down the stairs.

'What kept you?' he called out and heard her laugh.

They went out the front door together. It seemed incredible, but the rain had stopped though dark clouds hung over the town to the east. It was nice to clatter down the street without having to duck his neck into his collar to avoid the rain.

Nearing the bottom of Princes Street he said, 'I'm surprised you're still here. Compassionate Leave in the Met must be very generous.'

'I'd some leave due.' He could feel her search for the words, even wonder if she should say what was on her mind. 'Now I'm home again it might be nice to stay.'

'If you want to transfer into the RUC, you only have to say the word.'

'I think I've had my fill of being in the police. I only joined to please my father.'

He made himself sound anxious. 'But you'll stay anyway?'

'Yes, I'm getting a friend to send my personal things over.' She brushed impatiently at her skirt. 'I've worn this so often now I'm sick of it.'

'There's nothing wrong with it,' he said as they swung onto the Galgorm Road.

He hardly heard her say "Typical man" because Louise wasn't at McCann's pub. He supposed he'd expected too much off her. Then he saw the edge of her yellow coat flap. She was in the doorway of the sweetie shop across from McCann's. *Of course! She wouldn't stand outside the pub itself in case people got the wrong idea.*

Mary Jo linked her arm solidly into his. 'You've no idea how much I appreciate you calling. It's nearly impossible to rebuild old friendships.'

'And I appreciate your company,' he said.

Out of the corner of his eye he could see Pierson's moon face at the window of the Enquiry Office. *If that man ever does a day's work I'll die of shock.*

Mary Jo still held his arm and was hugging her shoulder into his when they came level with the sweetie shop.

Louise stepped out of the doorway. She was white faced, her mouth set tight with fury. She didn't speak, merely swung her hand. The blow hurt. The backhander caught his nose and he felt blood trickle.

Louise stalked past him. There was nothing he could say to bring her back.

Mary Jo had let go of his arm. 'Oops, that was my fault.'

He put a handkerchief to his nose to catch the blood. 'If you don't mind, I'll skip that drink.'

Chapter 55

Barlow went home. There was no use in trying to talk to Louise until she had calmed down, and even then he didn't know what to say to her. To explain. *Explain what?* He felt his mind was in a big steel ball and being tumbled this way and that. Everything was happening and nothing was making sense.

Back in the house he wiped off the blood from around his nose and held a damp towel to his burning cheeks. *That bitch has some swing.*

There was one cooked meal left in the fridge. Public transport in the Province was disastrous on a Sunday, so Vera had planned to come back home on the Monday. 'And I'll be here first thing, Dad, so make sure the house is the way I left it.' He made himself a cup of tea and left the meal untouched.

He'd done it in previous cases and it had worked. He thought he'd try again – make a written list of the people involved and see how they interacted with each other.

He sat at the kitchen table with pencil and paper and wrote out the names:

> Fetherton, Granny Cosgrave and Mary Jo.
> Vera, Louise and Maggie.
> Edward, Geordie and Harvey.

No matter what way he looked at it the list still seemed incomplete.

Distance from a problem tended to give things perspective. He made himself a fresh cup of tea and wandered into the sitting room.

He walked carefully because, 'Hell hath no fury like a daughter when she sees stains on the good carpet.'

He said it out loud because he was weary of a house empty

of other people. *Of my own life.*

'What to do about Louise?'

He stood at the window and sipped tea and watched rainwater run down the road. If he stood to the side and looked to the left he could see Mount Street, named probably after the steep slope it ran up. On the far side of Mount Street from him was a long stretch of waste ground. Water from the little stream at the top of that waste ground was pouring down the street, creating an interesting white-water effect.

A bell started to ring. It startled him and for a moment he couldn't think what it was.

'The telephone, someone's ringing.'

I'm talking to myself. I'll be answering next.

He went out into the hall and picked up the receiver. It was Wilson on the other end. Barlow knew it had to be bad because Wilson tried to make light of his news.

'Sarge, it's terrible, Sergeant Pierson is singing.'

'I didn't know he could.'

'He can't, and he's identified your lady friend.'

'Has he now?'

He says it's Mary Jo Cosgrave. He saw the two of you link arms down the street. Inspector Foxwood is away up to speak to her.'

The fact that Barlow had been with a lady the night Fetherton was murdered was supposed to be confidential, known only to senior officers. The only way Wilson could know was if someone had told him. And if Pierson had blabbed to him then he'd blabbed to the whole station as well. *That man needs sorted.*

Meantime he had Wilson on the phone. Try as he might to hide it the young officer was amused at his Station Sergeant being caught out in a bit of hanky-panky.

'Don't worry about it, son. Did WPC Day enjoy the trip to Belfast yesterday?'

'It turned out that my mother was working. WPC Day was on her own and it was pouring with rain so we went to the pict…

How did you know?'

Barlow had never actually used the word "naive" but he was thinking it then. 'Is there any other earth-shattering news or can I go and make my lunch.'

Wilson laughed, probably in relief that he wasn't going to be teased any further. 'There was one thing, just the coincidence of the Cosgrave name. I came across it in an old letter. Totally unrelated of course.'

Rusty cogs in Barlow's memory stirred. 'Go on.'

'In 1940, that was during the war you know.'

'I remember reading about it in the papers.'

'Sorry, Sarge.' Wilson didn't sound sorry. 'Well anyway, a DCI Cosgrave was sent over to Ballymena from the Met. It had to be Mary Jo's father.'

There was a pre-set fire in the fireplace. Barlow wished he'd lit it earlier because he suddenly felt a chill that reached deep inside him. 'What was he doing here?'

Wilson's voice changed pitch and slowed as he paraphrased an entry. 'He was to see that all enemy aliens had been taken into custody. Being local himself he was also involved in identifying Fifth Columnists and people likely to be pro-German.'

Barlow said, equally slowly, 'So the District Inspector was requested and required to give DCI Cosgrave all necessary co-operation and assistance, including unrestricted access to the station's records.'

Wilson was full of admiration. 'Sarge, you must have seen that letter at some time. You were nearly word perfect.'

'Son, I didn't know it existed.' He chose his words carefully. 'Immediately, and I mean immediately Inspector Foxwood returns, you personally are to put that letter into his hands. I also want you to dig out an old file relating to a Chris Cosgrave and give that to Inspector Foxwood as well.'

He got Wilson to repeat his orders to make sure they were clearly understood.

He could sense a glow to Wilson's cheeks as the young officer said, 'Sarge, about Susan… WPC Day, we're all trying to jolly her along after that fiancé dumped her. There's nothing more to it than that.'

That boy couldn't lie to save his own life.

'Of course not, son.'

Barlow went back into the sitting room and put a match to the fire. He closed the heavy drape curtains against the chill of the day outside and cuddled a cushion to his chest.

He thought the room would never warm.

Chapter 56

Barlow roused himself in the end because sitting waiting for things to happen wasn't in his makeup. If Deputy Commander Cosgrave, then a mere Detective Chief Inspector, had seen Chris Cosgrave's file then Mary Jo had to know about it as well. Which explained why she always latched on to him anytime Louise was about. It also moved her off the list of threes onto a column of her own. One warped bitch out to get her revenge by driving him and Louise apart.

He'd seen the poison plant, the Wolfsbane, in the garden before Granny Cosgrave was killed. *Mary Jo was still in England then.* As for that bit of candle, the broken heart. That could have been there for days, weeks even. He didn't believe that.

But the petrol can?

The petrol can had to be a straight plant by someone determined to have him blamed for Fetherton's murder. So someone was coming and going freely around his garden. How did they know they wouldn't be spotted, that the house was empty? The only way that could happen was if someone was spying on him and Vera. They'd see her go off in her Woolworths outfit and him heading down to the station for his shift. Which gave the watcher more than enough time to do some mischief and be well away before either of them got back.

Tomorrow morning, first thing, he'd have a good look outside. Meantime, making things right with Louise was more important than worrying himself silly over mere harassment.

He fetched the book on Wicca that Louise had given him and began to read through it, paying particular attention to colors and their significance. On the section – admittedly short, he noted – dealing with Skyclad, Louise had marked the subheading with an asterisk guiding him down to a note in her handwriting at the bottom of the page.

**There are some things you have to experience to understand their significance.*

Explanation and, perhaps, self-justification, he felt. All the same he had no intention of going Skyclading with the group. Neither did he feel the urge to try drugs to see what effect they had on people.

When his mind popped a sideways thought like that it had to be important. Barlow frowned and looked again at his list. *Should I put drugs on a fifth line?*

He read and re-read the book on Wicca and put more coal on the fire to keep his toes warm, then added damp slack. Any watcher seeing the increased smoke coming up the chimney would know that he was at home.

At heavy dusk he switched on the light in the hall and went into the scullery. He finally heated the meal left by Vera and ate it at the kitchen table. From there he could see beyond the yard to the back garden. Pulled on a coat against the renewed rain, and went out to refill the coal bucket. Apparently forgetting to turn off the yard light on his return.

He thought an early night would be in order because he was supposed to be recovering from the poison. That meant him reversing the role, going around switching off lights and making sure doors and windows were secure for the night. When pulling down the blinds in his bedroom he resisted the almost overwhelming compulsion to stare in the direction of Mount Street.

With the main light on in his bedroom he made sure his shadow crossed and re-crossed the blinds while he changed into his pajamas. Except the pajama top was the shirt he had just taken off and the bottoms a pair of slacks.

He read for a while, he'd got into that habit since Maggie had left, then turned out the light. Boots, socks and reefer jacket in hand, he crawled out the bedroom door and slid along the corridor in case anyone was watching in through the glass panels at the front door. He opened the kitchen window and crawled out into the yard. With the blade of a penknife he did the reversal of a burglar's trick, locking the window again from the outside.

Everything he wore was dark. He held an arm up to cover his face and crept along his neighbor's boundary hedge until he reached the convent wall. There he crouched and watched to see if he had been spotted. If a watcher could see him in the reflection of the street lights on the road, then he could see them. After fifteen minutes, and confident that he was in the clear, he jammed his toe onto an outcrop of lava stone and hauled himself up and over the wall into the convent grounds.

'My apologies,' he mouthed to The Sisters of Saint Louis.

Nuns being nuns, the grass was kept cut short even if the ground was soggy. He squelched across the lawn and through a line of trees to the wall on the Cullybackey Road. He could either climb the wall and give some innocent passer-by a heart attack at his sudden appearance, or... The heavy front gates were held closed by a simple latch. Barlow knocked up the catch, stepped onto the pavement and quietly closed the gate behind him. It didn't squeak. He'd depended on that, nuns did everything for the Glory of God, even if it was only oiling a squeaky gate.

He crossed the road into Clarence Street and found the entrance to a rat-run across the fields favored by the Dunlops. One of them was coming along the rat-run now, a short, thin figure, who whistled under his breath. Barlow stayed deep in shadow until the Dunlop-by-blood-not-name had passed.

The fields were a quagmire and he muttered his disgust as he trudged through sticky mud. Another rat-run brought him onto the Galgorm Road by Beechfield Close, almost across from Leighinmohr Avenue. The long hard slog over walls and through hedges and across fields had tired him to the point of irritable exhaustion.

Louise's house was in darkness. Barlow rang the bell. If it hadn't been for the tenants above he'd have kept his finger on the bell until Louse appeared. As it was it took a third ring before a light came on in the hall.

Louise's said, from behind the solid outer door. 'Who's there?'

'John.'

The door didn't open immediately, she'd thought about it first. She wore a red dressing gown, her hair sleep tossed. She looked utterly beddable.

Barlow said, 'You are one bad tempered bitch.'

Chapter 57

Barlow went face to face with Louise, close enough to smell her breath. When she failed to invite him in he shuffled his boots against her bare toes until she retreated back past the inner door.

The colors of the miters on the stained glass were the primary colors of red, green and blue and represented the three strands of the She Goddess. This he'd learned from the book on Wicca. The black and white runs of glass in the edging, the colors Louisa had worn when she'd visited him in hospital, denoted: energy, purity and light. Now he knew these things – *God only knows what else is in the house* – it felt like desecrating a temple, but he was determined.

With Louise trapped in the hallway he kicked off his boots and gave his trousers a second turn-up to keep mud off the carpet. Why she didn't pick up something and hit him with it, he didn't know. She looked mad enough, standing there arms folded, a stubborn look on her face.

In his stocking feet he grasped her shoulders and guided her by gentle pushes towards the sitting room.

With the first push he said, 'On our first date you wore green for physicality. When you took me into the oak grove you were offering our physical union, the Great Rite as you call it, to the She Goddess.'

On the second shove he said, 'When I called at this house unannounced you were wearing blue, denoting emotions and when you looked in Caulfield's window you wore the yellow coat. That's rational thought.'

Now he had her right on the doorstep of the sitting room. 'Green was for the unknown but possible future relationship. Blue, hope for a future together and yellow because it had started to happen.

He gave her that final push into the sitting room and turned on the light.

She said, 'I'm wearing red now.'

'Aye, red. Red for will power and courage. Red to suit the mood you're in: stubborn as hell and thick as champ.'

If she was going to make a run for it she'd have done it by now. He left her standing in the middle of the circle of roses and scooped up the cushions from the settee. Trapping the four small cushions to his chest he picked up the poker from the fireplace and handed it to her. 'Make your magic circle.'

There was an implied threat in the way she stood, poker in hand.

'Make it.'

She did, holding the poker high as she turned, but low enough for it to brush his hair. When she had completed the circle he took the poker off her, then he lobbed the cushions into their four quadrants.

She said, 'I don't know what you're planning to do, but there's nothing worse than an amateur who thinks he knows it all.'

He said, 'Strip.'

'Certainly not.'

He could feel millennia of outraged blue blood in that refusal.

He went nose to nose with her. 'If you don't strip, I'll do it for you. And if you fight back you could be bruised. I don't want that, but strip you will.'

She breathed out at him, angry puffs through clenched teeth. Reluctantly her hands loosened the tie of her dressing gown and let it fall away.

Now he could see her nightdress, three-quarter length in silk that clung to her curves. He could only catch his breath at her beauty even as he said, 'Off.'

Again there was the silent confrontation before she crossed hands at her thighs and lifted the material above her head. It was done so slowly she could have been teasing him. From the look on her face he thought it sheer defiance.

Her breasts were succulent, with a slight stretch from age.

He kept his eyes locked on hers. 'And the rest.'

She said, 'This is rape.'

'Call it what you will.' He was deliberately crude. 'Get your knickers off.'

She pushed them down and stepped out of them. Stood defiant, not even covering herself with her hands.

She could try to run and didn't. Could scream and arouse the sleeping tenants on the first floor. She didn't do that either. Relieved that whatever happened was between them he stepped back from her and undressed. Jacket, shirt, trousers, socks and new underwear for the occasion. Finally naked he stood before her.

'Damn,' he said.

'You deserve to be for this,' she said.

He ignored her catty comment. He'd forgotten to bring his laces and now they'd started he couldn't break the circle to go fetch them. The dressing gown tie was too big for what he had in mind. For a moment he panicked thinking it was all ruined. *The knickers!*

He picked them up, took one of her hands and slipped it down one leg. Twisted the material tight so that it wouldn't fall off.

She held out her second hand without being asked. 'I'm surprised you didn't think of handcuffs.'

He took her second hand, held if for a moment then released it again. Slipped his own hand into the second opening of her pants.

They stood close, joined hands at chest height. He could finally cup her breasts, kiss unresponsive lips.

'Now what?' she asked

He said, 'Under the laws and auspices of Wicca I join with you, Louise Carberry, in the union of marriage for the Wicca term of one year and a day.'

She said, 'Not if hell froze over first, would I marry you.'

Chapter 58

Louis pulled away from Barlow. He quickly put another twist in the pants so that she couldn't easily slip her hand free.

'Who do you think you are, John Barlow, coming in here and laying down the law?'

He had thought her angry before, that was only froth to the fury that now burned in her eyes.

'I'm a woman so obviously I need a man to tell me how to run my life.' She pointed at the door. 'You forced your way into my home, and the first thing you did was check my breath for drink. If I had been drinking, what would you have done then? Run?'

He would have, he knew it. 'I've enough problems with Edward.'

It sounded like an excuse even to him.

Now a hand was against his chest, thumping it with every word. 'Let me tell you, John Barlow.' The pointing hand aimed in the direction of the kitchen. 'I opened a bottle of wine tonight. Then I thought, why suffer a hangover because of another useless man? It's in the fridge, untouched.' He got a final hard thump on the chest. 'I've got the occasional problem with drink, fair enough. But what's your problem, John Barlow, other than the fact that you play God with people's feelings?'

'No I don't.' he hated himself for giving another weak reply, but he didn't know how to defend himself.

'Oh, no? So I am supposed to accept you pawing that Cosgrave woman and any other piece of skirt that you fancy…'

He thought he'd better interrupt before she started screaming at him to get out. 'I wasn't pawing her.'

'So you have another word for what I saw? Sweet innocence? No harm done?'

'She was pawing me.'

He was beginning to realize what Harvey went through when he steamrollered his superior.

'And that's different?' she hissed.

'She grabbed me anytime she saw you come. She wants to break us up.'

Louise paused to consider this. 'It's not like you're the greatest catch in the country.'

He ignored the insult. Just getting breathing space was enough.

He said, 'Her uncle drowned because of me. I think she wants her revenge.'

'When?'

'Long before she was born, but the Cosgraves have even longer memories.'

It had to be the row and the raw emotions it generated but he could see it again in his mind's eye. Chris Cosgrave diving into the river to avoid the police and being caught in the swirl of floodwater. And him standing there, still a child, a runaway from the Workhouse, and unable to help. His fault, because he'd seen the three youths break into the castle when Edward and his sister were away at a party, and had called the police.

He said, surprised at the shake in his voice, 'I thought I was doing the right thing. All my life I've had to find my own way. I never had anyone to share decisions with.'

He tried to pull his hand free of the binding material. To dress and apologize, to walk away and promise never to bother her again.

She grabbed his wrist and stopped him with his hand still trapped in the material. 'Under the laws and auspices of Wicca I join with you, John Barlow, in the union of marriage for the Wicca term of one year and a day.'

For a moment he thought she was teasing him or, worse, mocking, but she was smiling her sweet smile.

Reassured he said, 'I give you my love and my gratitude for your gift to me, of a greater understanding of people and the generosity of their actions.'

She said, 'I give you my love and my gratitude for your gift to me of forgiveness for wrongs done.'

He didn't want to think of what she'd done over the years to keep a roof over her head. That was a different woman in a different lifetime. Hopefully he was a different man.

There was a pause while he wondered what to do next. He hadn't thought much beyond the mechanics of the marriage ritual.

Not knowing if he was doing the right thing he untangled his hand, retrieved her dressing gown and draped it over her shoulders. Instead of retying the girdle she moved her body against his and wrapped the dressing gown around them both. Their kisses were gentle, deliberately not building passion.

At a pause for breath she asked, 'What now, John?'

Chapter 59

Barlow had learned his lesson about sharing, 'I was going to take you to my house. Then when Vera arrived home tomorrow you'd be a…' There was a phrase, he couldn't think of it.

'Fait accompli,' she said and he nodded.

It was difficult to break off kissing a second time because by now their bodies were joining in. The dressing gown lay forgotten, puddled around their feet.

'So what now?' she asked.

'Stay here…' He corrected himself. 'I suggest we stay here tonight and I'll speak to Vera myself in the morning.'

She shook her head, smiling. 'You've stood on your own long enough. I think we should go with the first option.'

Now a tear really did fall. It took all his willpower not to scrub it away with the back of his hand. Years of loneliness, of staring at blank walls at night, fell away.

A Wicca wedding had seemed erotic. Now he understood the true meaning of Skyclad. Of a total giving of oneself with nothing held back.

They broke contact, stepped apart.

She moved towards the door. 'I'll throw a few things in a case.'

He called softly, 'Mrs. Barlow.'

She turned back. He'd intended to say "You won't need any night things" but the pleasure in her face at being called "Mrs. Barlow" stifled the words.

'Mr. Barlow,' she said softly.

'Mrs. Barlow,' he repeated.

Her eyes were gentle on his. Again that smile. 'I take it I won't need any night things?'

She can read my mind.

'Only if it snows.'

She left. He redressed, went back into the hallway and retrieved his boots. Put them on. He could hear her move about in the bedroom: the swish of hangers, drawers opening and closing. Guessing that she'd want a little time to herself he stood on in the hallway.

Eventually she reappeared. She was wearing the green turquoise dress, the "giving" dress he thought of it. He took the overnight case off her and helped her pull on her yellow overcoat. Stood in the rain while she secured the front door behind them. Went to the car, deliberately choosing the passenger side. He felt he was watching someone else do these things. Someone very like him but different. A kinder, gentler person. They settled in the car.

He put a hand on her knee, well below the panic line. 'Mrs. Barlow.'

She took her hand off the choke and touched his leg. 'Mr. Barlow.'

It took an effort for him to say, 'I love you.' The depth of what he was feeling made them sound like meaningless, made-up words.

They stretched for more kisses before she drove off. Up Leighinmohr, down the Galgorm Road past the police station. Lights were burning in offices where there should have been darkness. *Something's up.* If a policeman was down, someone would ring the house and tell him. Other than that he didn't care.

The Pentagon, then they were on the Ballymoney Road. He could see blue lights and people moving near the top of Mount Street. *This could be serious.*

He caught Louise looking at him. 'If you want to go,' she said.

'They'll shout if they need me.'

He loved her for that understanding of what it was to be a policeman and responsible for a town of people.

She turned into his – *OUR* – driveway. Only then did he notice that the hall light was on and that lights showed around the edges of the sitting room curtains.

He said, 'Vera's home, she must have got a lift.'

He'd hoped for time to readjust to their new life together before the row, *and row there will be,* started.

Louise said, 'I'll be right behind you.'

'That's what the staff officers used to say.'

He had to put it that way, to build resistance for the arguments to come.

Louise took the night case off him while he hunted out his front door key. As he pushed open the inner door a dog, a Jack Russell, came snarling out of the sitting room, hackles raised. It stopped in its tracks showed its teeth and wagged its tail. Kept snarling.

Vera appeared in the doorway. The three of them looked at each other. Barlow with his key still in his hand. Louise with the suitcase, obviously come to stay. Vera with her mouth open for words that didn't come.

Eventually she said, 'Dad, Mum's home.'

Chapter 60

Barlow stood stupid. *Maggie's home?*

But this wasn't her home, never had been. She'd walked out of the old house taking the dog and her knitting bag, and leaving her wedding ring on the dressing table.

It's not fair!

He could see on Vera's face a look of disdain for Louise, the interloper. And he remembered her words "Dad, you promised Mum, for better or worse. For better or worse".

Louise couldn't stay. He couldn't let her go.

He turned back to speak to her, but she was already gone, walking out the door.

'Louise.'

It was only a whisper. If she heard him she ignored it. She got into the car and reversed out the drive. He could see her white face looking his way. If he held out his hand, would she come back? Then her car was on the road and it was all too late.

He stumbled past Vera to his bedroom. She saying something about being sorry, the dog still growling. Only when he was at the bedroom door did he realize that Maggie might be there. She wasn't. *There's a third bedroom of course.*

He kicked off his boots and crashed onto the bed. His heart cried out for her. *Louise!*

He fell asleep lying stretched across the bed, still fully dressed. A restless sleep haunted by images of fleeing from a towering wave of darkness that pursued him no matter where he turned.

Chapter 61

Near dawn a thundering knock at the front door wakened Barlow. He lay on. *Let it go away.*

The knock thundered again throughout the house. He heard Vera's frightened voice saying, 'Dad, who is it? What's wrong?'

He managed to get his head off the pillow, his feet on the floor. If something didn't hurt it wasn't part of his body. *Give me a minute.* He was sitting on the side of the bed where Louise would have lain. *Oh my poor darling.* There was a crash as the front door burst open. *That Yale lock, I never got it fixed.*

Concern for Vera got him to his feet. He stumbled to the door, his feet not coordinating in any meaningful way. The bedroom door burst open. Harvey and Foxwood stood there, pistols drawn.

'On the ground,' Harvey screamed.

'What?'

Foxwood yelled, 'Hands behind your head. Kneel.'

They came close to him, their pistols pointing straight at his head. Pierson stood in the corridor, a Sterling sub-machine gun pointed his way.

Barlow's brain started to click into a semblance of sense. 'What's got in to you?' he asked Harvey.

He wasn't ready, still wasn't properly balanced when Foxwood hooked a leg out from under him and pushed. The floor vibrated under the impact and his ribs hurt. Someone grabbed his arms and wrenched them back. He heard handcuffs clicking secure, felt hands searching his body. Pierson stuck the barrel of the Sterling in his face.

Barlow got his breath back from the fall. He said to Pierson, 'Put that gun on safety before you shoot yourself.'

'Back off, sergeant,' said Foxwood as he stood up from searching Barlow. Pierson retreated onto the landing. Foxwood hooked an arm under Barlow's and hauled him to his feet.

Barlow could see Vera's frightened face in the doorway and behind her Maggie. Maggie wore only a full length Winceyette nightdress. She'd be affronted when she realized how naked she'd been in front of strangers.

'Dad!' said Vera.

Harvey closed the bedroom door in her face. 'Damn you, Barlow. Jailing you for being a crooked policeman is one thing. But murder makes everyone in the station look bad.'

Chapter 62

Travelling in a police car, with his hands uncomfortably secured, helped Barlow get his mind back in gear. Two policewomen accompanied Vera and Maggie in a second car. They had instructions to make sure that the two women had no opportunity to concoct a collaborative story. The clothes Barlow had worn had been pulled or cut from his body and fresh ones, straight out of the hot-press, pulled on or hooked over his shoulders. He wore his slippers, no socks. His fingers hurt from dirt being scraped out from under his nails.

Rather than worry about Vera and Maggie's feelings, he concentrated on what was happening at the house. A highly uncomfortable Detective Sergeant Leary was carrying out a forensic examination. As for his pistol that Harvey kept shouting about. If it wasn't in his locker at the police station, it had to be in the secure box at the bottom of the wardrobe. Yet when they looked it wasn't there.

The police car pulled into the station yard. They splashed through even more encroaching water to the back door. The whole building vibrated with the presence of men on duty yet not one showed as he was marched to an Interview Room. The Federation Representative waited them there, the man unkempt and haggard from lack of sleep.

Harvey and Foxwood came into the Interview Room with Barlow. A disappointed Pierson was told to wait outside.

Barlow said to him, 'Bring us a cup of tea and those chocolate biscuits you keep hidden in your locker.'

'Go to hell,' said Pierson.

'Tea, yes please,' said the Representative.

'Good idea,' said Foxwood.

Barlow felt that he was back on form. Pierson had to bring them all tea – and he wouldn't dare not bring the biscuits.

Before Pierson could close the door he called after him, 'Tell Wilson to get in here now.'

Pierson slammed the door shut before Harvey could tell him to ignore that order.

The handcuffs were taken off and Barlow was allowed to pull on his vest and shirt.

Now that he'd taken the initiative he was determined to keep it. Whatever was going on, had something to do with those lights and police cars at the top of Mount Street.

He asked Harvey, 'Who am I supposed to have killed?'

'I ask the questions around here,' said Harvey.

Foxwood asked, 'How do you know someone's been murdered?'

'Because some dickhead told me instead of me letting it slip during the course of the interview.'

The dickhead of course was Harvey who looked both furious and uncomfortable.

'Keith Ingram,' said Foxwood.

'Him? What for?'

'That's for you to tell us,' said Harvey.

Keith Ingram? Yet somehow Barlow felt that he shouldn't be surprised at Keith being killed. *Now why's that?*

Harvey said, 'Barlow, it always surprises me how the professionals make the most elementary mistakes when they turn crooked.'

The Representative said, 'Don't answer that.'

It hadn't been a question as such but Barlow kept the Representative's point in mind when he said, 'I can sit here forever and not answer your questions, or…' He let that "or" hang a moment, giving Harvey a chance to remember other pointless interviews between them. 'Or you tell me what you know and I'll give you the answers you're looking for.'

'I'll agree to that, with reservations,' said the Representative.

At the same time he gave Barlow a disbelieving look. He'd

never heard Barlow give a straight answer to the simplest question and didn't expect it to happen now.

'Certainly not,' said Harvey.

Foxwood said, 'Sir, we already have several irrefutable facts about this case. If Barlow's guilty…'

'What do you mean "if"? Of course he's guilty.'

Foxwood shrugged, 'It's worth a try.' Harvey didn't say yes or no. After a pause Foxwood leaned towards Barlow. 'This is the way we figure the murder happened.' He paused and glanced at Harvey who obviously disapproved but said nothing.

'I'm listening, sir,' said Barlow.

Foxwood started slowly, still waiting for Harvey to silence him. 'You decided to kill Keith Ingram, the reason why is currently unknown. You took him or arranged to meet him at the waste ground on Mount Street, where you shot him. Right so far, Barlow?'

'I'm listening, sir.'

Unexpectedly Foxwood almost smiled, giving Barlow the impression that Foxwood wasn't as convinced of his guilt as Harvey.

'Well keep listening, because after you shot Ingram twice – we believe with your own pistol though Forensics still have to confirm that – you took out the used shells and threw them away.' He paused for effect rather than expecting a confirmation. 'Shells with your fingerprints on them, that's how we traced you so quickly. In addition, you didn't replace the two used shells or clean the pistol itself before hiding it at the back of the settee.'

'What!' Barlow couldn't hold his shock and surprise back.

He'd forgotten about bringing the pistol home in the grip, let alone dumping the grip at the back of the settee.

Foxwood continued. 'After you murdered Keith Ingram and placed or replaced the pistol in your grip, you went out again. Where to and why is still a matter of conjecture. Your daughter and your wife arrived home before you. You spoke to your daughter and then went straight to bed, where you fell asleep without undressing.'

They had to get most of that from Vera. *Good girl, she never mentioned Louise.*

The thing that got to him was that he'd been out-maneuvered by someone. Somehow, in spite of all his precautions, someone had known that he'd left the house. *The stream!* The stream at the top of Mount Street crossed the street by means of a culvert and ran along the back of the houses across from him. Over the years the bank of that stream had become one of the rat-runs of the town. Someone had to be standing on that rat-run where they could see down the length of the garden.

They'd seen him leave the house and slip over the convent wall. Then they'd taken the gun, killed Ingram and then returned it. Not only did the whole thing seemed planned, whoever it was had to know that the gun was there in the first place. To do that they must have been in and out of the house at least once before.

What gave him the shivers wasn't so much the cold-blooded murder as the realization of the amount of personal hate that someone had for him. *Who? Why?*

'We're waiting, Barlow,' said Harvey. He sat back in his chair, arms crossed, a pleased look on his face. 'Frankly I don't care whether you answer or not.'

Barlow let the Representative do the asking. 'Why do you say that?'

'Because Barlow either hangs for the murder or he gets fired for failing to secure his personal weapon. A weapon that was used in a murder.' Harvey thumped the table for effect. 'Either way I've got rid of him at long last.'

Chapter 63

Up until then Barlow had merely been annoyed and upset. The murder charge was nonsense. It couldn't have happened before he left the house and the police were already on the scene when he got back. All he'd wanted to do was to keep Louise's name out of it.

How could he tell people that he'd gone to her house, and that they'd become Skyclad and gone through a pagan marriage service? Then they'd then left for his house intending to have consensual sex only to find that his legal wife had arrived home unexpectedly? They'd be a laughing stock and he'd caused her enough hurt already.

The charge of not properly securing his pistol he hadn't seen come, and Harvey would make the most of it.

He knew he should say something, had more or less given his word he would. *But what?*

Someone knocked the door and came in. Wilson's voice said, 'You wanted to see me, sir.'

'No, get out,' said Harvey.

'Stay,' said Barlow. He turned round in his chair to face the young officer. 'I want you to head out straight away and arrest young Peter Slane.'

'Who?' asked Wilson.

'Take Gillespie with you. He will know who Slane is and where he lives.'

'I told you to get out,' snapped Harvey.

Wilson sidled slowly backwards and managed to get trapped in the doorway with Pierson trying to bull past him with a tray of steaming cups.

Good lad.

Barlow added, quickly, 'They might not know it yet but someone on the Cullybackey Road was burgled last night. Ask

Slane what time he went through Clarence Street. And tell him to stop whistling "Dixie" under his breath, it's a dead giveaway.'

Harvey said, 'Barlow would you answer our questions.'

'I am, sir.'

'In your own sweet way,' said Foxwood. 'So what time did you meet Peter Slane?'

Barlow asked, 'What time was Keith Ingram killed?'

Pierson put a cup of tea in front of him, the first cup to be put down. *I'll lay odds he spat in it.* Barlow passed the cup to Harvey and helped himself to another off the tray. Not by a flicker did he betray his enjoyment at the look of horror on Pierson's face.

Nobody had answered Barlow's question about the time of the murder so he sipped his tea and took his time selecting one of Pierson's chocolate biscuits.

Harvey said, 'I presume this Slane youth will confirm that you were in Clarence Street?'

'And with a bit of coaching he'll tell you a time that suits you.'

'I resent that,' said Harvey.

'And I resent your presumption of guilt.'

Harvey looked furious. The Representative smiled, he was starting to enjoy himself. Foxwood sat back and folded his arms, content to watch a row develop that had nothing to do with him.

The Interview Room had no window and they'd taken his watch. Barlow could only assume that it was daylight outside. He refused to answer any more questions about his movements the previous night. 'See what young Slane has got to say,' he told Harvey.

However, to buy time he agreed to make a formal statement about how the pistol had been left improperly secured. At the Representative's suggestion Harvey and Foxwood left the Interview Room while Barlow and he worked on the statement.

Chapter 64

Barlow's first draft of his statement read:

I was just out of hospital and feeling really ill. The same day I collected some dirty clothes and the pistol from my locker in the station.

No way would he mention Gillespie's involvement, in case it got him into trouble as well.

When I got back home I was exhausted so I threw the bag behind the settee and fell asleep. I don't normally keep a gun at home so I never thought about it again until District Inspector Harvey came looking for it.

The Representative worked on the initial statement, padding it out very nicely. He placed great emphasis on how Barlow had nearly died, poisoned by person or persons unknown.

'It also gives us grounds for claiming that the use of your gun in the murder was another attempt on your person. In this case your liberty if not your life.'

'Aye,' said Barlow. He'd already thought of that but wanted the Representative to feel that a loss of a night's sleep wasn't entirely wasted.

The senior officers may have left them in peace but the writing of the statement was constantly interrupted by callers.

Gillespie popped in. 'I'm just taking Maggie and Vera home. Leary's mob have finished searching the house and found nothing incriminating.'

'They missed the bodies in the cellar then?'

'Maggie's fine, but very concerned about you. She saw nothing, heard nothing and slept like a log until our lot came battering at the door. I took her statement myself. Vera told WPC

Day even less.'

'That's because she knows nothing.'

Gillespie snorted. 'She's a chip of the old block. She thinks the time of day comes under the Official Secrets Act.'

'What time is it anyway?'

Just to annoy, Gillespie wouldn't tell him.

Pierson followed soon afterwards. He looked like he'd dropped a penny and found a hundred-pound note.

'Your friend's for the high jump,' he announced. 'Two years at least.'

'That's one more friend than you have.'

Pierson waited for Barlow to ask "What friend?" Barlow wouldn't oblige so he had to tell him anyway. 'Your old Commanding Officer, Edward Adair. He's admitted to stealing that lorry load of drink from the brewery.'

For a moment Barlow's mind went blank. He'd been expecting Pierson to say Geordie Dunlop.

'Your head's a marley,' was the best he could manage.

'And we've got the proof. We found some of the stolen whiskey in that shack of his.'

'Shut the door on your way out.'

It was a weak come-back and Pierson knew it. He left, gloating at finally getting one up on Barlow.

The Representative was speaking, looking for confirmation of facts before writing them down. The words didn't make sense to Barlow. *Edward under arrest? For stealing*?

He forced himself to put Edward out of his mind. The important thing was to get himself released and then go check that his family was all right. Edward and his problems would have to wait.

All the same he found himself thinking of himself and Edward as they struggled to disarm a bomb in an armaments factory. For some reason, when everything seemed to be going well, Edward's head popped up from the other side of the bomb. 'Sergeant Major, I am of the opinion that one should evacuate the area with alacrity.'

Barlow had never heard of the word "alacrity", but he and Edward were tumbling behind a sandbag barricade when the bomb exploded.

Someone gave the door a scratch of a knock. The Representative sighed at another interruption.

Barlow shouted, 'If it's more bad news, clear off before you come in.'

Half of Wilson's body invaded the Interview Room, the rest remained in the corridor, watching out for senior officers.

'Sarge, I thought you should see this.'

"This" was a handful of faded papers clipped together.

Way back, when Barlow was still at war, one Ezekiel Fetherton had been accused of raping a young girl called Anna Somerton. Anna refused to testify in court and the case was dropped for lack of evidence.

Chapter 65

Fetherton raped Anna Somerton? thought Barlow in wonder.

Of course the young girl, as she had to be then, wouldn't have dared testify in court. Not when she had to stand in a public dock and recount in intimate detail what Fetherton had done to her. Then have the Defense Counsel try to paint her as a young lady of easy virtue. Some of Fetherton's friends might even claim that they'd slept with her.

No way would I let Vera go through that.

Barlow heard footsteps out in the corridor and recognized them as Foxwood's. He slipped the faded papers among the working drafts of his statement just as Foxwood came in.

Foxwood had taken time to shave and put on a fresh shirt. He looked tired but invigorated.

'Barlow, we were still interviewing young Slane when a couple on the Cullybackey Road rang to say they'd been burgled. All we had to do was tick the items they claimed were stolen against a list of things found in Slane's home.'

'They must be delighted, sir.'

Foxwood acknowledged that dry remark with a raised eyebrow. Barlow wondered why he could sometimes irritate Foxwood but had never succeeded in annoying him.

'Young Slane also confirmed to the minute the time he was in Clarence Street. He is very proud of his watch with its luminous dial, and keeps checking the time.' Foxwood smiled. 'Or should I say "was very proud" and "kept". It was stolen of course.'

Barlow decided that silence was better than a snide remark because Foxwood was building up to something.

After a pause waiting for Barlow's remark that didn't come, Foxwood seemed almost disappointed as he continued. 'I was curious, Sergeant, as to where you were going when you passed Peter Slane in Clarence Street. I knew you won't tell me, so Gillespie and I took the police dog for a walk.'

Barlow hadn't seen the charge come of not properly securing his personal weapon, or this. Once he'd given Foxwood the starting point the rest was easy. 'Shit!'

Foxwood said, 'The dog led us half-way across town, over fields and ditches. Did you know that Gillespie has flat feet and a bad back?'

'Don't forget his weak chest, sir.'

'He moaned constantly while we were following the dog. To the house belonging to a certain lady.'

Foxwood produced a copy of Louise's statement. Barlow grabbed it before the Representative could take it. In the statement Louise said that Barlow had called at her house to discuss personal matters. He was in the house for approximately forty-five minutes, after which she ran him home because it was raining. She had added, probably at Gillespie's insistence, that there had been no sexual intercourse. It saved him from possible charges of "Inappropriate Behavior" and "Bringing the Force into Disrepute", but what had it done to Louise?

The fact of his late call at her house would become common knowledge. Foxwood was being as tactful as possible and Gillespie wouldn't give a man the time of day. But Harvey? Harvey would make a laughing stock out of him and not care who he hurt in the process. He'd make Louise sound like a slut.

Foxwood picked up the statement about the pistol prepared, by Barlow and the Representative. He read it carefully, checked their signatures and then added his own.

That done he turned to the Representative. 'I am pleased to inform you that Sergeant Barlow has fully accounted for his movements during the relevant period of last night. He therefore is no longer a suspect in the murder of Keith Ingram. However, he is suspended from duty for failing to properly secure his weapon. We will of course keep the Federation informed regarding the date and time of the Disciplinary Hearing.'

The Representative took that as a polite dismissal. He

shook Barlow's hand, promising to stay in touch, scooped his papers into his briefcase and left.

Barlow reckoned it would be the next day at least before the Representative came across the faded papers dealing with the rape of Anna Somerton. Assuming he posted them back to the station that would buy another couple of days.

It's surprising what a man can accomplish in that time.

Barlow stretched to show his casualness and was surprised at how stiff his body had become. He needed a bath and a shave and something better than carpet slippers to go home in.

'What now, sir?'

Foxwood said, 'You can go anytime you want, Barlow.' He made to shake hands and then changed his mind. 'I'm sorry about the gun thing. I'm going to miss you around here.'

Harvey wanted him jailed or dishonorably discharged. Senior officers from Headquarters visited the station when they thought he was off duty. And Foxwood was going to miss him?

Barlow said, 'I've been missing tricks all day, sir, but you missing having me around has left me stunned.'

Foxwood laughed. 'When this current unpleasantness is sorted, you're coming to dinner. My wife is dying to meet you.'

Barlow said, 'There's no accounting for a women's taste.'

Foxwood sat back, smiling. 'Every night I get home she asks, "What sort of day did you have?" What she actually means is "what has Sergeant Barlow done today to annoy Mr. Harvey".' He dropped his voice against anyone listening outside the door. 'She doesn't like Mr. Harvey.'

'He thinks he's God's gift to women,' said Barlow, catching on.

'And takes some convincing otherwise,' said Foxwood, and now he wasn't smiling. There was a pause then he said more cheerfully, 'Anyway, you and Mary Jo Cosgrave walking past the station together fooled that idiot Pierson.'

Barlow said, 'Pierson acts long before he thinks. Mary Jo was in England the night of Fetherton's murder.'

'I know, I checked with BEA. She flew into Belfast on the Sunday afternoon.'

Barlow pretended to look surprised.

'Standard procedure,' Foxwood reminded him. 'Most murders are committed by family or family friends. So we check all their alibis.'

Barlow nodded in agreement. He could always depend on Foxwood to follow basic procedures.

'She's a nice girl,' added Foxwood. 'She works in a unit specializing in Organized Crime and her father of course was a Deputy Commander. Quite a tradition to uphold. In a way I can see why she wants to make her own career path.'

Barlow nodded at that. Not because he was agreeing with Foxwood but with another possibility. He wasn't convinced that Mary Jo's attempts to put a divide between him and Louise was misjudged humor. The Cosgraves had a lot of bad blood in them and they were vindictive, which was why his part in the death of Chris Cosgrave had never been let out. Vindictive enough to plant a poisonous plant in his garden? He thought so. *But how to find out?*

'Sir, it might be worthwhile checking to see if a Mary Jo Cosgrave flew in and out of the Province in the week leading up to Granny Cosgrave's death. Or caught the Liverpool boat.'

Foxwood started in surprise. 'Are you telling me that you distrust a fellow officer?'

'Just covering every option.'

Foxwood stood up, no longer friendly. 'Before you go, Solicitor Moncrief wants a word with you.'

Barlow said, 'If Moncrief came to my funeral, it would be to spit on my grave.'

Chapter 66

The previous day Barlow had felt strength and vigor come back into his system. The lack of a proper night's sleep, the loss of Louise and the whole thing about being arrested and treated like a criminal had taken its toll. He'd laughed inwardly when the doctors said he needed a month to recover from the poisoning. Now the whole idea of being suspended for an indefinite period seemed like a good idea.

He thought he'd get Johnny Scullion and his taxi to run him home. Make sure Vera was okay and then take to his bed for a week. *God only knows what this morning has done to Maggie and her nerves.*

Barlow pushed the chair back and stood up. He knew he looked as haggard and unkempt as he felt. He said to Foxwood, 'Tell Solicitor Moncrief to come and gloat another day.'

'He said "please".'

Even walking to the front door and the taxi seemed like too much effort, let alone dealing with Solicitor Moncrief. The man who treated him like dirt to be walked on.

Foxwood said, 'Moncrief's waiting for you in my office.'

'With Mr. Harvey?'

He could see the two of them, heads together conspiring against him.

Foxwood laughed. 'I think Moncrief's hoping you can abracadabra something to get Edward off.' He tried to make his shrug appear casual. 'Just because he tried to hang you doesn't make Harvey a total…' He cut off the word. 'Someone very clever set you up for a murder. Now he knows it's not you the DI is out at the crime scene looking for anything that will help us catch this man.'

'Right.'

Searching for clues was a good excuse. Harvey had no

intention of being in the station when Charlie Denton charged in, roaring like a bull at his old Commanding Officer being arrested.

Barlow pulled open the door into the corridor. After the fetid air of the windowless Interview Room the rest of the building felt fresh. The slippers were too big for his sockless feet and he had to slide along like an old man.

Pierson was waiting in the Enquiry Office to gloat. Barlow ignored him, stretched across the counter and pulled the telephone closer. He dialed home. Vera answered on the third ring. She was so relieved to hear his voice that she started to cry. If only he could be there to give her the big hug she needed.

'It's all right, love, they know now that it wasn't me who killed Keith Ingram.' Telling her about the suspension and the probable loss of his job could wait.

According to Vera, Maggie was fine, though she'd gone very quiet – something that worried Barlow – and she kept asking if he was all right.

'She's not in bed or anything?'

When Maggie went into one of her depressions she retired to bed and wouldn't get out.

'No, she's making a brown stew for lunch.' Vera sounded just as surprise as he felt. 'You will be home for lunch?'

He glanced at the clock in the Enquiry Office. *Near twelve.* He ached to say "I'll be home in ten minutes" but there were things to do first. There was an enemy out there who wished him harm.

Checking Mary Jo Cosgrave's movements, for the week the Wolfsbane was planted in his garden, was purely procedural. He wanted to eliminate her from the enquiry and then go looking for the real villain, and the only way he knew to trap the man was to solve all the current crimes. Whoever was targeting him personally had to be responsible for more than Keith Ingram's death.

He told the now much calmer Vera. 'I'll be home at one o'clock.' And he would, if only to touch base and make sure everything was all right again in her little world. Spend time comforting her instead of collapsing into bed. Sometimes it was hell being a parent. *And the best job in the world.*

He signed for the envelope containing his personal items. Pierson made great play of shouting them out as he ticked the items off his list: Wallet, sundry bits of paper, one folded envelope, one ten-shilling note…

Pointedly, Pierson held back his police notebook. 'You'll not be needing that again.'

What Barlow really needed was pen and paper and ten minutes to himself to work up his own list of who and what. Somewhere in there he'd find the why.

Rather than give Pierson another opportunity to gloat Foxwood escorted Barlow to the locker room. When Barlow undid the padlock and opened the locker door he found only his spare uniform and a pair of boots. Gillespie had stuffed everything not actually uniform into the grip to conceal the pistol.

Conscious of Foxwood watching his every move, he went over to Gillespie's locker, spun the dials of the combination padlock and opened the locker door. Took out a fresh pair of socks and an old Barber jacket that Gillespie used for fishing.

Foxwood raised an eyebrow in query rather actually question Barlow.

Barlow said, 'We use the same code numbers so we're never stuck for dry gear.'

'It must be the only thing you two agree on.'

'Only because it suits Gillespie.'

With socks and boots on, everything properly tucked in and his hair combed he felt ready to take on the world again. Foxwood started to lead him to his office and the waiting Moncrief. Barlow turned in the opposite direction and the cellblock.

At the cellblock Barlow told the Custody Officer. 'I want into Major Adair's cell.'

'You can't share a cell, Sarge, it's against the rules.'

The Custody Officer had put in nearly as many years of

service as Barlow. He parried Barlow's glare with a glimmer of amusement, then indicated gracefully for Barlow to proceed.

Edward was in the cell held reserved for him during periods of what he gracefully referred to as "inclement weather". Against all regulations the door was on the push. Edward sat on the edge of the bed, tie hauled loose, fingers working in and out of each other in a restless arc.

'It's good of you to call,' said Edward.

'You're a bollocks,' said Barlow.

Chapter 67

Barlow folded his arms and leaned against the frame of the cell door. Edward looked frighteningly frail. Even so Barlow kept all sense of sympathy out of his voice when he said, 'Where you're going they lock the doors. How will you like that?'

Edward swallowed and had no answer. They looked at each other, Edward from his seat on the bunk, Barlow still leaning against the doorway. Edward ran a hand over dry lips.

'And there's no booze there, either,' said Barlow. He straightened and brushed dust off his sleeve. 'So what's this all about?'

Edward coughed gracefully into a knuckle. 'The Royal Ulster Rifles…'

'What has the regiment got to do with it?'

'They're in action, my dear chap. Borneo, one of those funny little places at the end of the Empire.'

'And?'

'The Comforts Fund was running done, and when you're in the jungle those little extras make all the difference.'

Barlow had enough problems of his own without getting involved in Edward's troubles, but he needed him out of that cell.

He stepped back and said to Edward, 'Out, and don't argue. My lunch is waiting and I haven't had a square meal today.' As an afterthought he looked at Foxwood who stood in the corridor, anxious at a suspect being questioned without their solicitor present. 'With your permission, sir.'

'My office, where Solicitor Moncrief is.'

Edward straightened his tie and finger-combed his hair tidy as they went. Moncrief's twisted jaw twisted even more in surprise as they all walked in. Edward took the only free visitors' chair, leaving Barlow standing. Which suited him.

What also suited him was the case of whiskey sitting on

Foxwood's desk.

First Barlow spoke to Moncrief, 'I'm surprised Captain Denton isn't in here, shouting?'

'He's in Belfast talking to the bankers.'

'He'll get nowhere with that lot. They only lend you an umbrella when it's dry.'

'He'll be back as soon as possible,' said Moncrief.

Which meant that Denton was having no luck in getting the bankers to extend his overdraft. The business was still in trouble and economies would have to be made, *like jobs*.

Barlow turned his attention on Foxwood. 'Sir, how do you know that that case of whiskey forms part of the load stolen from the brewery?'

Foxwood had gone round to his own side of the desk but hadn't actually sat down. He stayed alert, his eyes going from Barlow to Moncrief to Edward in a restless arc. 'Firstly, Major Adair admitted that it formed part of the load.'

'And if he hadn't admitted it?'

'Then, Sergeant, if you ever noticed, there are little nicks on the label of every bottle of spirits.' He produced a plastic card with teeth, miniature but otherwise like that of a comb. 'By matching this to the nicks on the label you are able to ascertain which batch the whiskey came from.'

Barlow knew he was taking a chance but the idea seemed right in his head. 'Did you check all the bottles with that card thing?'

'Only three, but…'

Foxwood stopped. He couldn't see what Barlow was getting at but he knew there was an angle.

'Sir, this may be one for the wife.'

One by one, Foxwood pulled the bottles out of the case and matched the labels with the plastic card. *Batch, batch, batch* came in a restless litany until the tenth bottle. Foxwood checked the label, double checked it and checked again. 'This isn't from the same batch?' He finished checking the last two bottles and put eleven back in the case. The non-batch bottle he left on his desk. 'How did you know?'

Edward said, 'How dare you doubt the word of a gentleman. I have pleaded guilty, isn't that enough?'

'Shut up,' said Barlow.

'Sergeant!'

Barlow ignored Foxwood and looked at Moncrief, the one man who should have been shouting about police aggression and bullying tactics. Moncrief was apparently deeply engrossed in reading the duty rosters.

Barlow glared at Edward. What he really wanted to do was to grab him by the lapels and bang him off a couple of walls. 'Charlie Denton will have to fire people because the insurance company won't compensate him for the loss of the whiskey. Right?'

Edward stuck his Adair nose in the air and refused to acknowledge the question.

Barlow stuck his face close to Edward's. 'Right?'

'An unfortunate and unforeseen outcome of ones actions.'

'So if "one" admits to switching off the alarms after they had been properly set? And if "one" admits to being the inside man in the theft, then the insurance company will pay up and the jobs will be saved?'

'One must face the culpability of ones actions rather than see others suffer.'

Barlow nodded. 'Don't worry, you will.' He counted the charges off on his fingers. 'Wasting Police Time, Making a False Statement, Withholding Information which may be of assistance in an ongoing investigation, Accessory After the Fact, Attempted Fraud of an insurance company. Annoying my bloody head.'

Moncrief had given up reading the rosters. He sat poised like he did in court when anxious to make submissions, which might get a guilty client off. Even so he remained silent.

It was Foxwood who spoke. 'Barlow, I wish you could prove that.'

Barlow didn't blame him. Charlie Denton in a blazing temper was not a pleasant experience.

Barlow perched on the edge of the desk so that he could hold eye contact with Edward.

'Recently you've come into money, a salary from the brewery, which Mrs. Anderson doesn't let you near. Every Friday she gives you an allowance which you take to the Bridge Bar and buy rounds for everyone there until it's done.'

'One may entertain ones friends.'

'Aye, and when the money's done those self-same friends do what they've done for fifteen years. Buy you enough drink to satisfy your need for the devil brew, but not enough to make you incapable.'

'Ones' friends, former comrades in arms…' Edward began.

Barlow talked on, not acknowledging the interruption. 'I met you the morning after the whiskey was stolen. You hadn't been drunk, you'd been legless and you were running late for an important meeting.'

Edward vibrated indignation. 'One does not run, one proceeds with alacrity.'

Edward's attitude annoyed Barlow, there wasn't even a hint of him admitting the truth. He snarled, 'Well "one" was late and "one" is never late because "one" considers being late the worst of bad manners.'

'True, but there were exten…'

'Shut up, Edward,' said Moncrief. He said to Barlow, 'If Edward is still in custody when Denton gets back I'm likely to lose a valued client.'

It annoyed Barlow having to help Moncrief in any way – *For "valued" read "best paying"* – but Edward's freedom was what counted.

The final decision was Foxwood's so Barlow turned to speak to him directly. 'Sir, the way I see it is this. The night the whiskey was stolen, Edward was in the pub and got his usual top-up of alcohol. Mrs. Anderson's house is strictly "dry" so he went to his hut under the arch to sleep it off.

'There Edward found a full case of whiskey waiting for him. Whiskey stolen by person or persons unknown from the brewery and left by the same person or persons unknown…'

'The Dunlops,' said Foxwood and Moncrief together.

'The Dunlops, specifically former Rifleman Geordie Dunlop,' agreed Barlow. 'Edward, being half-pissed already, doesn't question his good fortune but broaches a bottle of whiskey and drinks himself insensible.'

'Really, my dear chap, you make ones imbibing of alcohol appear excessive.'

'Edward, you're a drunk.'

It hurt Barlow to say that bluntly, but he had to get home. Vera could be struggling to cope with a Maggie who had slipped back into her schizophrenia.

'You replaced the bottle you drank but didn't know what to do with the full case. It wouldn't help you telling the police about the crate because everyone knew it was the Dunlops. At the same time, you couldn't just carry it into the brewery and put it back in the store. Then you had this bright idea of saving those jobs by claiming that you stole the whiskey. After all you had a case of the stuff as proof of your guilt.'

'Really, my dear chap,' said Edward.

'Really,' said Barlow and continued to concentrate on Foxwood. 'Edward didn't steal the whiskey, had nothing to do with the theft of the whiskey.' He chose his words carefully. 'Right now we're up to our necks in three murders. I suggest we give Edward bail subject to certain terms. That way we can sort out him and the relevant charges when things settle down a bit.'

'Terms?' asked Moncrief.

'That you take Edward straight home. That he doesn't speak to anyone, doesn't phone anyone, doesn't see anyone, doesn't stand at the window until tomorrow morning at the very earliest.'

Foxwood gave a half nod while he thought over this

unusual restriction on a suspect's movements. Barlow took it as agreement and left the office, heading for the Enquiry Office and the necessary forms.

He glanced at his watch as he went. If didn't hurry he'd be late home for lunch and he'd things to do before that. *People to sort.*

Chapter 68

Pierson was not pleased when Barlow marched into the Enquiry Office and demanded Edward's envelope of personal possessions. He leaned on the counter-flap to stop Barlow getting through. 'You have no right to give orders, you're a disgrace to the Force.'

What Barlow thought of Pierson he kept to himself because Wilson was there and able to listen in. He went eyeball to eyeball with Pierson while Wilson searched out the envelope and slid it into a bundle of files on the counter.

Once Wilson was safely back at his own paperwork Barlow appeared to give up. 'Have it your way. Major Adair is being bailed. Take the bail forms down for him to sign.' He gave the bundle of files a flick as he turned away. 'I keep telling you, don't leave files lying around like that, it makes the place look untidy.' He apparently noticed the envelope for the first time and pulled it out. 'Well, well, Major Edward Adair,' and walked off with the envelope under his arm.

Back in Foxwood's office he said that Pierson would be straight down with the bail forms, which made Pierson sound like the office boy. He opened the envelope and spilled the contents onto the table. 'We'll do this now.'

Foxwood said, 'You're rather rushing things, Sergeant.'

'I know, sir, but it'll speed things up.'

He asked Edward to check his personal items and sign the form: watch, wallet, sundry small coin, diary and a Parker pen. A couple of envelopes with their contents pulled out and not replaced.

Edward put everything back in his pocket except for a folded piece of paper. 'Yours Sergeant Major.' He nodded reassuringly. 'One prevailed in the end.'

Just then Pierson bustled in with the forms. Barlow scooped up the piece of paper and let Pierson's bulk squeeze him into the doorway. Once Pierson was safely in Barlow stepped into the corridor and closed the door. He apparently didn't hear Foxwood call, 'Sergeant,' as he headed up the corridor.

As he went he checked the piece of paper. He reckoned it had to be Pierson who had gone through Edward's personal possession. Anyone else would have picked up on the Fethertons' names appearing on the list.

Edward's "prevailing" had added ticks identifying the unknown devil worshippers. Barlow now knew the name and address of every man and women involved in the pagan rituals. What he now needed was a telephone and a room where he wouldn't be overheard.

Harvey's out at the murder scene.

He went into Harvey's office and made himself comfortable on Harvey's over-padded chair. Picked up the phone and buzzed through to the WPCs' office. 'Get me Mrs. Fetherton on the line.'

The WPC's voice went up in pitch. 'Sarge, what are you doing in there? Mr. Harvey will go spare if he catches you.'

'You get me Mrs. Fetherton. I'll worry about Mr. Harvey.'

Next Barlow buzzed Wilson in the Enquiry Office. He at least didn't dare question what Barlow was doing in Harvey's office.

'Wilson, those reports on the movements of the Dunlops. You gave me a copy and gave another one to Inspector Foxwood.'

'Yes, Sergeant.'

'I'm guessing you kept a copy for yourself?'

'I did.'

Wilson sounded surprised that the obvious would be questioned.

'Son, all my stuff's at home. I need your copy right away.'

'I'm kind of stuck, Sergeant. I'm manning the Enquiry Office.'

Which suited Barlow, at least until after he'd made a couple of phone calls. He rang the switchboard and asked the WPC to hurry up with Mrs. Fetherton's number. In the meantime she was to give him a second line.

He rang Louise's house and found himself mentally crunching down on a brandy ball while he wondered: she's in, she's not in; she won't answer, she will.

Louise picked up.

He could say that he was heartbroken or that he could happily wring Vera's neck for encouraging Maggie to come home. Or lots of other things that were only excuses.

He said, 'I'm sorry.'

'So what do you want?'

He wanted her, but without all the baggage he'd collected through the course of his life. 'I hurt you.'

She said, 'We were wrong even thinking it could work.'

'We can still work something out.'

'I'm not going to be the "other woman". I'm not going to sit in all day hoping for a phone call or having you slip in by the back door for a quick shag.'

It could have been anger at him but her words were all hurt.

He struggled for something positive to say. 'It wouldn't be like that.' Hated the note of pleading in his voice.

'John, you didn't let me leave last night because Maggie was there. You let me go because of Vera. You would give that child your heart's blood, and right now that means allowing Maggie back into your life.'

'I love you,' he whispered, a final desperate plea.

'You were the right man at the wrong time. Please don't ring me again.'

She hung up.

Chapter 69

Barlow hung up slowly after his phone call to Louise. "Don't phone me again" she'd said and meant it. He wished he could find it in his heart to hate Maggie for the years of grief she had caused him. He dreaded the coming years, of slipping into retirement and old age without Louise there to give his life real purpose.

He sat back and waited for the Fetherton call to come through. Lots of interesting files sat on Harvey's desk but he wasn't in the mood to investigate them. The top drawer contained a selection of antacid tablets and a packet of digestive biscuits. Barlow opened the packet and helped himself to a couple of biscuits. It gave him something to do while he waited, even if it was only eating.

The WPC put the call through.

Mrs. Fetherton was at her snottery best. 'What do you want, Barlow?'

In reply Barlow read out the names on the list, then he added. 'I want to see all those people in your house at seven-thirty tonight.'

'I've better things to do, and how dare you make demands…'

'Seven-thirty.'

'People have other commitments. You can't just…'

Barlow said with studied patience, 'If anyone is not there at seven-thirty, a police car will be at their door at seven-forty. They will be brought to the police station where the absolute minimum charges will be: Obstruction and Withholding Information in Relation to an Ongoing Investigation.'

He could hear asthmatic breathing at the other end of the line but otherwise silence.

He said, 'My way we should be able to keep things confidential. Nobody else need know a thing.'

'Please,' she whispered.

They disconnected as Wilson knocked the door and came in. Barlow helped himself to another of Harvey's biscuits. They were Jacob's digestives. That surprised him, he didn't think Harvey had the intelligence to go for quality over price.

Wilson had brought his copy of the Dunlop Report and a big mug of tea. Barlow blessed the boy for his intelligence in thinking of the tea. He'd make the sort of inspector that Barlow would only be rude to on occasion, and he could think of no higher accolade than that.

He told Wilson to pull up a chair and help him separate the reports between young bucks and the older men like Geordie and his son. Wilson kept an anxious eye on the door as he worked, terrified in case Harvey should appear unexpectedly.

He said, 'Su.... WPC Day is manning the Enquiry Office for me. She'll buzz through if Mr. Harvey appears.'

'Then you can relax.'

Barlow was beginning to think that Harvey's expensive chair wasn't a total waste of money. *There must be a way of getting my hands on it, permanent like.*

With the reports separated into their two piles, Barlow pushed the one dealing with the young bucks aside and gave Wilson half of the reports on the older men. 'Now date order.'

They put their respective halves into date order and then amalgamated them. It would have been quicker to do it on his own but Barlow wanted to keep Wilson with him. He needed Foxwood to see that Wilson was already involved in the investigation into the missing drink.

There was something he had noticed in his first reading of the reports but it hadn't properly registered at the time. It was so vague, so obscured by the other things happening in his life, that he couldn't clearly say what it was.

Having Wilson seen to be working with him was one thing, but actually there...?

Barlow needed a few minutes to himself. He scrawled a

note on a piece of Harvey's expensive notepaper and gave it to Wilson. 'Leave that in with Inspector Foxwood...'

'What if he asks where we are?'

'If you read the note, it tells him where we are and asks him to join us ASAP.' He grabbed Wilson's arm to stop him from shooting off immediately. 'Find Gillespie. Tell him I need those old army sleeping bags we use when we go fishing.'

Wilson repeated his orders to make sure he had them right. 'Give the note to the Inspector and ask Gillespie...'

'You never ask Gillespie for anything, he's too twisted to say yes. TELL the man.'

'Yes, Sergeant.'

With Wilson gone, Barlow read and re-read the reports on the older Dunlops. He was right, there was a pattern of movement up until the point when they realized that they were being monitored. He formed a sense of them drifting to and from the northern end of the town.

That satisfied him that one of his problems tied in nicely with his need for the sleeping bags. He helped himself to another sheet of the expensive notepaper and started to do his long delayed listing.

Fetherton, Granny Cosgrave, Keith Ingram
Vera, Louise, Maggie
Edward, Geordie, Harvey.

It took the form of three groupings of three: The murdered people, the women in his life and the men causing him the greatest grief. Reluctantly he had to accept that Louise was no longer part of his life so he regrouped again.

Fetherton, Granny Cosgrave, Keith Ingram
Edward, Geordie, Harvey
Vera, Maggie, Mary Jo
Louise, Wicca, Whiskey.

This gave him the murder victims, the three men and the three women currently causing him problems and a fourth line as what he could only think of as leftovers.

He checked his watch, *nearly ten to one,* and not a chance of Pierson allowing him a lift home in a squad car. He rang Johnny Scullion for his taxi and threw his lists into the bin. Wrote a note to be left with WPC Day for Wilson.

Look out two pairs of binoculars and the old army walkie-talkies. Put fresh batteries in the walkie-talkies.

Harvey came tip-toeing down the corridor just as Barlow was leaving.

'What were you doing in my office, Barlow?'

'Inspector Foxwood will explain, sir.'

He walked on.

Chapter 70

A herd of policemen searching a house was bound to leave their mark. Barlow arrived back at his bungalow at one o'clock expecting to find every room in a mess, with things strewn higgledy-piggledy across the floors.

The smell of Mansion Polish assailed his nose as he walked in the door. Mirrors and glasswork sparkled in the watery sunlight, the sitting room had never looked cleaner or tidier. From the kitchen came the rattle of pots and pans and Vera's voice saying, 'Dad's home.'

He walked into the kitchen. Instead of the usual oilcloth the table was spread with a linen tablecloth. The best crockery, matching knives and forks. And serviettes. Vera stood at the fireplace. She wore a summer dress in place of her usual jeans and tee-shirt, and had her hair pinned back instead of allowing it to flop around her face.

God bless them but they're making a special effort. Only Toby, the dog, appeared unchanged. It snarled at Barlow from Barlow's own chair. *So what's different there?*

Maggie bustled in from the scullery, carrying plates. 'Sit down, Mr. Barlow, your dinner's ready.'

He was still "Mr. Barlow" to his own wife but her cooking, when the tablets were working, was something special.

'Sit down,' she repeated, fluttering a tea towel at his place.

He did as he was told and used his knife and fork to dig into a plateful of stewed beef barely visible under a mound of boiled potatoes. A jug of buttermilk sat beside his glass.

Maggie brought in her own plate and they all started to eat. He couldn't believe that Maggie didn't have to be cajoled and bullied into eating. Admittedly her plate held a quarter of what his held, but it was disappearing.

Maggie paused in her eating. 'I'm sorry it's not something

better but we had so many visitors this morning.'

'Visitors?'

'All your friends from the station, and Mr. Barlow do you really think Vera should be wearing those jean things?'

'I agree with you there,' he said and winced when Vera kicked his ankle.

Visitors from the station? What sort of tablets is she on?

'Your friends are lovely people,' continued Maggie. 'But they're really curious, they had a good look in every room.'

He looked at Vera. She didn't know whether to laugh or cry.

'In every room, you say?'

'And that big man, the awkward one, broke that glass thing in the sitting room.'

'Pierson?' he said and hardly bothered to make it a question.

Vera said, 'We'll have to replace the jar but I kept all the stones.'

'Aye, the good-luck stones.'

Not that they've brought me much luck.

Maggie made a little fuss of collecting the plates. 'I'm afraid we'll have to hurry dessert or I'll miss my train.'

'What train?'

'It's apple sponge and custard, your favorite.'

She disappeared into the scullery.

Barlow looked at Vera. 'What train?'

'She's going back to Donaghadee.'

Vera's lip trembled.

He took her hand in his and lied as convincingly as he could. 'But this is her home.'

'She's grateful to us for letting her come and stay overnight. She's very pleased with the new house you've got for me, though it could be cleaner.' Her glower of irritation at her household skills being questioned was spoiled by tears glistening on her eyelashes.

Maggie came back with dessert.

Barlow let her settle again before asking, 'Why the rush back to Donaghadee? You've hardly got here.'

'The honeymoon couple will be back and I have to get the house ready for them.'

'Surely Mr. Granger has staff to run that big house?'

'Not his house. Our family home, he's coming to live with us. He says that grandchildren wanting to play with him at six in the morning has lost its charm.'

The look of hurt on Vera's face put Barlow off his food. They both struggled to finish the dessert rather than offend Maggie.

'Should I call the taxi?' he whispered to Vera when Maggie had carried off the dirty dishes and was busy at the sink.

'I'll do it,' she said and ran off.

He heard her crying down the phone. He went into Maggie and pleaded with her to stay for a few more days at least, that they needed her here. He felt dirty at being so two-faced.

But Maggie would go. She put on her coat, picked up her case and called the dog. Toby lay on in Barlow's chair, his head buried between his paws.

'Now don't be silly,' said Maggie and forced Toby's head up while she put on the lead.

Barlow lifted Toby off the chair. Maggie dragged him to the front door, Barlow followed with the case. Vera stood in the hallway, snuffling tears. Toby shook his head clear of the collar and trotted back to the kitchen.

Barlow said, 'Maggie, he's trying to tell you that this is your home.'

'Mr. Barlow, the things you say. I live in papa's house in Donaghadee. I always have.' She handed him the lead, 'Toby is your dog after all,' and climbed into the taxi.

The taxi drove away. Barlow went back into the house and tried to take Vera in his arms.

She fought off the hug that he needed. 'You should have

made her stay.'

'Vera, love.'

'You didn't want her to stay. That's why she left.'

She ran down the corridor. Looked back. 'I hate you.'

Her bedroom door slammed. He heard sobs and shaking gobs of breath.

Barlow choked with hurt for Vera. *Big boys don't cry,* he told himself fiercely and went into the kitchen. Toby was back in his chair. He snarled when Barlow came near. Too bone-weary to fight with a dog, Barlow went into the sitting room and crashed onto the settee. Toby followed and jumped up beside him. Rested his head on Barlow's leg, still snarling.

Barlow used his finger and thumb to caress Toby behind the ears. 'With you around, who needs enemies?'

Chapter 71

The doorbell rang, jerking Barlow out of a stupor of exhaustion. Toby still lay with his head on Barlow's leg, breathing in soft growls. Barlow slid out from under Toby and went to the door. Gillespie stood there, a police car parked in the drive behind him.

Barlow said, 'Police at the door can give a house a bad name.'

'The Inspector wants to see you.'

'I'm sick and I'm suspended.'

'And my feet are still sore from guarding the Hibernians, but you don't hear me complaining.'

Toby had followed Barlow to the door. He ran past the two men and piddled on the car's wheels. 'I knew that dog had a use,' said Barlow and went to fetch his jacket. He also put his head around the door to tell Vera where he was going. She was asleep or pretending to be. He closed her door gently and tip-toed away.

Toby lay on the floor, paws paddling the air while Gillespie scratched his stomach.

He told Gillespie, 'You put him in the kitchen. If I tried to do it he'd probably bite me.'

'Well don't bite him back or you'll give him rabies.'

Barlow went out to the car, leaving Gillespie to pull the front door shut behind him.

'You've been busy,' said Gillespie as they drove off.

'Aye.'

'And Foxwood's having palpitations wondering what you're up to.'

Barlow said, 'This evening, put on a civilian overcoat and hang around the entry to the Bridge Bar until Geordie and his son appear.'

'Then what?'

'Use your initiative.'

'That's what I like: clear, unambiguous orders.'

They arrived at the police station. Wilson was in the Enquiry Office fussing over three walkie-talkies. Barlow nodded his approval and headed purposefully for Foxwood's office.

Harvey was already there, sitting grim faced. 'Barlow, you are withholding information likely to…'

Barlow picked up the phone. When the WPC answered he said, 'Ring the Federation. Tell them I need that Representative fellow back here ASAP.'

He let Harvey snatch the receiver out of his hand.

Harvey told the WPC. 'Do not make that call. Repeat, do not make that call.'

He hung up and sat with a hand on the phone to prevent Barlow from using it again. Acid reflux made him burp.

Foxwood said, 'Barlow, what the District Inspector is trying to say is that you appear to have information relating to ongoing cases. Information not included in any official report filed by you.'

This was going to be a long interview. Rather than not be invited to sit down, Barlow pulled up a chair for himself.

With toes crossed against a series of lies to come he said, 'With the greatest respect, gentlemen, a lot of information has been withheld from me. However, I have a feeling in my waters that tonight we may, with a lot of luck, recover most of Captain Denton's missing whiskey.'

He explained about the pattern of Geordie's movements in the days before he spotted the police patrols taking an interest in where he was going. 'We know the bulk of the whiskey hasn't been sold, Captain Denton saw to that, so it has to be stored somewhere, probably to the north of the town.'

Harvey's temper had disappeared. Now he was the savior of the hour, returning the missing whiskey to Denton. 'How do we plan to do that?'

Barlow noted the "we" but ignored it as he explained that

Geordie had a great loyalty to Edward and he'd feel guilty at Edward being arrested for the theft of the whiskey. So guilty that he might decide to return it. But Geordie had never done anything quietly. There was no way he'd walk into the police station and tell them where to find the whiskey, he'd have to deliver it personally. Either way he was likely to go sit among the bottles while he wrestled with his conscience.

'If he has one,' finished Barlow.

Harvey was back to looking furious. 'So you're depending on some sort of honor among thieves?'

Barlow said, 'Geordie and I and a lot of other men are still alive because Edward got us through the war. That's not easily forgotten.'

Harvey still looked ready to argue.

Foxwood quickly intervened. 'Tailing Geordie hasn't worked before. What makes you think this time would be any different?'

'As you say, sir, we can't follow Geordie, he's too wily for that. He won't be taking the main Ballymoney Road, there's too many cars passing and he'd be seen. I'm guessing he'll use the Old Ballymoney Road and head out along the river from there.' He stood up because he was restless and wanted to be away doing things. 'Instead of trying to follow Geordie we get ahead of him by posting people on the hill on Arthur Somerton's land. You can nearly see the next county from there.'

'It's a chance,' Foxwood told Harvey.

'Manpower,' said Harvey. 'You're talking about detailing six to eight men for the operation.' He looked impatiently at Barlow. 'Typical of you, Sergeant, you never think ahead. With all the recent murders we're shorthanded as it is.'

'Aye you'd be right there, sir,' said Barlow as if the manpower problem hadn't occurred to him. 'Now what we could do is have one man on lookout and put…' He let his voice brighten as the solution seemed to occur to him. 'One man on lookout and a WPC sitting beside the phone in Arthur Somerton's kitchen.

When the lookout spots Geordie he uses one of the old walkie-talkies to alert the WPC who rings the station.' He looked innocently at Harvey. 'Surely in those circumstances you could spare four men for an hour to make the arrests?'

Harvey was back to dreaming of glory. 'Foxwood, detail the officers. Send them to my office, I'll brief them personally.'

He marched out.

Foxwood said, 'Barlow I authorized the withdrawal of two pairs of binoculars and three walkie-talkies from stores, an hour ago.'

'You must be psychic, sir.'

Foxwood pointed to the chair. 'Sit.'

'A minute, sir.'

Barlow put his head out the door and shouted up the corridor. 'Wilson. Day.'

WPC Day appeared from her office. 'You growled, Papa Bear?'

'Wilson and Day, report to the DI immediately.' He scowled at her. 'And if you're Wilson, get that haircut.'

Chapter 72

Barlow sat down again in his chair.

Foxwood folded his arms and tried to look stern. 'All right, Barlow, what are you really up to?'

'I'm not sure, sir.'

'You can do better than that.'

'No, I mean I don't know who killed Fetherton, not yet. But give me until tomorrow morning and I might have the answer.'

Foxwood shook his head. 'Not good enough, Sergeant.'

Foxwood hadn't let on to Harvey that Barlow had the stakeout planned before he'd left for lunch. That put him partly on his side. All the same, he felt uneasy at having to trust an Inspector.

Reluctantly he produced the list of devil-worshippers and handed it over. 'Do you really want to start a witch hunt with that lot?'

"That lot" were related to half the "County" families in the Province. Even the threat of holding them up to public ridicule could destroy a man's career.

Foxwood said, 'Mr. Harvey will have to be told.'

It sounded like a plea for an easy escape from his responsibility. He didn't object when Barlow pulled the list out of his hand and put it back in his pocket.

Barlow thought, if he hasn't got it, he haven't seen it and therefore he knows nothing about it. Barlow didn't mind. He was used to senior officers looking the other way. The best thing to do was to keep them busy with other worries.

He pulled out the envelope that he'd carried in his pocket for a couple of days. Opened it out and passed it over. 'Do you remember the envelope of drugs they found at the docks the other week? The ones they couldn't figure out who they were intended for?'

Foxwood held the envelope by his fingertips, wary of the grime that had collected along the folds. ‘Yes?’

‘I was wondering what use an old woman like Granny Cosgrave would have for padded envelopes.’

Foxwood was already reaching for the telephone. ‘She’s hardly likely to post the drugs to herself.’

He got himself put through to someone in Headquarters. They couldn’t be sure without actually seeing the envelope themselves but it sounded exactly the same.

Foxwood hung up and gave a puff of held-back breath. ‘Okay, Barlow, let’s start with the Cosgraves. You made sure that I saw Colin Cosgrave’s file, now I want you to put into words what I don’t want to hear.’

Barlow coughed as if clearing a tickle from his throat. ‘Sorry, I’m getting a bit dry.’

‘So you want a cup of tea?’

‘You wouldn’t have any of those Jacobs’ biscuits that Mr. Harvey favors?’

Foxwood buzzed the WPCs’ office and ordered tea for two, and if DS Leary had any buns leftover from that morning’s trip to Matthews Bakery, to bring them along as well.

Barlow relaxed back in his chair. There was nothing like a cup of tea and a bun to make a man susceptible to suggestions.

Chapter 73

Barlow said to Foxwood, 'As you say, let's start with the Cosgraves, and in particular Mary Jo. Was she here the week her granny died?'

Foxwood nodded. 'A Mary Jo Cosgrave was on the evening flight to Heathrow on the day Granny Cosgrave was last seen alive. That was the Friday.'

So she was here and could have planted the Wolfsbane in my garden. But why after all these years?

'The ticket?' he asked though he'd no hope there.

'Bought at the airport for cash.'

'What does Mary Jo say about all of this?'

Foxwood gave a dry smile. 'I've learned a lot from watching you and Mr. Harvey. You need more than supposition when you accuse a policeman or, in this case, a policewoman of anything.'

Barlow helped himself to one of his imaginary sweets while he thought things through. In this case a bitter lemon. Mary Jo Cosgrave had been home when Granny Cosgrave died. The autopsy had been indeterminate. She might have been pushed, she might have fallen. Either way Mary Jo had done a runner, which implied guilt.

He gave the bitter lemon a final suck and put it away for future use. 'Whatever's going on with the Cosgraves isn't recent. Or at least it started way back.'

Having got that out, things settled in Barlow's mind though there was still a big gap in the "why".

'I was on the run from the workhouse and made a living by doing odd jobs, by nicking vegetables from abandoned gardens and selling them.' He smiled remembering his own forays outside the law. 'And poaching of course.

'One night I was setting rabbit snares on the Adair estate

when I saw three youths break into the castle. Edward and his sister, Grace, were away that night and they didn't have any live-in servants.

'But because I was only a kid and because they were shorthanded the Duty Sergeant sent only two men to investigate. The policemen came on the youths as they climbed out of the window again. They pursued one, the other two got away and were never traced.'

Foxwood touched a file. 'Chris Cosgrave,' he said softly.

Rather than dwell on Chris' final struggles for life, Barlow pushed on. 'Chris formed part of a trio of troublemakers: himself, his brother Jack, and a cousin Sammy Millar. Not that anything was ever proved. Anyway, soon after Chris' funeral someone tried to burn down Adair Castle. The next morning Jack was on the Red Bay boat to Scotland. From there he went to London and eventually joined the Met. Sammy Millar turned to religion and has spent the last thirty years in Africa trying to convert the Hottentots.'

One of the WPCs came in with the tea and a box of pastries. She pointed to the gravy ring. 'DS Leary says he spat on that one especially for you.'

'I like bitter,' said Barlow.

He helped himself to the gravy ring and pushed the box Foxwood's way. Foxwood took a shoe pastry, full of cream and covered in chocolate.

The dead: Fetherton, Granny Cosgrave and Keith Ingram could wait. Barlow was more concerned about Mary Jo who was very much alive and, for some reason, a threat against him and his family. Nor could he forgive her for causing Louise so much hurt. Besides he had a big void of unknowns about Mary Jo's life. He didn't like that. Mary Jo could be the nicest girl alive but with an unfortunate sense of humor. *Or she could be a Cosgrave.* He was betting a Cosgrave.

With the sugar starting to work on Foxwood, making him more relaxed, Barlow asked, 'Mary Jo, how are you going to approach her?'

Foxwood licked cream off his lips. 'I sent a request through channels to have a look at her file.'

'Channels you say?'

The only time Barlow used "channels" was when he wanted something buried and forgotten.

'I only have the first two digits of her number, which won't help.'

'The last three numbers are: three seven four,' said Barlow.

Foxwood grabbed for a pen. 'Are you sure?'

'When I saw her ID she had her thumb over the first two digits.'

For a moment Barlow was back in Caufields' café, with Mary Jo telling him that she was in the police and flashing her Warrant Card as proof. 'Sir, you didn't ask to see her ID, did you?'

'Of course not.'

So either Mary Jo was very proud of being in the police, which she wasn't because she intended to resign, or…'

Barlow reached for the phone and pushed it Foxwood's way. 'Forget "channels". You worked in the Met before you came here. You must have one friend who likes tittle-tattle and gossip.'

'Why didn't I think of that?' asked Foxwood.

Barlow didn't answer because at long last Granny Cosgrave's death was staring to make sense. Jack Cosgrave might have been a big man in the Met but he was still dirty. One side-line was posting drugs home to his mother, Granny Cosgrave, who then passed them on to people like the Saab driver. For cash of course. Granny Cosgrave kept her cut and posted the rest of the money back to Jack in the padded envelopes.

Jack takes ill and dies after a long illness. Darling Mary Jo, who had been reared with money no object, is suddenly struggling to live on a WPCs salary. She's buys drugs on credit to sell on but a batch is found and confiscated. Someone puts a knife to her throat and gives it a nick. They want their money and the next visit won't be so friendly. Mary Jo runs home in a panic to granny who, being a tight old bitch, refuses to help. A row develops and granny gets pushed. She falls and hits her head.

Mary Jo probably arrived at the Cosgrave home after dark and stayed out of sight during the day. No one knew she was there so she took the first flight back to England. Who'd even think that someone living in London had killed an old woman in Ballymena?

Only an old Sergeant who knew the family too well to be bluffed.

So Mary Jo had planted the Wolfsbane and the broken heart and worked at splitting up him and Louise. Distracted by illness and with his love life on the skids he wouldn't be thinking too clearly.

Clever girl.

Especially if it was her who shot Keith Ingram and planted the murder weapon on him.

Now why would she kill Keith?

Chapter 74

Eventually Foxwood hung up. His phone call had taken him up and up through the New Scotland Yard hierarchy until he was talking to a very senior Chief Superintendent. Barlow had listened to Foxwood's part of the conversation so he knew the gist of what had been said.

Nothing had ever been proven against Deputy Commander Jack Cosgrave, but he had lived suspiciously well for his salary level. His daughter, Mary Jo, was different. There had been more than a grave suspicion of her passing on information to certain criminal elements. The Met had accepted her resignation rather than face the adverse publicity of a court case.

Foxwood looked pleased with life. Who wouldn't when a written commendation was coming from the Met for his astuteness at being suspicious of a weary looking Warrant Card.? A few months back, Mary Jo claimed that she'd lost her ID when helping to drag a suicide out of the water at London Bridge.

Foxwood reached for his cap. 'I wonder how Miss Cosgrave will cope with being on the wrong side of a cell door.'

Barlow held his hand up. 'Let's think a minute. Mary Jo flashed the Warrant Card when she told us both that she was a serving police officer.'

'Yes.'

'You don't normally do that. Policeman to policeman in a social setting accept each other's word that they're in the job. Which made her over anxious to prove her… I don't know what.'

'Bona fides.'

'Aye, well. She also told me that she was getting her personal stuff shipped over.'

'Me too.' A light seemed to go on in Foxwood's brain. 'Drugs?'

'You could ask the transport people if they delivered

anything to Balmoral Avenue today.' Barlow kept thinking. 'If they haven't, there's a grumpy old fart who lives on the corner of Balmoral Avenue. His bathroom overlooks Granny Cosgrave's house.'

Now Foxwood was on his feet and ready for action. 'We could set up an observation post in his house and pounce once Mary Jo takes delivery of the drugs.' He looked at Barlow, embarrassed. 'With you being suspended… and of course there's a personal thing between you and the Cosgraves, which would exclude you anyway.'

'How come?'

'That time in fifty-three when you applied for promotion to Inspector, Jack Cosgrave made sure you didn't get it.'

'Did he now?' asked Barlow who had often wondered why he'd been turned down.

Foxwood pointed to a file on the floor. 'When he was here in forty-one, he filed a report saying that your loyalty was suspect. It appears that you helped two German nationals escape to the Free State before they could be interned.'

Barlow nodded in agreement. 'A real danger they were to the war effort. Their youngest daughter met them off the train, and she was in her sixties.'

Foxwood laughed, mostly in relief that Barlow wasn't going to argue about being stood down from the investigation. 'And you never tried again?'

'Well, sir.' Barlow settled himself comfortably in the chair. 'The first and last time I was ever at headquarters was for that interview. All I could see was Inspectors running here and there with bits of paper, each man trying to outdo the other. Common as muck, the rank, but there was only one Station Sergeant.'

Foxwood stabbed a finger at the door. 'Out! Out to hell!'

Chapter 75

Barlow was grinning as he walked up the corridor to the Enquiry Office. Pierson was there, automatically making himself look busy when Barlow appeared. Wilson was there too.

Barlow asked, 'Did the DI give you your orders?'

'He did, Sarge.'

Barlow indicated the walkie-talkies. 'One for Susan in the house. You take the other two to the Observation Post. You don't want to be without a radio when things happen.'

'Yes, Sarge,' said Wilson though he obviously didn't like the idea of tramping muddy fields with two heavy radios.

Pierson was fussing over an entry in the overtime schedule. He had his head down and was turned away from Barlow.

Barlow pointed a finger at himself and made a steering motion with his hands. 'Have an early tea and be out at Arthur's in good time. Geordie's hitting the stuff hard and might need an early top-up.'

Wilson glanced Pierson's way. Seeing it was safe he nodded. 'About half six, would that be soon enough?'

'Perfect time.'

Barlow went to walk off but Wilson raised his voice. 'Sergeant Pierson, wasn't there a message left in for Station Sergeant Barlow?'

'I'm nobody's messenger boy.'

Wilson hunted in through the "In" tray, found and handed Barlow an envelope, in nice quality paper.

From Louise?

He could only hope. He put the envelope in his pocket, by the way casual, and walked out. He was on the doorstep before he remembered that he hadn't ordered a taxi. For some reason it had stopped raining. Rather than face Pierson again he walked on, his step lighter because of the note from Louise.

Except it wasn't. He knew that as soon as he looked at the writing on the envelope. It was a request from Dr. Ingram to join him in the club that night for a drink. At eight o'clock, and please be prompt, the Doctor had written.

The disappointment at the note not being from Louise crushed what little energy he had left. The walk home became a conscious kick forward of weary legs.

He dropped his coat in the hall. 'Vera.' There was no reply, he tried again. 'Vera!'

Again silence. She wasn't in the kitchen or in the sitting room. Her pillow lay crushed to the shape of her head but she had gone out without leaving a note. A partly-packed suitcase lay on her bed.

'Oh Vera love.'

Chapter 76

The front door bell rang. From the settee Barlow could see Wilson's old Austin A5 in the drive. It took effort to get onto his feet. He wanted to forget about the people he'd planned to see. *Let the idiots sort themselves out.* He wanted to be there when Vera came home.

The coat he'd left lying on the hall floor snagged his feet. He picked it up and was putting it on as he opened the door. He had to go because someone had put Vera's life at risk with the Wolfsbane and they might try again.

Wilson waited at the door. He wore a fresh uniform and smelled of aftershave. 'Are you ready, Sarge?'

'Aye.'

Barlow slammed the door behind him and got into the front passenger seat. WPC Day sat in the back, her perfume equally strong. Barlow wound down the window to protect his sinuses.

WPC Day leaned forward and touched his shoulder. 'Are you all right, Papa Bear?'

'I'm fine.'

'Barely a week ago you were nearly dead...'

'I'm fine.'

He looked up and down the road as Wilson reversed out. *No sign of Vera.* He knew she was with friends somewhere, but she was stubborn – *wherever she gets it from.* He didn't know if he could talk her out of leaving home.

He huddled into his coat against the cold chill of the damp day and felt the note from the doctor in his pocket. He reckoned the old doctor had taken a brainstorm. Barlow had picked on too many members over the years for him to be welcome in that club.

Another night, Doctor. I'll be lucky to see bed as it is.

He roused himself. 'Did you bring the sleeping bags?'

'They're here beside me,' said WPC Day. She leaned

forward. 'Why two?'

'One for each of you to keep you warm in that open shed.'

'But I'll be in Mr. Somerton's house.'

'In your dreams. I'm the one in Arthur's house, you're on the hill.'

Wilson said, 'But Mr. Harvey…'

'Isn't here and I am.'

Lying beside each other in sleeping bags in an open shed might not be a leafy glade on a summer's day, but there was no more objections from the young couple.

Barlow added. 'You can ask each other exam questions to keep yourselves alert.'

With that he subsided into the collar of his coat until "Road Closed" signs blocked their way on the road along the river. A Road Man was busy putting up warning lanterns for the night. Wilson pulled up beside him.

The Road Man leaned in and recognized Barlow. 'The river's undermining the bank. It's too dangerous to use until we get it shored up.'

'We're trying to get to Somerton's farm,' said Wilson.

The Road Man jerked a thumb in the direction they'd come from. 'You'll have to go the long way round.'

Wilson pointed. 'The turnoff is only a hundred yards up the road.'

The Road Man said, 'See those puddles up there. They might be puddles proper, they might be caused by subsidence.'

Wilson's sigh saved Barlow from doing one.

They turned back and approached Somerton's farm by a maze of side roads.

Wilson recognized the abandoned farmstead. 'We could park here.'

'Go to the farmhouse itself.'

'But, Sarge, we're right beside the hill.'

'You don't go onto a man's land without permission.'

Wilson gave another sigh and drove on.

Barlow turned to WPC Day. 'He's a moaner, you can't say you weren't warned.'

She made a face. Wilson flushed from his neck up. They were silent until they turned into the farmyard. Arthur appeared at the door, pulling on his overcoat.

Barlow got out of the car. Before he could explain why they were there Arthur said, 'Mr. Harvey rang and said there'd be police calling this evening and would I be in.'

Barlow was shocked. 'I didn't know that.'

'I said to give me time to settle the stock for the night.'

Barlow quickly explained why they were there, without giving any specific details. Arthur kept nodding and saying "Aye" at regular intervals.

Barlow only allowed Wilson to take one of the walkie-talkies.

'But you said to take two in case one breaks down.'

'I've changed my mind. On you go.'

It was a long tramp across the field with the radio, the binoculars and the sleeping bags, but the young officers didn't seem to mind.

Arthur stood with Barlow to see them off. 'You're a smart man, Mr. Barlow.'

'Am I now?'

'You send two young bucks up there. When they spot whoever you're after they'll want to get closer to make sure it's them. Then they'll decide to make the arrest without backup and get into all sorts of bother. But him with the young woman, he'll keep their heads down and yell for help.'

Barlow said, 'You've more sense than a lot of senior officers I could name.'

He opened the car door and swung into the driver's seat.

'Are you not coming in, Mr. Barlow?'

'Later, Arthur. First I have to see a man about a dog.'

With the road along the river closed off to him, Barlow drove east over the hills until Slemish Mountain appeared on the horizon. He took the next right turn and arrived back in Ballymena by the Cushendall Road. The town was quiet. Everyone was weary of the constant rain and inclined to stay indoors. Gillespie was already huddled into the entry at the Bridge Bar.

Barlow stopped and handed over a walkie-talkie.

Gillespie looked at it sourly. 'It's too late for Workers Playtime.'

'If you see Geordie come over the bridge, let me know.'

'And then what?'

'When I know where he's going to, I'll let you know.'

'That's very kind of you. Not that I give a continental about Geordie or what he's up to.'

Barlow ignored the gripe. The problem with Gillespie was, you could either play along with his grumpiness or start a row. Barlow had neither the time nor the energy for a row.

He said, with studied patience, 'Once you get the message, you hotwire a lorry and come after us.'

Gillespie scowled. 'Why is it always my pension at risk?'

'It goes with your charming nature.'

Barlow got back into the car and drove off. He turned into Waveney Road and from there onto the Galgorm Road. That way he avoided the police station and the watchful Pierson at the window.

Chapter 77

The Fetherton home was a detached, cement-faced pile on the Galgorm Road. Barlow counted five cars parked in the drive or immediately outside on the road. He nodded in approval. Five cars meant four couples and Mrs. Fetherton. The right number according to Edward's ticks against the names on the list.

He jammed Wilson's car into a gap near the gateway and went into the house without knocking. A vibration of nervous talk ceased with his arrival.

A middle aged man, spine stiff and full of indignation stepped forward. 'This is ridiculous, totally uncalled for.'

He was the only man in the room that Barlow didn't know by sight, even if his English accent hadn't given him away.

Barlow said, 'You're Smythe-Harrington.'

'Major Smythe-Harrington.'

'Prisoner Smythe-Harrington if I have my way. You made a written statement to the police, knowing that it was false.'

Smythe-Harrington spluttered and backed off.

Mrs. Fetherton came forward. 'Sergeant, Mr. Barlow, you said if everyone came that you'd keep things quiet.'

'Aye, and I will if I get a bit of cooperation and the truth out of you lot.' He glared at the assembled company. 'All of you. One lie…' He left the threat unspoken.

He marched into the sitting room. The people parted before him. For a crowd of seasoned devil worshippers they looked more like a bunch of schoolchildren caught out playing doctors and nurses.

He made a sweeping gesture with his hand. 'All furniture against the walls.' Willing hands pushed settees and chairs back. Big and all as the room was, it was still tight for what he wanted to do.

He drew an imaginary line on the carpet, from the doorway

to the fireplace. 'From here to the bay window is the hayfield.' He stamped his foot on the imaginary line. 'The hedge.' He walked to the back of the room. 'The wheat field.'

He stood with folded arms praying he had them sufficiently cowed to obey. 'I want you to process into the wheat field in the same order you did that night.'

A woman's fingers played nervously with the buttons of her blouse. 'You don't mean…?'

'We're simulating, missis, if you know what that means. Pretending.'

They all retreated to the fireplace wall and fussed for a while as to who had preceded whom. There was an awkward moment when one woman remembered that Ezekiel Fetherton had been behind her. A grimace accompanied by hip tightening told Barlow that not all of Fetherton was behind her, and she didn't like it.

They processed into the designated wheat field and stood in a circle. All of them avoided looking at the gap in the circle where Fetherton had stood. One woman remained at the fireplace.

So far so good.

Now he had them cooperating he didn't want them time to think. 'You've done your song and dance, you've smoked your hashish.' There was a flutter of concern at him knowing that. 'Now bring on your virgin.'

Two men brought the waiting woman into the circle.

'Sit down, missis.'

She sat on the floor.

'And the man that shagged you first.'

A man stepped forward.

'Now the second man.'

The first man re-joined the circle as another man stepped forward.

Barlow felt guilt for the few times over the years when he'd betrayed Maggie. But to do it in front of your wife? To watch her do it? For a moment the woman on the floor was a young Louise, forced to prostitute herself in an attempt to save her marriage.

The image blurred and cleared. He wanted to castrate every man in the room and shove it down their throats.

He pointed to the copulating lovers. 'You two stay there. The rest of you…' He made a sweeping arc with his arm. 'That's the hayfield. Move to where you went with your partner.'

He noticed that the Smythe-Harringtons stayed together and moved to the fireplace. They had obviously headed for the far hedge and the parked cars.

Nobody had stayed with the copulating couple. He pointed to them. 'There was a man waiting his turn?'

'Ezekiel,' said the woman.

The rest had paired off. One woman stood on her own at the door leading into the hallway. Mrs. Fetherton. The equivalent of what, on the night, had been the solitary haystack and the handy drinking trough. Everyone else was looking at her, wondering.

'I didn't,' she said. 'It wasn't me?'

She put her hands over her face and started to cry.

She was a slab of a self-indulgent woman who never had a good word to say about Barlow. Even so he went over and pulled her hands away from her face and held them in his.

She said, 'I loved him. Times he was so annoying I could have killed him, but I didn't do it.'

'I know you didn't.'

He pushed her into an armchair. 'You sit there, missis.'

Behind him a row was developing. A woman was saying, 'I told you not to go with that bitch.'

A woman screeched back. 'You're one to be talking. When Mike was in the army, not even the postman dared go near your door.'

'SHUT UP,' roared Barlow, afraid the row would develop into more than name calling. 'Right the rest of you. Second positions.'

The two women bashed shoulders in passing. The virgin got up and moved to stand beside a chastened Mike. The Smythe-

Harringtons stayed together.

Barlow said, 'I thought Ezekiel was waiting his turn.'

'I told him I had to go pee first.'

And didn't go back.

'Third positions.'

'You've got to be joking,' said one of the men.

'That's it then, we're finished.'

He watched as husbands and wives came back together and stood sheepishly, not looking at the other. Maybe, when fueled by drink and drugs, an orgy seemed like a good idea. Simulated in the comfort of a home it had become something else.

'Right the lot of you, shift the furniture back then head back to your butter-wouldn't-melt-in-my-mouth lives.'

The furniture was shoved back and everything roughly realigned. The Smythe-Harringtons were first out the door. Two other couples filed out, got into their cars and drove away without speaking. The virgin and her husband remained.

Barlow said, 'I appreciate you staying with Mrs. Fetherton. Would you mind putting the kettle on while we have a private word?'

He listened to their footsteps go down the hall and made sure the sitting room door was tight shut before he hunkered down beside her.

'There was a man at the haystack, wasn't there?'

Her tear-stained face nodded.

'Was he waiting or did he come soon afterwards?'

She whispered as if afraid of even overhearing herself. 'Soon afterwards.'

Which meant one of the couples in the "first position" could be lying. Especially the Smythe-Harringtons who had stayed together the whole evening.

'Do you know who it was?'

'We didn't speak and there was no moon at that point.'

Nor had there been one for him and Louise. He remembered her gentle encouragement, letting him know that it was him she wanted. He couldn't understand Mrs. Fetherton and her friends. *Bitches in heat and not particular who they got.*

Mrs. Fetherton was looking at him, frowning. He realized he had gone silent and blurted out, 'Then what?'

'I saw Ezekiel come so I…'

'Avoided him?'

'If I hadn't, he'd have been all right.' She started to cry again.

This time the crying was defensive against him and his questions. He needed one more piece of information.

He took her hand and squeezed it hard enough to get her attention. 'Describe the man you were with.'

'Muscular,' she said, and rolled the word around her mouth like a favorite sweet. 'Muscular.'

Barlow nodded as the final piece slotted into place.

He stood up and made his insincere thanks for the cooperation of her and her friends. In spite of her protestations of love, the loss of Fetherton hadn't gone that deep. However, she'd soon learn that her social life had changed for the worse. A single woman on the prowl is not welcome near husbands.

In a way he felt sorry for her.

Chapter 78

Time was flying. Barlow had a million things to do before he could even think of Geordie heading for a lorry load of stolen drink. He was shooing the Austin A5 down the Galgorm Road when Dr. Ingram not so much popped into his head as resurfaced in his conscience.

He remembered a young boy turning up at the doctor's door in the middle of the night, his leg sliced open by a rusty piece of metal. Dr. Ingram had brought him into the surgery, cleaned the wound and stitched it. Then he'd carried the young Barlow to a spare bed. Dr. Ingram and his late wife made him stay in the house for a couple of days until they were sure there was no infection in the leg.

Barlow checked his watch, *after eight.* Dr. Ingram had lost his brother that day in a brutal way. The least he could do was share a glass of something with the old man. The car seemed to agree with him because it turned right at the Pentagon and went up through the town.

Outside the club Barlow shone his shoes against the back of his trousers and wondered if he would be allowed in without a tie. *Allowed in at all.*

The front door opened. Judge Donaldson stood there. 'Barlow?'

'Dr. Ingram…'

'Come in, man. Am I glad to see you.'

Barlow stopped in the hallway, puzzled at this almost effusive greeting.

Donaldson ushered him on. 'On you go. Quick.'

Whatever it was had to be urgent. Barlow took the stairs two at a time and hurried into the clubroom.

Dr. Ingram sat beyond the snooker table yet well back from the bar area. Members were gathered around him. Their looks of concern turned to relief when they recognized Barlow.

The old man's had a heart attack. He rushed forward.

Dr. Ingram sat in a leather armchair with padded arms. He held a glass of brandy in his hand. His face wasn't flushed, one of the signs of a heart attack, he wasn't white and yet Barlow could see why the other members were concerned.

'I'm sorry about your brother,' he said.

'Young Barlow, you've had a busy day but I knew you'd come if you could.'

'Anything for you, Doctor, you know that.'

Barlow was holding the old man's wrist and getting a steady pulse. A bit faster than he liked, but nothing to worry about. The old man seemed to like the physical contact so he held onto the hand.

Dr. Ingram said, 'There's nothing you can do about old age.'

'Except thole it.'

'But not the mistakes, Young Barlow. It gets so you can take no more. I want you to know that I meant well.'

'There's no better doctor in this country.' The doctor's hand was clammy in his, sweat sheened his face. 'Are you in pain?'

'Pain?' said Doctor Ingram, his words becoming harder to hear. 'I relieved their pain thought I knew it was illegal.'

'What did?'

Barlow mouthed at the gathered members, 'Ambulance.'

'On its way,' said Donaldson.

'The hashish,' said Doctor Ingram. 'But don't blame Keith for that. I encouraged him. I paid him to get it. I didn't know about the rest, the money that he took.'

'Hashish?' Barlow was convinced that the old man had sunk into some sort of dream world.

'For the old dears with their aches and pains. The cancer patients with no hope.'

Now Barlow knew who had killed Keith and why.

'You meant well, Doctor.' He eased the brandy glass out of Dr. Ingram's hand. 'What's in that?'

Dr. Ingram indicated a water glass on a side table. 'It's to take away the bad taste.'

The water glass was empty except for a smear of something up the side. Barlow leaned over and sniffed, got the smell of chemicals.

An overdose!

Panic blocked all his training on what to do with a chemical suicide.

Now Dr. Ingram's hand held his. 'It's too late. Just stay with me, friend.' His eyes closed, his breathing became shallow.

Barlow stayed. All he could think to talk about was the young Workhouse runaway whom the doctor had befriended. Attending to his cuts and bruises, giving him paid work around the house and garden, having him in for meals.

By the time the ambulance arrived Doctor Ingram was deeply unconscious. The ambulance men brought in a stretcher to man-handled him down the narrow, winding stairs. Rather than have him suffer that indignity Barlow scooped the old doctor into his arms and carried him to the ambulance.

He watched the ambulance drive away. He couldn't say that he himself was in pain but everything in his life was being stripped away: Vera, Maggie, Louise, his career. Now it was an old man whose goodness had stopped a young boy from taking his angers out on the world.

Judge Donaldson said, 'Barlow, come back into the club, you need a drink.'

He needed a drink, he needed a bottle and he needed a lorry load of stolen whiskey. He needed a dose of that chemical in the water glass.

'Thanks, Judge, but the pain's only starting.'

Chapter 79

The light was beginning to fade when Barlow again drove into Arthur Somerton's farmyard. As he got out of the car the radio crackled his name for the umpteenth time.

'Barlow, would you answer.'

Gillespie was definitely tetchy.

'Aye, what?'

'I've been trying to get you for this last half hour.'

'I was busy.'

Busy trying to stay ahead of his demons and knowing he was running into more.

The microphone at the other end rattled as it was snatched out of Gillespie's hand.

District Inspector Harvey's voice sounded sharper than usual. 'Barlow, you're suspended. How dare you involve yourself in an ongoing investigation.'

If Gillespie had been trying to contact him then Geordie had to be on his way. Barlow switched off the walkie-talkie, rather than listen to a tirade from Harvey, and left it in the car.

The blood red of the setting sun seemed appropriate for what he had to do.

This time Arthur hadn't come to the door. Barlow knocked and entered. Arthur sat at a dying fire, the only light in the room. He still wore the overcoat he'd slipped on hours back. A battered suitcase lay on the butcher's block.

Barlow sat in the chair on the opposite side of the fire and listened to the tick of the old wall clock. Neither man spoke as the day darkened into night. Occasionally Arthur bubbled a cough.

Arthur finished the dregs of a glass of whiskey. 'You know, don't you Mr. Barlow?'

'I do, Arthur.'

'It annoyed me, them-ones forever making free with my

land. I grabbed a knife and stabbed the first man I came to.'

'Arthur, a confession like that. You'll hang before the lung cancer can kill you.'

Arthur coughed and spat into the fire. Embers hissed as he poured himself another dram. 'I suppose I should pad it out a bit.'

'Like the haystack closer to the house than the rest. Like the woman you met there every year. Like the husband who knew where to find her.'

Arthur said nothing.

Sometimes Barlow hated his job. This was one time when the law had nothing to do with justice. 'It was Willie, your brother in law, wasn't it?'

'No.'

'Aye.'

Arthur sunk into his coat. 'Things are never that simple.'

'It never is when your wife's bothered with her nerves. Times you'd do anything, anything for peace. But killing a man? No.'

'What do you know about it?' Arthur was edge of his seat, stabbing a fist at Barlow.'

'I know that Fetherton raped Anna and after that, for thirty years, she couldn't bear a man to touch her. I know that her daughter, your niece, is about the same age now. I'm guessing she was one of the kids who got gastroenteritis from Fetherton's contaminated milk. I'm guessing that it brought all the old horrors back, especially with coming of Lughnasa and the ritual sacrifice of a maiden's virginity.'

They sat in silence watching the fire turn to ash before Arthur spoke. 'Willie caught up with her well down the road. She threatened to kill him if he tried to stop her. I don't know how but he managed to get her to come into the house and talk things over. Even so there was no calming her. She kept trying to dart off with that knife. In the end, to calm her, we agreed to help. Anyway, Fetherton deserved it, he ruined all our lives.'

'And it had to be Willie,' said Barlow.

'The state she was in she might have killed anyone and with my cough they'd have heard me come.'

Barlow nodded though Arthur couldn't see it. 'That's why I knew it wasn't you.'

And the fact that Mrs. Fetherton didn't recognize the muscular Willie.

He kept that to himself though he supposed Arthur guessed that Willie had been unfaithful.

Arthur said, 'The way Anna's nerves are, she needs Willie around. And the bairns, don't forget the bairns. Better then it's me that gets taken.'

'I can't do it, Arthur.'

Arthur's voice sounded tired. 'Then you're no longer welcome in my house.'

Barlow stood up. Stretching the kinks out of his body didn't make him feel any better.

He stopped in the doorway. 'We'll send a car for you in the morning. In the meantime don't do anything silly.'

Chapter 80

Outside the farmhouse there was no rain, no clouds. The sky was awash with a bucketful of spilled stars and a full moon guided Barlow's footsteps to the car. He climbed into the driver's seat and switched on the walkie-talkie.

He keyed the "Transmit" button. 'Gillespie, are you there?'

'I'm here and the DI's going to gut you for cutting him off.'

'I didn't cut him off. I was in a dead zone but I'm out of it now.' Barlow ignored Gillespie's "hump" of disbelief. 'So where are you?'

'On the Carniny Road, near the abattoir.'

'Have you got a lorry?'

'I borrowed one from the brewery. Captain Denton's in the squad car behind with the DI.'

Barlow told Gillespie how to get to the abandoned farm buildings at the back of Arthur's farm and warned him to be careful, some of the roads in the area were washed out. He trusted Gillespie to get the message "Take your time".

Next he ordered Wilson and WPC Day to come down off the hill.

'But, Sarge, we can see two people on the road. If it's Geordie and his son we'd need to see where they're going.'

'Son, you've been guarding the drink all evening. Now come on down.'

He switched off the walkie-talkie, started up the car and drove along the farm track leading to the wheat field. Using sidelights only he drove over the lumpy field to meet the young officers.

Wilson piled WPC Day and the equipment into the back and swung into the front passenger seat. 'What do you mean, we've been guarding the missing whiskey all night?'

Barlow asked, 'How many totally abandoned farm

buildings do you know that are watertight?'

WPC Day started to laugh.

'It's not funny,' Wilson shouted.

Barlow looked back at her. 'He's also bad tempered.'

Wilson slunk down in his seat, tight-lipped.

At least this time Barlow was on the farm side of the flooded road. It didn't take him long to drive out of the field, then the farm and along the county road to the abandoned homestead. He parked in the layby Louise had used that first night and got out.

WPC Day clambered out on his heels. 'I'm coming too.'

'I'm relying on you to subdue Geordie.'

She giggled nervously and stayed close behind him as they walked single-file into the abandoned farmyard. A vague light showed on the ground floor of the old house.

Barlow nudged Wilson and pointed to the gates. 'Open those wide for the lorry.' He didn't bother to keep his voice down.

The front door was stuck. Barlow kicked it open and walked in.

Geordie Dunlop and his son, Young Geordie, sat on up-ended whiskey cases, sharing a bottle between them. Behind them were stacked row upon row of whiskey cases.

Barlow had a good look at Geordie in the poor light and was shocked at the change of the man in even a couple of weeks. 'You look like death.'

'It's only a touch of blood pressure,' said Geordie.

'Try adding blood to the alcohol in your system,' said Barlow, and made himself comfortable on a stray case. Young Geordie got up and fetched one for WPC Day. She nodded her thanks, tucked her skirt demurely behind her knees and sat down.

She was still nervous, especially with Young Geordie towering over her, but determined not to show it. Barlow caught her eye and nodded approvingly. This was one reason why he'd wanted her along. For some reason she brought out the best in people, nearly even in himself.

Wilson appeared and filled the doorway as best he could. He waived his truncheon about threateningly.

'Put that away,' Barlow told him.

Geordie found a glass at his feet. He swilled it out, poured a generous measure of whiskey and held it out to WPC Day.

'I only have the occasional gin and tonic,' she said. She didn't even blush as she said it.

Wilson beamed his approval at her abstinence.

Geordie handed the glass to Barlow who passed it on to Wilson, saying, 'Drink it, son. Don't insult the man.'

Wilson struggled to get the neat spirits down. He shook his head and blinked and stumbled without moving his feet. Barlow accepted the refilled glass and sipped at it. He said, 'We're all off duty until I finish this.' He took another sip. The whiskey burned heat into his tired body.

He leaned against the stacked cases. 'I was thinking, if you can't sell the stuff because all the barmen are too frightened of Captain Denton to buy it, and if you can't drink it without killing yourselves then maybe you should hand it back?'

Geordie raised the bottle to his lips. Barlow leaned forward and pulled it down again. 'A spell in jail would dry you out.'

The son said, 'Jail will kill him.'

Geordie wrenched the bottle from Barlow's grip and took a slug. 'I'd rather die a free man.'

'Talk's cheap,' said Barlow. 'Anyway you've an alibi for the night it was taken: you and Connie were at The Thatch for her birthday treat. The way I see it, Young Geordie stole the whiskey when he was drunk and annoyed at District Inspector Harvey for arresting his sons, your grandsons. By the time he sobered and came to his senses all hell had broken out and he didn't dare take it back.'

Young Geordie nodded vigorously in agreement.

Geordie took another swig of whiskey. 'There's all those suspended sentences still hanging. Accessory or not, Judge Donaldson will throw away the key.'

This time Barlow took the bottle off Geordie. 'Donaldson owes me a couple of favors. I'll make sure he doesn't forget it.'

'You'd do that for me?' asked Geordie.

'I would.'

'Why?' asked the son.

Barlow finished his glass of whiskey. It had been a long day, the need for sleep was overwhelming. 'Because the war made us all slightly mad, and the courts don't allow for it.'

They heard a lorry come along the road outside. Saw its lights swing round in an arc as it turned into the yard.

Barlow said, 'That's Corporal Gillespie. Captain Denton's in the squad car following.'

'He'll gut me,' said Geordie.

'Too good for you.'

Geordie lumbered to his feet and lobbed the first case of whiskey to Wilson. Wilson and the case somersaulted out the door.

Chapter 81

Captain Denton charged into the old farmhouse, roaring like an enraged bull. Geordie roared back and District Inspector Harvey gave orders that no one could hear.

Barlow walked out of the house and out of the yard and down the road. He felt as if his body had been sucked dry. His hands twitched up and down his chest looking for a pain that wasn't there. He folded his arms on top of a stone wall and leaned his chin on them to stop the twitch. Stared into the moon-lit darkness of a countryside asleep.

In spite of the dour, dome-shape of Slemish Mountain showing hard against the horizon, Barlow felt content. At least today was over. Tomorrow morning would finish things. Vera would be safe and he could finally rest.

Footsteps sounded on the road, the delicate heeltaps of a woman. WPC Day's shape appeared beside him. She too folded her arms on the wall and stared out across the countryside. She didn't say anything, one of the things he loved about her. She knew when to speak and when not to.

'Wilson?' he finally asked.

She gave him a grateful nudge with her shoulder. 'There'll be no more talk of me being on the rebound.'

'You'll be an asset in his career,' Barlow said.

'But he'll never match up to an old Station Sergeant I know.'

She kissed his cheek and walked away as Foxwood came down the road.

In the farmyard, he could hear the voices of Captain Denton and Harvey arguing bitterly. *Lord, all I want is peace.*

Foxwood asked, 'Well, Barlow, any more miracles?'

'You could shut those two up to start with.'

'Denton naturally wants his whiskey back and the DI is

insisting on holding it as evidence.' Foxwood rested his back against the wall. 'Johnny Scullion is bringing out brewery men to load the lorry. When he's going back, why don't you go with him? After all you're not here officially.'

'Tomorrow morning, sir?'

'Is all set up. The transport people have already identified the parcel and will deliver it first thing. Pierson and a couple of men have taken up position in the old man's house. We watch the parcel being delivered, give Mary Jo a few minutes to open it and then we pounce.'

It sounded easy, too easy.

Barlow asked, 'What if she says she didn't know the drugs were there until she opened the parcel? That they must have been slipped in by someone without her knowledge?'

'That's a problem for the courts.'

'Maybe not,' said Barlow. The dryness he felt in his body had ignited a mild burning sensation in his guts. 'It's a pity we can't get her for "Supply" as well as for "Possession".'

'What? How?'

'We suspect that Granny Cosgrave was supplying drugs wholesale, probably to someone in Belfast.'

'The Saab driver?'

'The Saab driver. She was also supplying locally to Keith Ingram who sold them on to certain people.' He had given his word to Mrs. Fetherton and the rest so he couldn't name them. 'Keith also gave hashish-laced cigarettes to old ladies with pains.' *No need to mention Dr. Ingram's involvement.* 'Keith didn't do it because he was kind. He did it to gain their confidence then he talked them into letting him invest their life savings in some great paying scheme of his.'

'A scam? Have you names? That could be the motive for his murder.'

'Mrs. Cosgrave for one.'

That silenced Foxwood for a moment. 'Are you saying that Mary Jo killed him?'

‘With my weapon. That way she got double revenge with one stone.’

A flicker of an idea started to work slowly through his exhaustion. ‘We know or suspect that Mary Jo is living above her means and owes money to a scary drugs dealer in London. One who’s threatening to cut her throat if she doesn’t pay up.

‘We also know that she came to Ballymena to borrow money off Granny Cosgrave who wouldn’t lend it to her or perhaps couldn’t because Granny had given it to Keith Ingram to invest. Somehow Granny Cosgrave ends up dead, and now Mary Jo’s in serious trouble.’

Barlow paused to think things over. Decided that it really did make sense, and continued. ‘The driver of the Saab is in trouble as well. Those drugs discovered at the docks were intended for him. He’s running short and if he can’t supply his regular customers they’ll go elsewhere. Without cash up front Mary Jo can’t resupply him. So she does a deal with Mr. Saab. He advances the cash, she buys the drugs and has them shipped over with her clothes.’

Foxwood made a fist and punched his other hand. ‘You’re right. With that sort of money involved, he’ll be there first thing to collect, and then we can catch them both dead to rights.’

He started to re-jig the planned operation against Mary Jo. Barlow hardly bothered to listen. If only Johnny Scullion would come with the brewery men, he’d be gone.

Chapter 82

At long last the taxi arrived with the brewery workers. Four stout men loud in their relief at their jobs being saved. By then the moon had sailed behind the oak trees, making their leafless forms stark but not threatening. The brewery workers got quickly to work. Case after case of whiskey thumped onto the lorry bed. Its springs sang under the increasing weight.

Barlow roused himself from an almost slumber against the wall and walked back to the farmyard now bright with eye-burning car lights.

Things at the farmyard were as they should be. The criminals had been separated. Young Geordie stood beside Gillespie arguing the continuous battle of opposing football team supporters. Would England ever be good enough to win the world cup? As for Northern Ireland – forget it. Geordie senior was loud in his insistence that he be arrested by the "charming young lady". Barlow had almost reached the taxi when Harvey stepped out of the shadows. 'Barlow, I won't ask what you're doing here. It's quite obvious that you chose to ignore a specific order not to interfere in ongoing cases.'

'Go away, little man,' said Barlow.

'What?'

'You heard.'

Harvey's chest puffed out. 'That's insubordination.'

Barlow leaned into the angry face. 'No it's contempt for an officer who doesn't know basic police procedures.'

'What do you mean? How dare you.'

The brewery men had stopped loading the lorry. Faces turned their way, attracted by Harvey's raised voice.

Barlow kept his low, he was too tired to shout. 'You told Arthur Somerton that we were coming.'

'And why not? It's good manners when setting up an

observation post on the man’s land.'

Foxwood came sidling over, anxious to stop a slanging match, news of which would be around the town the next morning. 'I was there when the phone call was made. Mr. Harvey gave no details of the operation itself.'

That was the one thing Barlow despised about Foxwood. He was terrified of an adverse report from Harvey blighting his career. So much so that he wouldn't stand up to the man.

Barlow wished he hadn't got into this row. It was draining what little energy he had left. 'Then the two of you should have known better. You do not, repeat not give any information of any sort to a suspect. Particularly a suspect in a murder case.'

Harvey bristled. 'Arthur Somerton a suspect? Ridiculous! Let me tell you Arthur Somerton is a past Grand Master of the Black Preceptory. Arthur Somerton...'

Barlow let Harvey rant on. He looked at Foxwood who wouldn't meet his eye. Foxwood knew he was right. Everyone involved in a murder case or who knows the victim, no matter how remotely, was a suspect until proven otherwise.

Eventually Harvey ran out of steam.

Barlow said, 'I told Arthur we'd send a car for him in the morning.'

'What for? How dare you.'

Annoyed with Harvey belittling him in public, Barlow raised his voice so that everyone could hear. 'For the murder of Ezekiel Fetherton.'

'Don't be ridiculous.'

Foxwood asked, 'Are you sure?'

‘Arthur will try to convince you that he killed Fetherton. He didn't. Arthur was an accessory but it was actually Willie Standish, his brother in law, who did it.'

He said nothing about Anna's involvement, sure that the two men wouldn't either. Bad enough the woman ending up in the mental hospital without the countryside knowing about the rape as well.

Harvey made a quick recovery from his put-down. 'If Somerton is guilty you should have arrested him straight away.'

'I'm under suspension, sir. Forbidden to get involved in ongoing cases.'

'But he could run.' Now Foxwood was on Harvey's side.

'When the DI rang, Arthur thought we were coming to get him. He had his bag packed ready for jail.' Barlow looked out over the moonlit countryside. 'I never spoke to Willie but I'm sure Arthur did. He'll be packed as well.'

Stray lights showed in the windows of scattered farmhouses and from cars passing on the far road. Barlow checked his watch. Late but not that late. *Early enough for a couple of teenagers to be up still.*

He found himself screaming the words. 'Wilson! Day!'

They came running. He pointed across the fields in the direction of Willie's house. Could only phrase his question positively, anything else was unthinkable. 'What time did Willie Standish and his family put out the lights and go to bed?'

Chapter 83

Barlow's question about the lights at Standishs' farm hung in the air.

Wilson said, 'Sarge, I don't remember.' He looked at WPC Day. 'Do you?'

She shook her head.

Barlow swung round, panicking, looking for the nearest vehicle. *Johnny Scullion and his taxi.* He ran to it, his leaden legs unable to keep up with the horror in his mind.

He crashed into the passenger seat. 'Drive.'

'Where to?' asked Johnny.

Barlow pointed. 'Straight ahead.'

Someone jumped into the backseat. Johnny put the car in first gear and they moved off.

Barlow implored, 'Faster. This is an emergency.'

"The DI's in the way,' said Johnny at his laconic best.

'That's what bumpers are for.'

Harvey jumped clear and Johnny accelerated. Foxwood and the other officers were running for the police car.

Barlow instructed Johnny to take the first right turn and looked back to see who was in the car. Geordie's face beamed back at him in the near darkness.

Barlow said, 'You're now a fugitive.'

Geordie said, 'The way you're looking, you could be dead before me.'

Barlow could only pray that he was panicking over nothing. 'You know what we're likely going into?'

'We've done it before, in the war.'

'Aye.'

They took the right turn into the laneway running between Willie and Arthur's lands. Willie's farmyard lay unlit under the dark shadows of trees. Not even the porch light glowed from the house.

Barlow jumped out of the taxi as it came to a halt. His weary legs took longer to follow and he stumbled heavily on the way to the front door. He rang the bell. It chimed through the dark house. He rang again. No lights came on, no one came to the door.

Geordie put his shoulder to the door and burst it open. 'You were always too honest, Sergeant Major.'

During the war, they'd shared worse black humor as they scraped enough of their friends together to justify a funeral.

Barlow found the switch and clicked on the hall lights. 'Police, Sergeant Barlow,' he shouted.

Geordie pointed but he was already looking at drag marks on the carpet. They stretched from the kitchen to the sitting room.

Barlow went to the bottom of the stairs and shouted 'Police,' one last time, then he pushed his way into the sitting room. The girl lay on the over-stuffed settee, her twin brother on the mat in front of the fire. Both had a rug wrapped around them. The pillows that had been used to smother them, placed lovingly under their heads.

They were obviously dead. Even so Barlow touched their alabaster necks to be sure. Inside he was churning but his hand was surprisingly steady. *No pulse, no breath.* He pushed a stray lock of the girl's hair back into place and heaved himself onto his feet.

Geordie appeared in the doorway. 'The husband's in the kitchen.'

'I'll come look.'

They both spoke softly.

Willie lay on the kitchen floor. Like the children he was happed-up in a rug, his head resting on a pillow. The side of his face around the eye had a livid bruise. Instead of death in the air Barlow smelled spicy cooking.

'What do you think?' asked Geordie. At least shock had drained the burn of blood pressure from his face.

Barlow said, 'A woman like that she'd have Valium 5 or

something stronger to make her sleep. She put it in a spicy dinner to take away the bitter taste, and waited. Poor old Willie went down hard and he was too heavy for her to drag. The twins – well she was a loving mother right up to the end.'

'The place is spotless,' said Geordie.

He was looking around the kitchen rather than the body on the floor.

And it was. Every surface shone, every dish and pot washed and put away.

Barlow rubbed the scars on his chest and arm. He'd got those the night Maggie had gone mad with a knife. Even in the middle of the madness she had been non-threatening with Vera. Anna had looked at the world and saw only threats, and thought her children safer in the arms of God.

So where is Anna?

With a history of sexual abuse behind her, he knew it wouldn't be the bedroom. Nor would it be tablets. She'd have used every last one on her family to ensure they didn't suffer. He walked back down the hall and took the stairs one at a time. Found his hand hauling on the bannisters to help himself up.

Three doors were slightly ajar. *The bedrooms.* He opened the bathroom door and was assailed by a cloud of steam. Something rattled behind the door. He checked there rather than look directly at the bath. Anna had taken off her dress, put it on a hanger and hung it on a hook on the back of the door. Once Barlow had examined the steamed up mirror and the widow and the tiled walls, he had to look at the bath.

Anna had run herself a hot bath and got into it wearing a slip and her underwear. A woman wouldn't cut her throat and make herself ugly. Bandaged wrists in a coffin look unsightly. Coming from a family who killed their own meat Anna knew how to bleed-out an animal. A gouge out of the femoral artery in the thigh brought unconsciousness in seconds, death in short minutes. In her death-throws, blood and water had splashed onto the floor.

Barlow walked out of the bathroom and down the stairs.

Harvey was already in the hallway, the rest of the police piling in the door behind him. No one dared speak to Barlow as he forced his way out into the fresh air. He didn't know where he was going. He just knew he had to get away from people and their problems. Wilson's Austin A5 was parked on the road. Barlow searched the spare key out of his pocket, got in and drove away.

Chapter 84

The house was in darkness when Barlow arrived home. Toby ran out of the kitchen to join him, teeth luminous in the dark, a growl rumbling in his throat. He came up to Barlow and stood tight against him, still growling.

Barlow didn't know if Vera was in bed and asleep or whether she and the suitcase had gone elsewhere. He didn't want to know, couldn't bear another hurt that night. He went into the sitting room and sat facing the window, not that he saw anything. Toby jumped up beside him and edged his nose under Barlow's arm and rested his head on Barlow's thigh.

I need help. He could express it in his head, but doing something about it? Dr. Ingram was dead and had no junior partner that he could call on. The other doctors in the town? *Good men all of them.* Getting up and searching through the phonebook for their emergency numbers seemed like too much effort.

It wasn't all to do with the poison still in his system or the cycle of violent deaths that had come his way. The big, bullying Station Sergeant had always someone who needed him: Maggie, making her eat and get up occasionally; Vera to rear; Geordie was ageing and finally getting a bit of sense; Edward had Mrs. Anderson to keep him in line. And Louise? *God forgive me there,* but he'd selfishly put his needs before what was best for her.

He didn't sleep, wasn't aware of time passing but suddenly it was daylight. It took another half hour to make himself ready to go out because every move had to be thought through in advance.

He needed to be sure that Mary Jo Cosgrave had been arrested and charged with something. Anything that would keep her well way from Vera for a long time to come. After that, *at least this bit's clear in my head,* Vera could go and live with her mother and aunt. As for himself, he'd borrow a rod from Gillespie and go fishing until his discharge papers came through. He might even end up living the life of a tramp in Edward's old hut under Curles Bridge.

Barlow got into the Austin A5 and drove over the tin bridge and out along the Antrim Road as far as Cromkill Orange. There he turned the car so it was facing back into town.

The two walkie-talkies were still in the back seat. He pulled one to him and called in.

Gillespie answered. 'I thought you couldn't keep your nose out of it.'

'So where is everyone?'

'I'm hiding in the builder's yard at the top of Princes Street. There's another car at the railway station in case they head out that way and the third car's in Mill Street.'

'What about the tin bridge and the road back to Belfast?'

'There's a brewery lorry parked outside Kerr's foundry. First sign of trouble they'll swing across and block the bridge.'

It all looks too easy, too sweet.

Gillespie said, 'Foxwood, Pierson and a couple of thickos are in the observation post, ready to make the arrests.'

He'd forgotten about the officers on the ground, the ones at risk. *I'm past this sort of thing.*

'Aye, well, I'll call you when the Saab passes and you can put everyone on alert.'

He got out of the car and lifted the bonnet. Pretended to work on the engine while watching the road.

Cars and the time passed. He found his attention slipping.

Gillespie called him up. 'Sarge, you were right. Mary Jo ran to the phone box the moment the parcel was delivered.'

'Right then, give the Saab man an hour to get from Belfast.'

His back ached from leaning over the engine. He flexed it straight against the side of the car while using a rag to wipe oil off his hands.

The Saab was passing him before he recognized it.

He was waiting down the road.

Once the Saab crested the hill he grabbed for the

microphone. 'Gillespie, he's on his way, he just passed me.'

'Right.'

Energy was flowing back into Barlow. He jumped into the car and set off in pursuit of the Saab. In an old Austin A5 there was no chance of catching up, but he put his boot to the floor and urged the car on. The police were up against a double killer and a ruthless drugs dealer. Suspension or not it was his job to be there when his men moved in.

When he crested the hill the Saab was at the end of the next straight. By the time he got to the end of the straight the Saab was out of sight. The Austin A5 was doing fifty and wheezing like a bellows as he thundered down Queen Street into town. The message hadn't reached the brewery lorry because it still sat outside the foundry. Barlow stood on the brakes. The cables to the brake pads worked at different times in different ways. The car slewed sideways, all but raking the side of the lorry as it came to a halt.

The driver was Captain Denton himself with Edward in the passenger seat. Denton waved to indicate that he understood the purpose of Barlow's emergency stop. Time to close the bridge. He also displayed a couple of shotguns – strictly illegal in the circumstances – which Barlow chose to ignore.

He drove on over the bridge, took the left hand turn onto Waveney Road and cut diagonally across the Galgorm Road into Princes Street. The old Austin A5's speed dropped steadily on the long, climbing hill. At the top of the hill and the entrance to Balmoral Avenue the car seemed to breathe in relief.

Four officers were advancing in line-abreast down Balmoral Avenue to make the arrests. Before Barlow could get out of the car the line hesitated. A shot rang out and the men ran for cover. Pierson turned Barlow's way.

I knew it sounded too easy.

A second shot echoed along the street. Pierson fell to the ground.

Chapter 85

Barlow found the Austin A5 moving forward though he'd no memory of putting it in gear. Inspector Foxwood and one of the thicko constables were already edging out to pull Pierson to safety. Somehow he had to give them cover while they did it.

One handed he drove into Balmoral Avenue while he keyed the mike. 'Shots fired, officer down,' he yelled to Gillespie as he passed Pierson.

The Saab's tires screamed as it came around the corner. Its path would take it directly over Pierson. Barlow edged to the right forcing the Saab to the left and away from Pierson. He'd assumed the gunman was the drugs dealer and was shocked to find himself staring at Mary Jo behind the wheel of the Saab.

He couldn't afford to risk a head-on crash in case the heavier Saab drove the old A5 back over the fallen officer but she had to be stopped. He risked a sideswipe as the cars passed. She shot at him through the side window. The bullet thumped into the doorframe, the sideswipe favored the heavier Saab. The Austin A5 reared up over the pavement, sailed through a wooden fence and crashed down onto an ornamental rockery. Steam and the smell of hot oil filled the air.

Barlow flung himself out of the car and ran after the Saab. It was already on Princes Street and racing downhill. Gillespie's car was bombing towards him from the builder's yard. Barlow stopped in the middle of the road.

Gillespie slewed to a halt and yelled. 'Get in or get out of the way.'

At the bottom of the hill the Saab turned towards the town. Barlow could hear a police car bell ringing from the direction of the railway station. *Quick response there.* The Galgorm Road and the tin bridge were now closed off to Mary Jo. She'd have to go through the town.

He jumped into Gillespie's car. 'Go back the way you came.'

'What?'

'Back.'

Gillespie started a frantic three-point turn.

Barlow grabbed the mike. 'Who's on Mill Street?'

'Kilo #2,' came the reply.

'Kilo #2 head for the Pentagon. Don't let the Saab up either Mill Street or Linenhall Street.'

'Right, Sarge.'

'And don't get brave. That goes for you too, Kilo #3.'

The last thing he needed was a dead hero.

They reached the top of Princes Street and the junction with the Cullybackey Road.

'Into town, lights, bell, the works.'

Gillespie made the speedometer needle zip upwards. The Cullybackey Road was narrow, with cars parked on one side but, by the grace of God, had no oncoming cars or mindless pedestrians.

Barlow's stomach muscles contorted in alarm as the Pentagon came in sight. Four speeding cars were heading for a roundabout already busy with traffic. He saw Kilo #2 reach the bottom of Mill Street and turn sideways, blocking both lanes. The officers jumped out and crouched behind the car, guns at the ready.

Barlow was back on the mike. 'Who's in Control?'

He meant at the station.

'I am, Sarge.'

Wilson, inexperienced but dependable.

He made his voice sound relaxed. 'Okay, son, use every phone line. I want an APB on the Saab. The driver is Mary Jo Cosgrave who is armed and dangerous. Tell every station that we have an officer down. That'll get them moving.'

'I'm on it, Sarge.'

'Get WPC Day to alert Antrim, Randalstown, Belfast and

Larne. A second person contacts the stations along the Bann River. I want a checkpoint on all the bridges. You personally deal with every station to the north of us: Broughshane, Ballymoney, Cargan, Clough and Rasharkin. Tell them to send their cars in this direction.'

They were still well off the Pentagon when they saw the Saab. It flew around the roundabout, swerved away from Kilo #2 blocking Mill Street and aimed for Linenhall Street. Kilo #3, which was following the Saab, got there first by taking the roundabout the wrong way round. It was going so fast that it couldn't stop before it crashed into the wall at the dentist's surgery. For a moment only the Galgorm Road and the roads to the North lay open.

Barlow said, urgently, 'Control, get guns to the front door. The Saab may be heading your way.'

Instead the Saab headed for the Cullybackey Road. Mary Jo seemed to spot Gillespie's car for the first time and continued the turn. The officers manning Kilo #2 on Mill Street hurried into their car.

Barlow breathed a sigh of relief. 'She's on the Ballymoney Road.' He nudged Gillespie and thumbed backwards. 'Right, back the way we came.'

Gillespie took his anger and confusion out in a handbrake-turn that had Barlow bouncing off the door. 'Would you mind telling me what you're trying to do?'

'If she heads south and west she might make it to the border with the Irish Republic, and that lot never extradite people to the UK. However, if we can force her to go north and east she'll be trapped against the coast and we can hem her in.'

'So why are we heading this way?'

'We can use the Carninny and Woodtown roads to cut across to the Ballymoney Road. If we get to the junction before her, we can drive her east into a maze of side roads that would take the heart out of a stranger.'

Gillespie muttered about lack of communication and weird

thinking. Barlow got on the mike and redeployed Kilos #2 and #3.

Gillespie's turn onto the Carninny Road was sharper than it had to be and car's four wheels were off the ground as it hurdled the hill outside the abattoir. Barlow said nothing rather than annoy Gillespie further and make things worse. On the Woodtown road, his teeth and bones rattled. He thought that Gillespie was deliberately choosing a route over every pothole.

He contacted Wilson. 'Any news yet on Pierson's condition?'

'Not yet, Sarge, but I'll let you know soonest.'

Not that he cared about Pierson as a man but he was one of his subordinates.

Kilo #2 was following the Saab and gave them regular updates. With a bit of luck and fingers crossed they might make the junction on the Ballymoney Road before Mary Jo.

'I thought you could drive this thing,' Barlow muttered.

'Any faster and we'd be taking shortcuts over the bends instead of going round them.'

Gillespie took the turn onto the Ballymoney Road in a four-wheel skid. The Saab was right ahead of them. Rather than be trapped between two police cars Mary Jo swung onto a side road, and eastwards.

'What now?' asked Gillespie.

'You could always follow her.'

'That would make a change.'

Now Barlow could relax. The chase was on.

Chapter 86

Mary Jo Cosgrave was obviously a trained police pursuit driver. The fact that she didn't know the roads locally didn't hamper her speed. The drug dealer's Saab was as souped-up as the police car and Gillespie was in his element on the narrow roads. Anything below sixty was like a full stop compared to the speeds they were doing.

Rather than dwell on his likely sudden death, Barlow stayed on the radio, directing cars in to cut Mary Jo off. The Clough car got there first. Mary Jo saw it coming and turned further east. She'd barely done that when she and Barlow spotted the Broughshane car hurtling down a far hill. Mary Jo turned again, left this time and away from Ballymena. Now she was on the river road, with brown floodwater lapping the edge of the banks.

Gillespie said, 'Isn't the road closed up ahead?'

'Aye, we got her now.'

Barlow wished he hadn't said that. Nothing was ever that easy, especially with the Cosgraves.

The reached a "Road Closed Ahead" sign. Mary Jo flew on past. Floodwater sprayed from under her wheels as she raced across a dip in the road.

'Anything you can do, I can do better,' muttered Gillespie, and accelerated.

Barlow closed his eyes. It would be just his luck if this particular part of the embankment gave way right then. They made it. Kilo #2 took a more sedate approach to the floodwater and fell behind.

On up the straight they went, with the floodwater occasionally spurting from beneath their tires. Around the bend there was a barricade across the road and a group of Road Men unloading sandbags from a trailer towed by a truck. They saw the cars come. One of the men stepped into the middle of the road and waved a red flag.

Mary Jo hit the horn as a warning for him to get out of the way. The man dived for cover and landed in a flooded ditch on the field side of the embankment. The Saab shunted the barricade aside and kept going.

Gillespie's blood was up. Barlow could feel his temptation to ignore the danger and stay in pursuit. Much as Barlow himself wanted to continue the chase the safety of his men came first. Never mind the road surface crumbling, one of the cars could aquaplane into the river. He put up a warning hand and they came to a halt just beyond the destroyed barrier.

He got on the radio, redeploying cars, while he watched Mary Jo speed away. He reckoned she knew they had her cornered, but wouldn't give up easily.

The Saab powered through the floodwater in the first dip on the road. The spray from under the wheels could have been the car itself giving them the fingers. At the second dip there wasn't so much spray as a splash. The Saab came to a sudden halt, the crunch of crumpling metal carried back to them.

Gillespie said, 'Sarge, do you fancy making a Citizen's Arrest?'

'I fancy putting my toe where it'll do the most good.'

Neither did they fancy getting their feet wet or approaching the Saab without being certain that Mary Jo was willing to surrender without a fight.

Wilson called them up. 'Sergeant Pierson, he was shot in the backside.'

Barlow didn't like the amusement in his voice. He snapped back, 'That could be serious, especially if a bone was hit.'

Now Wilson was laughing openly. 'It's a flesh wound – on both buttocks.'

They were laughing at Pierson's embarrassment and beginning to wonder if Mary Jo had been knocked out in the accident when the Saab began to drift, turning sideways to the road. There was no sign of Mary Jo in the driver's seat. They were out of the car in an instant. The men from Kilo #2 joined them.

Barlow said, 'She's hurt. I need a rope.'

One of the men ran to fetch a towrope. On Barlow's instruction he attached one end to a strut at the front of Gillespie's car. Barlow tied the other end around his own waist, paid out twenty feet of rope and took the rest in his hands.

He said, to Gillespie, 'Give me time to check that first puddle thoroughly before you drive over it.'

'For heaven's sake, Sarge.'

It could have been forty years back, a dark night on a different river, but the horror was the same. 'I let one Cosgrave drown, it won't happen this time.'

Barlow walked on the river side of the road, his eyes fixed on the tarmac surface. First sign of water bubbling up and he'd have to rethink his last actions as a serving policeman. The surface held firm, no sense of movement underfoot. Gillespie crawled the car along behind him. The Kilo #2 officers followed on foot, keeping to the middle of the road.

The first dip with floodwater looked natural. The fencepost on the field-side held firm when Barlow shook it. He risked stepping into the water and tested every step before allowing his full weight on that leg. He made it through to the far side, walked back along a different section of the dip, then did it a third time. Satisfied as best he could that the road would hold the car he waved at Gillespie and walked on.

He was concentrating so hard on watching the road for signs of crumbling that he hardly heard the shout, 'Look out, Sarge!'

He turned, sure the road was collapsing behind him. The Kilo #2 officers were ducked behind Gillespie's car, scrabbling for their guns.

A bullet whistled past Barlow's head.

He turned, crouching. Mary Jo was at the window of the car, taking aim at him for a second shot. He threw himself flat.

She fired, the bullet spurted tarmac close to his shoulder. One of the constables fired and a window in the car shattered.

Chapter 87

Mary Jo ducked out of sight. Barlow guessed that having stalled their approach she would exit by the passenger side and make a run for it. He knew he was right when the car tilted in that direction. He scrambled to his feet, ready to run after her. Could only watch in horror as the sudden change in balance caused the car to drift until its nose hung over the edge of the embankment. The force of the floodwater caught it and dragged it fully into the river. Mary Jo had still to be in the car, there was no sign of her on the road.

Barlow ran forward until the rope pulled taut behind him. There was a chance for her yet. The car was being dragged along the riverbank. If Mary Jo could get out of the car he could grab her. At worst, his men could use the rope to pull them both out of the water.

Coming level with him, the car caught on something. Its list increased until it was lying on its side. Mary Jo's head appeared at the window on the driver's side. Her hands scrabbled for leverage on the doorframe. She was screaming, unable to come any further.

Barlow stepped to the edge of the embankment.

Behind him, Gillespie shouted, 'Sarge, no. Sarge!'

He jumped, landed on a wheel. The car lurched under him and swung out into the full force of the current. Mary Jo disappeared. He lost his balance and fell, but managed to grip the frame of the shot-up window, and stopped himself from sliding off the car into the water.

He could see Mary Jo clearly now, lying crumpled against the passenger door. Only her head and shoulders showed above water. A stream of red, *blood*, rose from around her knees.

The car bounced and twisted under Barlow as he clawed his way to the front door. He glanced to the side. Gillespie was reversing the squad car, keeping level with him while the Kilo #2 men heaved the rope over snags on the embankment. Not far ahead was the Roads truck and trailer, the driver reversing up as fast as he could. The rest of the Road men were trying to clear the road of the pile of sandbags, hurling them into the flooded fields.

He stretched his arms as far into the car as he could. 'Mary Jo!'

She reached a hand up to him. He caught it.

'Now the other.'

He caught it as well and heaved her upwards. She seemed disorientated and unable to give more than token help. Her face was a bloodless white.

Arms burning with effort he got her up so far. 'Stand and take your weight.' But she didn't seem able to.

Up ahead he could see that the truck driver was having trouble keeping the trailer on the road. It had started to twist sideways. The truck stopped and then inched forward to get the trailer straightened.

'Take your weight.' Now he was shouting at her because they'd only so much time.

The burn in his arm muscles eased so she had to be trying to stand. Now her hands wouldn't let go of his. He fought one hand free and got his arm under her shoulder. He glanced to the side, the Roads truck was in trouble and had stopped again. The car was filling with water, he could feel the jars as it bounced along the bottom of the river.

She refused to let go of his other hand, held on tighter. 'No, no, no,' she kept saying.

He heaved and hoped, it was all he could do. He felt that his failure to save her uncle was finally laid to rest as her head and shoulders cleared the window. Then a leg became trapped between the gear stick and the handbrake. It had to be the injured leg because she screamed, let go of his hand and twisted sideways. His elbow dug into the edge of the door frame and his arm went numb. He lost grip and she fell back into the car.

The car caught on something underwater and flipped over onto its roof. The rope whipped taut.

Barlow found himself in mid-air, looking down on four wheels. He hit the surface of the river with a smash, it drove all the air out of his lungs. He could only think that he had failed again. It didn't seem important that he was breathing in water. Then he was lying on the road, too weary, too tired to even think of moving.

Chapter 88

The hospital released Barlow after two days. They sent him home with creams for the rope burns, Penicillin against infection from the dirty water he'd ingested and Valium 5 to help him sleep at night. Vera was home. He didn't know if she'd always been there or came back when she heard he'd been injured. He didn't ask and didn't care to know. She'd be gone again soon enough, he'd do something else to hurt her.

A new doctor called every day. He'd examine his chest and take his pulse, have whispered conversations in the hall with Vera and leave again. Visitors came and talked at him, drank tea and seemed grateful for Vera's worried face to talk to. Again the whispered conversations and the front door closing.

He hated it when she wrapped a rug around his legs. It reminded him too much of Anna's children. Toby gave him enough heat. Toby spend his days lying by Barlow's side, not even growling.

It's not that he wasn't capable of doing things, there just seemed no reason to bother. He'd no job, and that didn't matter. He'd break with his friends when he went away, *when I've the energy,* and he'd have no responsibilities there either.

The doctors called it delayed shock, but they were wrong. It had been coming on for a long time: names and graves and mangled bodies and all the things he could have done to prevent the deaths and hadn't. He'd look at his hands, constantly surprised they weren't red from the blood he'd caused.

The doctor came and left again after the usual whispered conversation. Vera came back into the sitting room, tears streaking her face.

'Dad, they're not helping and I can't take anymore.'

He said, 'Take your case and go. I'll be all right.'

'You need help.'

She ran out of the room.

Later he heard her make a phone call and her voice pleading. He wished she would leave, there was no reason for her to be stuck with him. She wasn't even going to work.

Later still the doorbell rang. Toby jumped off the settee and ran to the door, tail wagging.

Vera answered the door and there was the usual hushed voices. Toby barked, his nails scrabbled on the tiled floor as he circled the visitor looking for a pat. Gillespie got that sort of excited greeting, Foxwood less so.

Vera came in the door, hesitant, frightened. Hopeful. 'Dad, you've a visitor.'

Louise stood in the doorway, almost disdainful, declaring her neutrality with a black and white outfit.

She caught her breath when she saw him. In a moment she was kneeling at his feet, grasping his hands even as he tried to hide them and their invisible bloodstains under the rug. 'Oh my darling, what have they done to you?'

'I'm bucked.'

A tear stretched a line of mascara down her face.

His hopelessness was a solid lump in his chest. He felt that if he vomited it would be his guilt and despair. 'I've failed so many people.'

The weight of his failures had him doubled over. Louise leaned forward until their foreheads touched. Vera joined them and rested her head against both. Louise eased a hand free of his and put it around Vera.

'You've been so brave,' she said.

Other than that she remained silent until he whispered, 'Forgive me for the hurt I caused you.' He gave Vera's head an extra press. 'And you too, love.'

Louise said, 'There was a full moon last Tuesday. Wicca teaches that during a full moon, what we give in faith is rewarded threefold. What we give in bad faith is repaid a hundredfold.'

Her tears dripped onto their hands and he felt her

forgiveness.

Vera whispered, 'Dad, you risked your life trying to save a woman who hated you. What would you not do for me and Mum?'

Louise said, 'You taught me to trust again. That there are decent, well-meaning people out there.'

He could holdout against despair and guilt and against people needing him, but: goodness, forgiveness, love?

Barlow began to cry. A seep of tears he hardly noticed, then drips that joined Louise's on their hands. The first sobs came easy, then built until his chest hurt and they tore his throat.

When he was done crying Vera and Louise helped him to his room and into bed. He felt drained of energy. But this feeling of being drained was different, it left space for rest and love to refill him.

Vera and Louise left the room. He could hear the usual whispered conversation outside the door. He knew he would sleep, this time without drugs, but where would Louise be when he wakened? He wanted to call out to her, ask her to promise to call again. Be his friend.

He heard brisk footsteps on the hallway. *Vera's.* He'd know them anywhere and she was humming. He hadn't heard that since before Maggie's visit.

Louise came back into the bedroom. She stood beside the bed and let him watch as she slid off her dress then the rest of her clothes until she stood naked before him.

Louise said, 'Skyclad I come to you.'

She slipped under the covers and nestled into him.

'John Barlow, you swore a Wicca oath, "For a year and a day", and I'm holding you to it.'

Chapter 89

A month later Station Sergeant John Barlow balanced his bicycle against the front wall and marched into the police station.

Barlow was suntanned from two weeks of frustrated fishing in Donegal. Frustrated because his Wicca wife dabbled her feet in the water while he was fishing, thereby scaring away the fish. Or insisted on dragging him – not over reluctantly – to remote clearings where they could sunbathe Skyclad.

Wilson and WPC Day manned the Enquiry Office in a manner not appropriate for two officers on duty. They shot apart as Barlow flung the door open.

He threw an envelope at them. 'Give that to DI Harvey.'

"That" was his written acceptance of an official reprimand for "Failure to properly secure his personal weapon", the only charge that Harvey had dared bring against him. Worse than that, from Harvey's point of view, was the Chief Constable's interference. The Chief Constable had made it quite plain that any officer who solved three murders, trapped a known drugs dealer and risked his life trying to save a fugitive, all in the course of a long weekend, was the sort of man he wanted in his force.

Barlow said, 'Get out of uniform, then do your hanky-panky.'

Wilson burned red. WPC Day's nervous giggle followed him as he strode down the corridor.

He had timed his arrival for the end of the Inspection Parade. The constables had been allocated their tasks for the shift. Pierson was now reciting what the constables called the Ten Commandments: what and (mostly) what not to do. Barlow shoved open the door and walked into the Squad Room. Pierson stopped in mid flow. Acting Sergeant Gillespie ordered, 'shun,' and the line of officers snapped to attention.

Barlow took the clipboard out of Pierson's hands and

lobbed it into a corner. Then he walked the line of constables. Shoes not shone, uniform creased, food on tie and, if all else failed, 'Get your hair cut.' Not one man or woman passed inspection.

Barlow stood back and ran his eye over them once more. 'You're a disgrace to the uniform, the lot of you,' he said.

Finished with the squad he turned his attention to Pierson and noted several defects. *I'll sort him out later*. As a senior sergeant Pierson deserved his bollocking in private.

Gillespie stood behind and to the side of Pierson. His uniform was perfect, shoes shinning and hair cropped. Lips tight together to hold down a smile.

'What's so funny,' demanded Barlow.

Gillespie nodded for him to look behind him. He turned. The whole squad was smiling, they could have won the YP Pools they looked so pleased.

Barlow said, 'I don't know what you lot are looking so happy about.'

Gillespie made it sound like the worst luck in the world when he said, 'Barlow's back.'

Acknowledgements

How do you properly thank people who have given of their time and knowledge and patience to answer myriad questions or to read and comment on various drafts of the work in progress?

My wife, Patricia, of course, and our two children, Lucie and Daniel, and if Kevin Hart ever charged minimum wage per hour for the time he has spent encouraging and monitoring my output, he'd be a millionaire.

Professor Ciaran Carson and the guys at the Creative Writing Group, the Seamus Heaney Centre, Queens University, Belfast for their weekly critiques. Andrew and Arlene of Portnoy Publishing for their constant encouragement, Caoileann Curry-Thompson for a masterful edit and Ashley Bingham of Dogtag Creative for the eye-catching cover.

Consultant Stella Hughes for her medical input, which I always appreciate but sometimes ignore. Neil from the RUC Museum, Belfast, who gave me a detailed tour of the museum and answered follow-up questions with great patience. The staff at the Armagh Historical Library and Ballymena Library and Elaine Hill of the Ballymena Museum.

My wider family and friends for their encouragement and support and Sammy Gillespie for the use/misuse of his name. It's a good thing Sammy has a sense of humor.

Dara Vallely and Anne Hart for 'edging' my writing in different directions. Hugh Woodcock my Ballymena spokes-person and various retired police officers who have tried to keep me right on facts and procedures, and Fabio & Luisa, Luigi & Nadia who keep an eye on me when I'm in Italy writing.

Mr. and Mrs. W Hamilton Thompson who very kindly showed my wife and myself around their historic and utterly fascinating house and regaled us with tales of the real Adair family of Ballymena.

(Barlow #1) The Station Sergeant

When local farmer, Stoop Taylor, is found dead, Station Sergeant Barlow has the sinking feeling his comfortable life is about to be turned upside down. While local hoods, the Dunlops, are stealing cattle to order, a traumatized German soldier escapes and roams the countryside. Barlow's personal problems multiply as well. He falls in love with another woman, his schizophrenic wife turns violent, his daughter is growing up too fast and the new Inspector wants him demoted. The Station Sergeant faces a battle to find a killer and save his career.

ISBN: 978-1-909255-00-5

(Barlow #2) Barlow by the Book

Station Sergeant Barlow is back, but if he thought life was going to return to normal after his last case, he couldn't have been more wrong. Barlow's house is bombed, and he is suspended from duty on suspicion of Perverting the Course of Justice. His problems mount when his schizophrenic wife is released unexpectedly from the mental institution and he learns the truth about her traumatic childhood; while his daughter, Vera, is shot during a robbery. Barlow is under strict orders not to interfere in the ongoing investigations, but shooting Vera has made it personal.

ISBN: 978-1-909255-11-1